John Murray

Voyage of H.M.S. Challenger during the years 1873 - 1876

Zoology - Volume VI

John Murray

Voyage of H.M.S. Challenger during the years 1873 - 1876
Zoology - Volume VI

ISBN/EAN: 9783741123481

Manufactured in Europe, USA, Canada, Australia, Japa

Cover: Foto ©Andreas Hilbeck / pixelio.de

Manufactured and distributed by brebook publishing software
(www.brebook.com)

John Murray

Voyage of H.M.S. Challenger during the years 1873 - 1876

REPORT

ON THE

SCIENTIFIC RESULTS

OF THE

VOYAGE OF H.M.S. CHALLENGER

DURING THE YEARS 1873-76

UNDER THE COMMAND OF

CAPTAIN GEORGE S. NARES, R.N., F.R.S.

AND

CAPTAIN FRANK TOURLE THOMSON, R.N.

PREPARED UNDER THE SUPERINTENDENCE OF

THE LATE

Sir C. WYVILLE THOMSON, Knt., F.R.S., &c.

REGIUS PROFESSOR OF NATURAL HISTORY IN THE UNIVERSITY OF EDINBURGH
DIRECTOR OF THE CIVILIAN SCIENTIFIC STAFF ON BOARD

AND NOW OF

JOHN MURRAY, F.R.S.E.

ONE OF THE NATURALISTS OF THE EXPEDITION

ZOOLOGY—VOL. VI.

Published by Order of Her Majesty's Government

PRINTED FOR HER MAJESTY'S STATIONERY OFFICE
AND SOLD BY
LONDON :— LONGMANS & CO.; JOHN MURRAY; MACMILLAN & CO.; SIMPKIN, MARSHALL & CO.
TRÜBNER & CO.; E. STANFORD; J. D. POTTER; AND KEGAN PAUL, TRENCH, & CO.
EDINBURGH :—ADAM & CHARLES BLACK AND DOUGLAS & FOULIS.
DUBLIN :—A. THOM & CO. AND HODGES, FIGGIS, & CO.

1882

Price Forty-two Shillings.

CONTENTS.

EDITORIAL NOTE.

THE first Memoir in the present volume is a Report on the ACTINIARIA of the Expedition, by Professor Richard Hertwig, of Koenigsberg.

This Report is not complete, in so far as it does not embrace the whole of the Challenger collection. A considerable number of specimens did not reach Professor Hertwig till some time after he had completed the examination of the collection originally sent to him, indeed, not till the present paper was in type. Professor Hertwig has kindly undertaken to prepare a short supplementary Report on the additional specimens here referred to.

The Memoir has been translated from the German by Miss Nellie Maclagan.

The second Memoir is the first part of a Report on the TUNICATA of the Expedition, by Professor W. A. Herdman, of University College, Liverpool.

As Professor Herdman had completed the examination and description of the Ascidiæ Simplices, he consented to the separate publication of this portion of his Report.

The second part of his Report, which will consist of a description of the Ascidiæ Compositæ and the Pelagic Tunicates, will, it is hoped, be ready for publication within a year from the present time.

The above Reports form respectively Parts XV. and XVII. of the Zoological Series. Part XVI. was published in Vol. V.. Zoology.

JOHN MURRAY.

THE

VOYAGE OF H.M.S. CHALLENGER.

ZOOLOGY.

REPORT on the Actiniaria dredged by H.M.S. Challenger during the years 1873-1876. By Prof. Richard Hertwig.

INTRODUCTION.

In investigating the Anthozoa the majority of earlier naturalists were content to give the most exhaustive description possible of the parts which are externally visible in the living animal, and of the skeleton where such a structure existed ; on the other hand, they only went slightly into more exact anatomical details, as the observation of these presented great difficulties. The majority of the Anthozoa are not sufficiently transparent to allow of the recognition of the form and arrangement of the organs in the living animal, whilst after death they are so contracted that all the parts become misplaced in many ways and pressed one against the other, and can only be demonstrated, with great care, by means of knives and scissors. Up to the present time the systematic survey and characters of the orders, families, and genera are founded upon external characteristics which are of less morphological importance.

In this way many errors arose, which have only become intelligible from the work of the last decades. Following the steps of Agassiz (Contrib. to the Nat. Hist. of the United States, vol. iii.), Moseley (Phil. Trans., vol. clxvi. pt. 1, p. 91, 1876 ; vol. clxviii. pt. 2, p. 425, 1878) has shown in the most convincing fashion that many hydroid polyps which form skeletons have been long placed among the reef-forming corals, and that, moreover, in consequence of the skeletal formation alone having been taken into consideration, many Octocorallia have been disconnected from their natural systematic place, and united to forms entirely remote. It cannot by any means be asserted that recent discoveries have led to the exhaustion of the more comprehensive reforms of the system of Corallia, as up to the present time we only know the structure of the soft parts of the body, especially of the septa, from a comparatively small number of species, and our knowledge, even of such forms as have been most thoroughly investigated, is far from satisfactory.

This also holds good for the soft-membraned Anthozoa, the Actiniaria or Malaco-dermata. In this section the structure and arrangement of the septa are of the highest importance for the proper comprehension of the structure ; they will probably require to be taken pre-eminently into consideration in the classification, not only of the Actiniæ but also of the other Hexacorallia. But how little do we know on this point. In a recently published work (Studien zur Blättertheorie, Heft i., die Actinien, Jenaische Zeitschrift, Bd. xiii. p. 457, 1879) my brother and I have tried to show that all the important charac-teristics have hitherto been properly estimated only in a treatise by Schneider and Rötteken (Ann. Mag. Nat. Hist., ser. iv., vol. vii. p. 437), and that, on the other hand, both v. Heider (Sitzungsber. d. Kaiserl. Acad. z. Wien, Math. Nat. Classe, Bd. lxxv., Abth. 1, p. 367, 1877), in his otherwise very elaborate anatomy of *Sagartia troglodytes*, and Jourdan (Annales d. Sciences Nat., Zool., ser. vi., t. x., No. 1, 1880), in his treatise on the Actiniæ of Marseilles, remain far behind the two first-named naturalists. As, however, we have only a short report in a preliminary publication on the researches of Schneider and Rötteken, which extend over a large number of species, it is impossible to make any systematic use of their material, and therefore the number of more detailed anatomical studies of Actiniæ, which, taken from different species, would enable us to form an exhaustive plan of the variations of the type common to all, is still incomplete. These anatomical studies we must have before we can deem it possible to settle an accurate point of view from which to determine the relations of the Actiniæ both to each other and to the other Anthozoa.

Since it appeared to me a grateful task to make a beginning myself in the direc-tion just mentioned, I accepted with pleasure the offer made to me to undertake the working out of the Actiniæ collected by the Challenger Expedition. I wish at the same time to express my most hearty thanks to the late director of the Challenger Commission, Sir Wyville Thomson, and his first assistant and successor, Mr. John Murray, for the great liberality with which they placed the rich material collected at my free disposal.

Before going into a description of the separate species, I think it advisable to determine in a few words the requisites, which, according to my view, ought to be fulfilled by the anatomical description of an Actinia if this is to be of any systematic value. I shall therefore preface the description by a sketch of the structure of this animal, in which I shall lay stress upon the points which are most subject to variation, and to which the special attention of the describer must be directed. Such an attempt is also to be recommended for the further reason that in this way the reader will at the same time become familiar with the nomenclature, which, taken partly from earlier authors, and founded to some extent upon my own observations, will be adopted in the following pages. I shall also be able to interweave short remarks upon the most serviceable methods of investigation.

The body of the Actinia is shaped like a hollow cylinder, which is usually very long in proportion to its breadth, but which can also be shortened to a discoid form under certain circumstances. It is limited by two terminal surfaces, the "oral disk" or "peristome," and the "pedal disk" or "base," whilst the body wall corresponding to the outer surface of the cylinder is termed the "mural layer," or shortly, the "wall"; the wall is usually separated from the pedal disk, always from the oral disk, by a sharp margin, the two surfaces here meeting at a right or even at an acute angle; the wall occasionally passes gradually inwards into the base, in such a way that we cannot speak of a separate pedal disk.

Towards its periphery the oral disk bears the tentacles, which are simply hollow evaginations of the disk. Besides these "marginal" tentacles there are also "circumoral" tentacles, which are united in a corona round the oral opening, and "intermediate" tentacles, which occupy a position between the oral opening and the margin of the disk. As the first are always present, and the last two only exceptionally, those may be termed the "primary" or "principal" tentacles, these the "secondary" or "accessory" tentacles.

The oral opening, placed in the middle of the oral disk, leads into a tube which hangs down a little way into the hollow space of the body, and in the older descriptions was held to be a stomach, a name which we may now suitably abandon and replace by the term "œsophagus." This ends before it reaches the pedal disk in a free margin, and communicates by a wide opening, the "gastric orifice" or "cardia," with the large hollow space which occupies the inside of every Actinia, and is developed from the primitive intestine of the gastrula, whilst morphologically and physiologically it replaces the intestine and body cavity (enterocœle) of the bilaterals. Leuckart's term "cœlenteron," or "cœlenteric space," is therefore specially appropriate to the Actiniæ.

The œsophagus hanging down in the cœlenteron is fastened to its place by the numerous septa (sarcosepta, Hæckel) which spring from the oral disk, wall, and pedal disk, and are attached superiorly to the œsophagus, whilst they end in a free margin below. They therefore divide the peripheral part of the cœlenteron into simple radial chambers, which are closed where they surround the œsophagus and where they pass into the hollow spaces of the tentacles, but which open downwards between the free margins of the septa into the "central stomach," i.e., into that part of the cœlenteron which lies under the œsophagus and is no longer divided into chambers by the septa.

All the above-mentioned walls and septa of the body of the Actinia are lamellæ of no great thickness, and in many species the wall only is a tough sheath. The firmness of the lamellæ depends upon their fundamental substance of connective tissue, which, according to the degree of their histological differentiation, may be homogeneous and not enclosing cells, homogeneous and enclosing cells, or, finally, fibrous and containing cells.   The framework of connective tissue gives us an accurate figure of the corporeal form of the Actinia even when the epithelial parts have been removed by maceration ; from the standpoint of the " Blättertheorie," it must be termed the middle layer of the body or mesoderm.

All the lamellæ of connective tissue are covered on either side by a single layer of epithelial cells, which are distinguished by extraordinary length and thinness, and may, moreover, be placed in different categories according to their different functions.   The most usual form is seen in the " supporting cells," in which, despite their fineness in an isolated condition, we can recognise a distinct, triangular, basal expansion.   The most common after these are the " urticating cells " and " gland cells."   In the former the body is expanded by the presence of the thread, in the latter it is distended by glandular secretion stored up in it.   The form of the nematocysts, and the nature of the thread contained in them is not the same everywhere, and may, perhaps, some day become of systematic importance.   The glandular secretion is also of different kinds ; it sometimes fills the body of the cell, as a homogeneous, glassy mass, sometimes it is deposited as a mass of closely compacted granules, greedily absorbing colouring matter.   The fourth form of cells is that of the " sense cells," which have the same fine, filamentous nature as the supporting cells, from which, however, they can be distinguished in an isolated condition by their central end giving off two or more fine nerve threads, which have a tendency to become varicose.

With the exception of the glandular cells, all the cells bear appendages at the peripheral end ; the sense cells, and probably also the urticating cells, have fine, long, tactile bristles, of which each cell usually possesses only one ; the supporting cells bear a bunch of cilia, or a simple flagellum.   Ciliated cells and flagellate cells may be present in the same animal, e.g., in most Actiniæ the ectodermal epithelium is made up of the former, the endodermal of the latter, whilst in Cerianthus we find only flagellate cells. We have as yet no satisfactory knowledge of the manner in which the two forms of cells are distributed among the Actiniæ.

The epithelial coverings are derived immediately from the two primitive layers of cells of the gastrula larva, the endoblast and the ectoblast, and in the developed animal are therefore to be distinguished as separate body layers, as endoderm and ectoderm, even when they hardly vary in their histological character.   The ectoderm covers the outer surface of the body and the inside of the œsophagus ; the endoderm covers everything else, i.e., the inner wall of the whole cœlenteron, and the inner spaces of the tentacles. The supporting lamellæ of the wall, of the œsophagus, &c., are therefore covered with ectoderm on one side and with endoderm on the other ; the septa only form an exception, as they bear endodermal epithelium on both sides.

Among the histological elements of the Actinia we must finally mention the muscle cells, nerve cells, and reproductive cells; we shall merely discuss the two former here from a general point of view. The muscles originate either from the ectoderm or the endoderm, and usually continue to belong to both these epithelial layers. They consist of flat, fusiform, muscular fibrillæ, to one side of which the cell from which they were originally produced is attached. This latter is usually at the same time an epithelial cell, and with the fibre belonging to it represents an epithelio-muscular cell, or it is a cell lying in the deeper layers of the epithelium, and no longer extending as far as the surface, an epithelial cell, whose peripheral end has undergone retrograde formation, or a subepithelial muscle cell.

The principle of arrangement of the fibrillæ is the same in both cases; they are placed on the borders of the epithelium and the mesodermal connective substance, and form a thickly apposed simple layer, a muscular lamella. The muscles are not strengthened by the deposition of new layers of fibres, but by the "pleating" of the single-layered lamellæ. The underlying connective substance also comes into play, supporting all the folds of the muscular lamella by fine leaf-like processes (Pl. V. figs. 7–10; Pl. VI. figs. 4, 6).

The pleating of the epithelial, or subepithelial muscular lamella, becomes in many cases the starting-point for the development of a third form of the muscular fibres, the "mesodermal" fibres. When the surfaces of the supporting substance, which borders a muscular fold laterally, approach so that here and there they touch and become fused, the connection of the lower part of the pleating with the epithelium is dissolved, and it becomes completely enclosed in the mesoderm (Pl. VII. fig. 8). In this way are found in transverse sections, circular figures, whose periphery is occupied by the divided fibrillæ, whilst the centre contains the muscular corpuscles belonging to it. The transformation of the epithelial muscular elements into mesodermal can go so far that considerable masses of muscles lie in the mesoderm (Pl. IV. figs. 5–8; Pl. VI. figs. 1–3, 5).

In describing the muscles of the Actiniæ we must, therefore, be careful to note whether they are ectodermal, endodermal, or mesodermal, whether they extend simply in a smooth lamella, or are disposed in folds; as we shall see, they present in this way many characteristics of systematic value. This cannot be said of the nervous system, which I only go into here for the sake of completing my description. Nerve fibres and ganglion cells are found, in thoroughly examined Actiniæ, in nearly all the epithelial laminæ, where they form a layer between the bases of the epithelial cells. The layer is extremely thin in the ectoderm of the pedal disk, and usually also in that of the wall, whilst it is very strong in the ectoderm of the tentacles, of the oral disk and of the œsophagus. Nervous elements are usually less frequent in the endoderm, and only produce visible cords in the mesenteric filaments and acontia. We may lay down as a rule, that, where muscular filaments are present, the layer of nervous filaments lies over the former, and is most easily found in that place.

I have as yet only given a general survey of the anatomical and histological parts composing the organisation of the Actiniaria ; it now remains for me to discuss the differentiations shown by the histological elements in their nature, distribution, and arrangements in the various parts of the body, and to show how we may thereby acquire a knowledge of the more accurate characteristics of these parts.

The pedal disk does not present much worthy of notice ; it has a slightly developed endodermal muscular layer, always running circularly, which is often even wanting ; in the centre there are sometimes, but rarely, one or more small openings, through which the water can find entrance and exit ; as yet, however, such openings have only been observed where the pedal disk and wall pass continuously the one into the other, which condition is usually described as absence of the pedal disk. Radial furrows may also run on the outside of the pedal disk, and usually correspond to the insertions of the septa on the inside (Pl. IV. fig. 2 ; Pl. IX. fig. 5). The wall is much more complicated both on its endodermal and its ectodermal sides ; on the former there often lies a layer of circular muscular fibres, which appears everywhere as a flat or slightly folded lamella, but is also often more strongly developed in certain places, and forms a special muscular cord acting as a sphincter. The sphincter or circular muscle usually lies immediately below the upper margin of the wall, which it draws together like a bag over the oral disk and the tentacles if the latter require shelter from any threatened danger. A second sphincter, lying further down, may also be added to the upper sphincter.

The nature of the sphincters varies greatly. We talk of a "diffuse" sphincter when it merely arises from repeated pleatings of the muscular lamella ; because in that case it is not sharply defined at the upper and lower margins (Pl. V. fig. 8), it does not strike the eye in looking at the surface, and is shown in transverse section only by the local thickening of the wall in whose substance it is completely embedded. A "circumscribed" sphincter is formed when the pleated muscular mass projects above the inner surface of the wall, with which it is connected only by a narrow band, so that an annular swelling arises which is easily observed both in looking at the surface and in transverse section (Pl. VII. figs. 2, 4). Finally, in the "mesodermal" sphincter, the muscles have left their original position in the epithelium, and are completely hidden in the supporting substance, which consequently increases doubly or trebly in thickness (Pl. VII. fig. 7 ; Pl. VI. figs. 1–3).

The complete absence of the sphincter is comparatively rare. I have only observed it in a few species (e.g., in the representatives of the genus *Corallimorphus*), almost invariably animals which are not capable of contracting the upper margin of the wall over the oral disk. This is, however, also the case in animals with a weak sphincter, such as the Anthcadæ. On the other hand, the existence of a strong circular muscle can often be inferred with tolerable certainty from a high degree of contraction. The capacity for concealing the oral disk plays an important part in the systematic division of the

Actiniaria; this is generally most inappropriately expressed by the term " retractile tentacles." It would be decidedly more rational to make the anatomical reason, and not the physiological appearance, of systematic value. We shall therefore talk of Actiniaria without sphincter, and of Actiniaria with weak and with strong sphincter, and further distinguish in the latter case whether the muscle is endodermal or mesodermal.

The systematic value of the circular muscle does not end here, as it furnishes a character not to be undervalued, for determining the species. The extraordinary variations of the circular muscle are shown by a glance at Plates VI. and VII.; in the endodermal forms the shape and mode of branching of the muscular folds vary, in the mesodermal the shape and grouping of the bundles formed by the fibres, and also their position in the more superficial or deeper layers of the wall. I lay stress upon this point, as the circular muscle can be examined in the preserved animals even when their state of preservation is not very favourable, and because, moreover, a small piece of the wall, which can be cut away without essential damage to the whole animal, is sufficient for such an investigation.

Muscles, especially longitudinal muscles, are rarely present on the ectodermal side of the wall, whilst, on the other hand, it is not unusual to find " marginal spherules " and different forms of papillæ. The marginal spherules (" bourses marginales," Hollard, Ann. d. Sci. Nat., Zool., ser .iii., t. xv. p. 257) follow immediately outside the tentacles, and are evaginations of the mural membrane, just as the tentacles are evaginations of the oral disk. All the layers of the body participate in the evagination, though the ectoderm alone undergoes modification of its structure, being extraordinarily rich in nematocysts.

The papillæ, to which such importance was attached in earlier investigations of the Actiniæ, are formations of very subordinate value; they are caused by mere local growth of the supporting plate, and are not distinguished by a single special property of the covering epithelium (Pl. VIII. fig. 4). Hence the observer often found himself on the horns of a dilemma when he had to decide whether papillæ were present or not. A smooth surface may become papillose in consequence of contraction, and, on the other hand, small papillæ may disappear when, as often happens, the Actinia becomes distended like a drum. It would, therefore, be better in future only to make the papillose or smooth nature of the membrane of value in distinguishing species, or at most of genera, and to disregard it in the formation of larger divisions.

The comportment of the epidermis appears to me much more important. The majority of the Actiniæ have a smooth surface, on which particles of mucus become secreted when the animal is irritated; histological investigation then shows an active ciliated epithelium composed of extremely long, thin cylindrical cells. Besides this, two varying modifications of the integument have already been specially observed. In the one case, in *Cerianthus*, the epithelium is covered externally by a tough membrane, consisting of mucus, nematocysts, and scattered foreign bodies, which can be stripped off, but which is rapidly regenerated, and in which the animal is concealed as in a sheath ; in the other case there is a membrane present which cannot be stripped off, and which gives the surface a rough, bark-like appearance ; this has received the very unsuitable name of " epidermis." In fact, we have to deal with a cuticular formation. In the most simple cases, where the epithelium does not bear cilia, it is covered loosely by a thin, irregular fibrous membrane, outside which is a layer of mucus, traversed by all sorts of foreign bodies (Pl. VIII. figs. 1 and 6). This cuticular secretion rarely becomes a broad, stratified mass resting firmly on the epithelium, and recalling completely the cuticula of the worms (Pl. XII. figs. 1 and 2).

The wall can also be traversed like the pedal disk by furrows, which run in a longitudinal direction from the base to the border of the oral disk, and likewise correspond to the septa.

The possible presence of " cinclides " must finally be taken into consideration ; this is the name applied by Gosse (Actinologia Britannica, 1860) to openings in the wall through which water and the acontia, which we have still to describe, can be ejected from the inside of the body. Such cinclides can be observed in *Calliactis parasitica*, even in spirit specimens, where they are arranged in a circle at a little distance from the pedal disk. In other cases, on the contrary, we see that acontia issue from the interior of the living animal through the wall, but it is impossible to find performed openings, even if we take a protruded acontium as guide. Whether the opening is difficult to find out, or whether it is not performed, but arises afresh each time by rupture, as v. Heider assumes, must still be regarded as an open question. That is a point which essentially lowers the systematic value of the cinclides. Gosse has certainly made light of the question, and assumed the presence of cinclides wherever he noticed the passage of the acontia, even though he did not find any openings. Such a method of treatment, however, can be properly carried out only in the living animal, as spirit material leaves the question undecided.

The oral disk is furnished on both sides with muscular fibres, running radially on the ectodermal side, circularly on the endodermal ; the latter are connected immediately with the muscular fibres of the wall, with which they form a continuous layer. Whilst the endodermal muscular fibres possess no further interest, and comport themselves, so to speak, in the same manner throughout, the development of the ectodermal muscular fibres is subject to numerous variations, which, like the nature of the sphincter, can be turned to good account for more accurate determination of the species. In all cases we must distinguish whether the muscular fibres maintain their original place in the epithelium, or whether they have passed wholly or partially into the mesoderm. We must, moreover, pay attention in the first instance to whether the muscular lamella is smooth or pleated, and in the second instance to the form and arrangement presented by the mesodermal bundles of fibres.

The same questions recur in the tentacles, which are merely evaginations of the oral disk. Here the endodermal circular muscular fibres are always uniform, whilst the ectodermal longitudinal cords vary. Moreover, there are usually, if not always, openings present in the tentacles through which water is ejected when the animal becomes contracted; they occupy the point of the tentacles, and are easily observed in the living animal. In order to find them out in the spirit material I fastened a tentacle, which had been cut off, to a tube and inflated it with air under water; if an opening were present the air bubbled out through it.

According to their shape the tentacles are distinguished as "knobbed," "club-shaped," "branched," "conical," &c., terms which do not require further explanation. Their mode of arrangement, of which I shall speak in connection with the septa, is also of importance. On the other hand, their length and shortness is a characteristic which is not capable of exact definition, and cannot be determined with any certainty in the spirit specimens, as it is impossible to judge to what extent the length has been influenced by a greater or lesser degree of contraction. This characteristic cannot, however, be dispensed with for systematic purposes.

Whether the tentacles in the Actiniæ may be entirely wanting, without being morphologically replaced in some way or another, seems to me questionable, as no such case is known up to the present time. The tentacles may, however, undergo a peculiar retrograde metamorphosis, progressing so far that only the terminal opening is left in the form of a fissure, which is enclosed by thickened lips, and, lying in the periphery of the oral disk, shows the spot where we might have expected to find the tentacle. I have observed different stages of this retrograde formation in species of Actiniæ coming from great depths. We see the beginning of it in *Polysiphonia tuberosa* (Pl. II. figs. 7, 9), also *Sicyonis crassa* (Pl. IV. fig. 4), and the advanced stages in *Polyopis striata* (Pl. II. fig. 11), and *Polystomidium patens* (Pl. V. fig. 6).

The oral opening is only exceptionally round; it has usually the form of a fissure whose longitudinal diameter lies in the same direction in all Anthozoa. It is therefore of the greatest importance for distinguishing the axes which may be drawn through the body of the Actiniæ. If the Actiniæ were animals possessing perfect radial symmetry, then the longitudinal axis, determined by its passing through the oral and aboral poles, would be the only constant one, and all radial axes lying perpendicular to the longitudinal would then be perfectly equivalent to one another. By the constant form of the oral opening, the radially symmetrical fundamental form becomes more definite, and is at least transformed into the biradially symmetrical form. In all cases, two of the radial axes strike us as specially distinguishable, the sagittal axis running in the direction of the oral fissure, and the transverse axis perpendicular to it. We can even exceptionally recognise a dorsal and a ventral side at the ends of the sagittal axis, and a right and a left side at the ends of the transverse axis, and hence the biradially symmetrical fundamental form is transformed into the bilaterally symmetrical. I lay great stress upon this apparently unimportant consideration of the form of the mouth, as it is the expression of a fundamental character in the architecture of the body of the Actinia, which is, moreover, the standard for the configuration of the œsophagus and the position of the septa.

The œsophagus is a sac, flattened in the transverse direction, and open below and above ; it is furnished with circular muscular fibres on its endodermal aspect, whilst it has exceptionally longitudinal fibres on the ectodermal aspect, the one turned towards the lumen of the tube. Its walls are solid, and only two instances have been observed in which they have openings leading into the radial chambers. In the typical Actiniæ the lower end of the tube is produced into two long lappets, which fall in the sagittal axis and consequently under the two corners of the mouth, or, what is the same thing, where the two wider sides of the tube meet each other. The inner side of the œsophagus is covered with regularly arranged longitudinal furrows, of which two, corresponding to the angles of the mouth, are conspicuous by their special breadth and depth. These furrows or grooves lead from the oral angles to the œsophageal lappets, on which they run up to the end ; they constitute half canals, which remain open, even when the two wider sides of the œsophagus are pressed firmly against one another, and then become two canals leading into the stomach (Pl. 1. figs. 2, 5).

As the œsophageal grooves pass at the one end on to the œsophageal lappets, so they are bounded at the other end by two lip-like swellings, which enclose the oral angle : these are simply strongly-developed papillæ, which are also found in varying number on the oral margin, and indicate the ends of the longitudinal ridges rising between the smaller longitudinal furrows of the œsophagus. The Zoantheæ and Ilyanthidæ form an exception to what has been said ; the former have only one distinct œsophageal groove, whilst in the latter there are none worth mentioning. We meet here with differences, which are correlated with the structure and arrangement of the septa.

The septa are supporting plates formed of connective tissue, which are covered on both sides by endodermal epithelium, bear muscular fibres on both sides, and thus become very important organs for the contraction of the body. In those Actiniæ, which still preserve the most primitive structure of the septa, e.g., the genus Corallimorphus, we can distinguish only two systems of muscles ; the fibres run for the most part longitudinally on the one side, transversely on the other, forming in both cases a smooth, only slightly pleated layer. Considered more closely, the former spring from the pedal disk and the lower parts of the wall, and converge towards the œsophagus and central parts of the oral disk, whilst the latter arise from the whole length of the wall and are inserted into the oral disk and the œsophagus. In the majority of Actiniæ the longitudinal layer is differentiated by local, specially rich development of muscular fibres and repeated pleating into a special more or less sharply-defined muscle, the retractor, which projects to a varying extent above the surface of the septum, and shows many variations in the details of its constitution ; a second specialised but much weaker cord stretches along the wall, close to the origin of the septum. As the retractor in transverse section is placed on the septum like a pennon, Schneider and Rötteken have given it the name of "muscular pennon." On the other hand, the "parietobasilar" muscle is differentiated from the transverse muscles ; it lies in the angle between the pedal disk and wall, into which it projects with a crescentic margin, like the plica semilunaris in the corner of the eye. It extends to different distances up the wall and towards the central point of the pedal disk. It originates from the transverse muscular layer, by a process of pleating which is beautifully shown in *Leiotealia nymphæa*. As the muscular fold here still lies loosely on the septum, we can pass a needle into the pouch-like interspace. Apart from the parieto-basilar muscle, the transverse muscles are most strongly developed in the upper third of the body of the Actinia (Pl. II. fig. 6 ; Pl. IV. fig. 9 ; Pl. VII. figs. 5 and 12).

As the two surfaces of a septum differ from and are unequal to one another in the arrangement of the muscles, there are predispositions to a peculiar arrangement of the septa which, with few exceptions, is found in all Actiniæ, viz., that the septa are united in pairs, so that we cannot speak appropriately of single septa but of pairs of septa. The equivalent sides of the septa of the pair, *i.e.*, the sides in which the muscles run in the same direction, are turned towards each other. As a rule, it is the sides with the longitudinal muscles, and only in two pairs the sides with the transverse muscles. These two pairs of septa occupy a perfectly fixed position in the body of the Actinia, and may consequently be used for fixing direction, on which account we shall name them the "directive" septa. The directive septa correspond to the œsophageal grooves, and are fastened to the œsophagus from the oral angle downwards to the end of the lappets of the œsophagus. They constitute the principal reason why such stress should be laid on the form of the mouth, and they themselves contribute very essentially to a more clear expression of the biradially symmetrical character of the body of the Actinia.

The history of the development of the septa will help us to understand some further characteristics of their arrangement. We see from it that the septa of a pair have generally a common origin, and that only the first six pairs form an exception to this rule. The most recent researches show that the septa of the first six pairs appear independently and at different times, and that they become united secondarily in pairs ; as they are placed first, and according to a special principle, it is appropriate to distinguish them as "principal" septa from the others, the "accessory" septa. In some cases (in *Sagartia, Phellia*, &c.) they are permanently recognisable from the fact that they only are inserted into the œsophagus ; usually, however, this peculiarity is shared by numerous accessory septa, and they are then merely distinguished by their somewhat larger size. The difference of size may, however, be almost equalised, which makes the determination of the principal septa difficult. This is, however, made easier by the fact that the two pairs of directive septa also belong to the six pairs of principal septa.   These are easily found as they lie at the opposite ends of the oral fissure, and thereby furnish us a fixed point for the determination of directions.   The remaining four pairs of principal septa are distributed in the space in such a way that each two are found right and left from the oral fissure at equal distances from one another and from the directive septa.   The six pairs of principal septa form together a regular six-rayed star.

In an Actinia with the first six pairs or the first twelve septa, the space round the œsophagus is divided into twelve radial chambers, of which six lie inside the pairs and six between the adjacent pairs.   The former are the "intraseptal" spaces or "inner" spaces, the latter the "interseptal" spaces or "interspaces."   Whilst the inner spaces remain unaltered, the interspaces grow, and the accessory septa develop in them in pairs, and in an arrangement which will not undergo any change.   This definite arrangement may be shortly characterised as follows :—A pair of septa lie in the middle of each interseptal space : if we term the principal septa septa of the first order, or shortly, "primary septa," these are the six pairs of septa of the second order, or "secondary" septa.   They nearly equal the primary septa in size, and, except in the Sagartidæ, are fused with the œsophagus ; they divide the interseptal spaces into three parts : (1) an intraseptal space of the second order, and (2) two interseptal spaces of the second order.   Then follow twelve pairs of septa of the third order in the interspaces between the primary and secondary septa, twenty-four pairs of septa of the fourth order in the interseptal spaces so formed, and so on.   The septa usually decrease in size, for whilst the first, which arise from the pedal disk and from the wall, are inserted into the oral disk and the œsophagus, as far as the lower margin of the latter, the succeeding pairs gradually extend to a less distance down the œsophagus, then fail to reach it at all, and finally are attached only to the oral disk at a distance from its centre.   The same process is repeated at the pedal disk.   The older septa project nearly as far as the centre of the pedal disk, the younger only a little way inwards from the periphery.   As the size of the septa undergoes very gradual modification, we can merely place them in two categories, " imperfect " septa, which do not reach as far as the œsophagus, and "perfect" septa, which are fastened to the œsophagus.   After what has been already said, it is unnecessary to add that all the pairs of secondary septa have longitudinal muscles on the faces which are turned towards one another, and transverse muscles on the faces which are turned away from one another.

Methods of inquiry, differing according to the size of the animal, are to be recommended in order to recognise the above-mentioned conditions.   Small specimens may be examined in transverse sections taken through the œsophagus, by which we survey the whole arrangement of the septa at a single glance.   Care must be taken, however, that the section actually passes through the œsophagus and not somewhat through the oral disk, which in contracted animals often reaches deep down into the interior.   For example, it appears to me not improbable that v. Heider gave too high a number of complete septa in *Sagartia troglodytes,* because he mistook sections through the oral disk for sections through the œsophagus. To avoid such errors it is only needful to bear in mind that the oral disk has strong radial ectodermal or mesodermal muscles, whilst the œsophagus is almost always devoid of muscles on its ectodermal side. Oral disk and œsophagus can be also easily distinguished by the different character of the epithelium.

There are, however, numerous other difficulties attendant on the interpretation of transverse sections, as the principles of arrangement are often not visible from the large number of the septa which are pressed together and displaced by contraction. Such sections are, therefore, unadvisable in large forms, and especially in those of which we have only a single specimen at our disposal ; in these cases dissection with knives and scissors is preferable. For this purpose we find out the oral angle, and open the intraseptal space of a pair of directive septa by an incision into the œsophagus ; when we have cut through the base of the septum along the œsophagus, oral disk, wall and pedal disk, we have a fixed starting-point, and are then able to detach the septa pair by pair, and arrange them in series one after another. Any one at all versed in the matter will soon know from the size of the septa, from the distance of the directive septa, and from the way in which the septa follow one another, when he lights upon the next pair of principal septa : he then knows that he has examined one-sixth of the body, and does not require to investigate the remaining five-sixths, as the same formation is repeated in the usual forms of Actiniæ.

Another mode of preparation, which takes still less time, consists in detaching the pedal disk in such a way that the bases of the septa still remain in it. By this means we can easily see the arrangement of the septa, but not distinguish, however, how many of them are complete.

When we have separated and prepared the pairs of septa in the manner described, we also get a view of the distribution of the tentacles which are evaginations both of the intraseptal and the interseptal spaces. As a rule, each intraseptal space has only a single tentacle, while the number borne by the interspaces may be greater. This is by no means remarkable, as the interseptal spaces are seats of active growth. In those Actiniæ, in which there is a continual increase in the number of septa in the interspaces, there is also a continuous evagination of new tentacles, and as the formation of the latter precedes that of the former, it may happen that numerous tentacles are already present, whilst the septa belonging to them are either entirely wanting or their rudiments only perceptible. In *Antholoba,* for example, the innumerable tentacles of the umbrella margin belong chiefly to the interspaces (Pl. I. fig. 9).

Like the septa the tentacles differ in age, so that we can distinguish tentacles of the first, second, third order, &c. This often causes distinction in size, which is best seen in the Corallimorphidæ, where the entire arrangement of the septa is reflected in the size of the tentacles (Pl. II. figs. 1 and 3). The six largest tentacles belong to the primary intraseptal spaces, the next six, which are only a little smaller, to the secondary intraseptal, then follow the twelve tentacles of the tertiary intraseptal spaces which are visibly smaller, whilst the twenty-four last tentacles communicate with the interseptal spaces. The difference in the size of the tentacles is, however, rarely so marked as this, for a partial or complete equalisation in their size usually takes place at an early period of development.

When there are a large number of tentacles there is no room for them in a single row, but they are forced to form several rows, of which the inner are the oldest, the outer the youngest. All the tentacles of the same circle are essentially of the same size, but a difference in size may arise between different circles, which is shown by the innermost, and therefore oldest, tentacles being the largest, the outermost and youngest the smallest. If uniform growth take place in all parts of the body of the Actinia, the whole of the circles are arranged, as may often be seen, in multiples of six. For example, twelve tentacles of equal size form the innermost circle, if it be composed of tentacles of the first and second order ; twenty-four, if those of the third order be added to the number ; the next circle would then be occupied by the twelve or twenty-four succeeding tentacles of the sequence. There are often, however, numerous variations, caused by unequal growth in the different sextants ; for example, the tentacles of the third order may have advanced into the innermost circle in one sextant, whilst in another sextant they remain in the next circle. In this way it may happen that the arrangements of the tentacles and of the septa do not correspond completely, even though they are not directly contradictory, since the tentacles of a later order are, at all events, not larger than those of a preceding order. I only know one exception to this rule, *Polysiphonia tuberosa*, to the description of which I refer the reader.

Hitherto I have only spoken of tentacles which are placed on the margin, and which always remain equivalent to each other even when, changing their position for want of space, they have retreated on to the oral disk, and become apparently arranged in several rows. I have already placed these primary tentacles in opposition to the secondary tentacles, which are associated with the primary in the Corallimorphidæ (Pl. II. figs 1 and 3). They form a system in themselves, and are placed half-way between the peripheral and oral margins of the disk. They correspond only to the intraseptal spaces, and their size is graduated according to the age of the latter. The above-mentioned rule undergoes an exception here, as each intraseptal space communicates with two tentacles, a primary placed on the margin, and a secondary placed on the disk. The Corallimorphidæ are the only exceptions which I have observed, for the Cerianthidæ, which are usually described as Actiniæ with a double corona of tentacles, cannot be considered here because of the aberrant arrangement of their septa, which are not united in pairs, thus rendering the distinction between the intraseptal and interseptal spaces impossible.

The septa bear the reproductive organs, the mesenteric filaments, and in many families the acontia. During maturity the reproductive organs lie in the supporting plate composed of connective tissue. They form follicles of spermatozoa in the male, separate ova in the female, and both together in hermaphrodite individuals ; the youngest ova lie in the endodermal epithelium, which therefore represents the germinal layer, but even older eggs—at least this has been observed in several species—are still connected with the surface of the epithelium, either by means of a conical cord of protoplasm, or by means of a bundle of epithelial cells, at whose base a process of the ovum passes transversely through the supporting lamella.

The mesenteric filaments occupy the free margins of the septa, beginning at the upper end—at the œsophagus in the complete septa—and finishing at a little distance from the lower end. They are formed by the supporting lamella (Pl. V. fig. 5) splitting at the free margin into three laminæ, a middle and two lateral ; the former is covered by a streak of epithelial cells, principally glandular, the latter bear extremely fine, small ciliated cells. A visible cord of nervous fibres, which is entirely wanting in the ciliated streaks, runs along the base of the glandular streak. The character of the filament changes lower down, as the ciliated streaks with their supporting plate of connective tissue disappear, and the median glandular streak only remains.

The acontia (Pl. 1. figs. 4 and 5) are long filaments, kidney-shaped in transverse section, which spring from the septa at a little distance from the lower end of the mesenteric filaments, lie coiled in the stomach during a state of rest, and are ejected through special openings in the wall (cinclides), or through breaches in the wall, or through the oral opening, when the animal is irritated. Their component parts are : (1) an axial band of connective tissue, (2) an epithelium, chiefly composed of nematocysts, (3) nerves, and (4) muscular fibres lying between the basal ends of the epithelial cells (Pl. XII. fig. 10).

Finally, there are special openings in the septa which connect the separate divisions of the gastric space. There are two forms of such septal stomata. In nearly all Actiniæ we find openings which pierce the septa just where the latter touch the margin of the mouth, and which form together a species of peristomial canal ; the upper part of these openings is limited by the membrane of the oral disk, the remainder by the septa, so that they are shut off from direct contact with the œsophagus. More rarely there are other septal stomata, which lie close to the wall, about the junction of the first and second thirds of the body (Pl. VII. fig. 12).

I have hitherto described the anatomical conditions of the septa, as they may be observed in the hexamerous Actiniæ, and probably in all hexamerous corals. It would, however, be very erroneous to assume that what has been said applies to all forms hitherto included among the Hexacorallia ; we find, in fact, sundry variations, which I shall place under five different categories, though I do not presume to say that these exhaust all the variations presented in nature.

Among the first group I place those Actiniæ in which there are two pairs of directive septa, in which the remaining septa are grouped in pairs, but in which six is not the fundamental number for the arrangement of the septa, *e.g.*, *Sicyonis crassa* with sixty-four pairs of septa, and *Polyopis striata* with sixteen pairs. The two directive septa correspond to two distinct œsophageal grooves.

In the second group we find two pairs of directive septa, the single septa are constructed precisely as in the true Actiniæ, but, with the exception of the directive septa, are not united in pairs. I name *Edwardsia* as a type of this group.

In the third division, to which only a single species of those examined by me, *Scytophorus striatus*, belongs, the variation from the typical condition runs in the opposite direction. The paired arrangement of the septa is preserved, but one pair of directive septa is wanting (Pl. XIII. fig. 3).

In the fourth division we can clearly recognise a single œsophageal groove on the œsophagus; the septa inserted at the bottom of the groove may also be defined as directive septa, but it is not possible to point out on them the muscular arrangement found elsewhere. They agree, however, with the other septa, in so far as they have a thin layer of transverse muscular fibres on both sides. This is the case in *Cerianthus*. The fifth division is formed by the Zoanthidæ, in which the septa are paired, but partially in a rudimentary condition.

The plan which I have drawn up here, partly from the observations of others, but principally from my own earlier and later investigations, of the structure of the Actiniæ, allows me to make a few criticisms on the more important systems of Actiniæ already published.

Ehrenberg in his system of the Actiniæ, has made use first and foremost of the presence or absence of the sucking papillæ, then of the openings in the mural membrane, and, finally, of the form, length, and arrangement of the tentacles. The sucking papillæ recur in Gosse's system, though they are made of subordinate importance; they are described by him as hollow papillæ, furnished with a muscular apparatus, by which a vacuum is formed. I have entirely omitted the sucking papillæ in the general description of the anatomy of the Actiniæ, as I have never observed them, even in forms which were capable of incrusting themselves with foreign bodies. I am the more justified in doubting their existence, as Gosse has given no proofs verifying his assertions. Jourdan has lately described something like sucking papillæ in *Bunodes verrucosa*, his "verrues glandulaires," epithelial cones, consisting almost entirely of glandular cells, which press into the mesoderm, and partly form entirely or almost entirely detached mesodermal islands of cells. Here, however, we must consider the fact that, in the case of an extremely papillose surface, the depressions and sinuses between the papillæ may often resemble glands in transverse sections, taken through the wall. I have never been able to convince myself of the existence of glands in *Bunodes minuta*, which does not, however, refute the assertions as to their presence in *Bunodes verrucosa*. It is safer anyhow to consider the adhesion of foreign bodies as brought about, on the whole, not by means of sucking-cups, but by mucous cells, and nematocysts, and to entirely obliterate the sucking papillæ from the list of systematic characters.

With regard to the cinclides or pores of the wall, which are so extensively used not only by Ehrenberg (Abhandl. d. Berliner Acad., 1832, Phys. Cl., p. 225), but also by Gosse, and still more by Milne-Edwards, I need only repeat what has been already said. They are only distinct in a few forms, are questionable in most cases, and therefore form a characteristic which is practically of no great use. The tentacles form a much more important characteristic than the two already discussed, less on account of their form and size, on which Ehrenberg lays such stress, than on account of their arrangement and relation to the intraseptal spaces, which have hitherto only exceptionally been taken into consideration.

Ehrenberg's system was first essentially improved by Milne-Edwards and Gosse. Milne-Edwards added, to those already made use of by Ehrenberg, some new systematic characters, which undeniably indicated progress. The extended knowledge of species which had meantime been acquired rendered it necessary to take the different nature of the pedal disk in the Minyadinæ, Cerianthidæ, and Ilyanthidæ into account in the formation of the system ; we owe to a more exact anatomical knowledge the appreciation of the systematic value of the marginal spherules. On the other hand, it is difficult to understand how Milne-Edwards came to found two great groups, " actinines vulgaires " and " actinines verruqueuses," on such a character as the papillose or smooth nature of the surface of the body, which is in itself unimportant and in no case clearly marked. His mode of expression is by no means well chosen with regard to another point. When, for instance, Milne-Edwards divides the tentacles into retractile and non-retractile, he lays stress upon a secondary point, and overlooks the much more important behaviour of the upper margin of the wall which can be drawn over the oral disk in the former case but not in the latter. This varying action of the wall is the only point of importance, because it is anatomically founded on the structure of the circular muscle.

What I have said about Milne-Edwards is also true, on the whole, of Gosse, as the same distinguishing characters recur in his system, although he uses them in a different manner ; in consequence of this last circumstance the genera of Gosse and Milne-Edwards are often not co-extensive. A step in advance is made, inasmuch as Gosse takes into consideration in his descriptions the acontia, which he himself had discovered, but, on the other hand, the inconsistencies of which he is guilty lay the English naturalist open to the gravest criticism. How, for example, does it happen that the smooth wall not pierced by cinclides is made the most important character of the Antheadæ, and in spite of this the genus *Aiptasia*, which has been separated from other genera chiefly on account of the presence of cinclides and acontia, is placed in this family ? How can the genus *Phymactis*, whose diagnosis rests upon the character " skin warted," be placed among the Actiniadæ in which the wall ought to be smooth ?

The more recent naturalists who have given systematic surveys of the Actiniæ, and among them Fischer, Jourdan, Klunzinger (Korallthiere des rothen Meeres, Heft. i.), and above all Verrill (Proc. Elliot Soc., vi., Comm., p. 69), sometimes follow Milne-Edwards more closely, sometimes Gosse ; none of them have brought forward new or comprehensive points of view.

Although the existing systems of the Actiniæ undeniably require a complete re-modelling on a new foundation, I have refrained from this at present, as the material investigated by me was insufficient.   I only considered it absolutely needful to form some larger divisions anew, in order to express in some measure the conditions of relation-ship among the forms.   I have taken the structure and arrangement of the septa as the fundamental principle, and distinguish six tribes of Actiniaria : (1) Hexactiniæ, (2) Paractiniæ, (3) Monauleæ, (4) Edwardsiæ, (5) Zoantheæ, (6) Ceriantheæ.

I have followed Gosse as far as possible in fixing the limits of the families, but my great endeavour has been to define more sharply the meaningless characteristics hitherto in use, by bringing more emphatically forward the anatomical characteristics predomin-antly developed in the separate families, such, for example, as the nature of the septa and of the circular muscle, the presence of secondary tentacles and acontia (the latter may appropriately replace the cinclides), and the distribution of the reproductive organs. Thus, I have characterised the family of the Sagartidæ afresh, as I have laid down as essential that they should possess acontia and a mesodermal circular muscle, and that the six pairs of principal septa should be distinguished from the rest by being alone perfect, and not bearing reproductive organs.   I found these conditions in a whole series of forms belonging to the *Sagartiæ*, and if other species hitherto placed among them do not agree in these respects, it is impossible that they should remain in one and the same family.

As regards the definition of the species, I found myself in a difficult position.   All the specimens of the Challenger material before me were in a strongly contracted condition, so that I could only form a very imperfect idea of their natural shape.   Many of them were, moreover, injured in being detached from the underlying substance or by the dredging apparatus.   The colour had gone entirely, almost without exception, and the only information on this point was that given by Moseley about the few forms described by him in the Transactions of the Linnean Society.   Thus, nearly all the characteristics on which former authors based their diagnoses of species were wanting.   Verrill, who has a most comprehensive systematic knowledge of Actiniæ, declares that in such a case all specimens only known in a preserved condition are scientifically of no use ; he has therefore laid down as a fundamental principle, that only living forms, or those from which drawings have been taken in a living condition, can be utilised for accurate systematic description.

From this point of view, the Challenger material would have been, on the whole, of no use. Notwithstanding, I undertook to work it out, and extended my operations over nearly all the specimens, because, according to my opinion, Zoology ought never to take up a point of view, the effect of which would be that she must remain excluded from a large field of knowledge. In such cases it is rather the bounden duty of those who are working out the material to discover characteristics by which the recognition of the species is rendered possible, and this I believe I have achieved. Whoever keeps in view all the points taken into consideration in the description, the structure of the tentacles, of the septa, of the oral disk, of the circular muscle, &c., should find no difficulty or doubt in identifying a form with a living species, taking for granted that he has gained a correspondingly accurate anatomical knowledge of the latter.

In conclusion, let me add a few words as to the state of preservation in which the material for investigation was handed over to me. As all naturalists who have had much to do with Actiniæ know from personal experience, the animals are difficult to preserve, and require special attention in putting up. As such attention could not be devoted to them in the Challenger expedition, many of the Actiniæ did not fulfil the demands made by any kind of accurate histological investigation. I regret especially that many of the specimens had been first placed in chromic acid or chromate of potash, and then in alcohol. These were so dry and friable that they fell asunder like tinder under the slightest pressure; methodical dissection was therefore impossible, especially as even letting them lie for some time in water did not restore flexibility to the body. Preservation in chromic acid and chromate of potash must therefore be avoided, as it offers no advantages for histological investigation.

In many of the Actiniæ, hardened in alcohol, the inner parts were likewise macerated, perhaps because a large number had been placed in too small a quantity of alcohol, or because dilute alcohol had been used. Anyone collecting Actiniæ for examination ought to attend to the following points. In the first place, it is advisable to keep the animals separate till they are completely hardened, in order to prevent them from being flattened while soft by pressing against each other. If this be not done, not only the form but the sculpture of the surface suffers, which was often the case in the Challenger material. In the second place, it is advisable to syringe the inside of the animal with alcohol, placing the nozzle of the syringe through the mouth, or through a hole made in the wall or the pedal disk. On the other hand, cutting or even halving of the living animal is to be objected to, as in that case it is impossible to avoid the destruction of many of the septa, and the parts will be displaced much more than in the ordinary contraction of the animal.

In order to fulfil all requirements exactly, the Actinia before being preserved should be subjected to a process which paralyses the muscles, such as has been previously described by my brother and myself. This, however, requires more time and care than can usually be bestowed by the collector on a single object.

DESCRIPTION OF SPECIES.

ACTINIARIA or MALACODERMATA.

Polyps with simple unpinnated tentacles and with septa, the number of which is usually a multiple of six ; without skeleton. Body moving freely or adhering to supporting substances by means of suction of the pedal disk, rarely firmly fixed. Animals usually solitary, rarely forming colonies.

In the foregoing diagnosis I have placed the nature of the tentacles first as the only thoroughly positive characteristic of the group ; it is by this that the Actiniæ are distinguished from the Anthozoa with pinnated tentacles, the Alcyonaria or Octactiniæ. I have been obliged to place second, and to limit the value of the hexamerous arrangement of the septa, to which the chief importance was formerly attached, as the number of the forms in which no settled number or even another number than six is the foundation of the distribution of the septa is continually increasing. I have included the want of the skeleton in the diagnosis, and therefore separated the Actiniæ from the Corals, for practical reasons ; the division is not a natural one. There can, however, be no doubt, and this has been settled for some forms by observations, e.g., for *Caryophyllia cyathus* and *Madrepora variabilis* by G. v. Koch (Morphol. Jahrb., Bd. v., p. 316, 1880), that many Corals have the septal arrangement of the Hexactiniæ, and therefore approach this first section of the Actiniaria more closely than the remaining sections, the Paractiniæ, Edwardsiæ, Zoanatheæ, and Ceriantheæ.

Tribe I. HEXACTINIÆ.

Actiniaria with paired septa. The septa of each pair are usually provided with transverse muscular fibres on those faces which are turned from one another and longitudinal muscular fibres on those faces which are turned towards one another, with the exception of two pairs of directive septa, which are placed opposite one another, and have longitudinal muscles on the faces turned from one another, and transverse muscles on the faces turned towards one another. The number of the pairs of septa is at least six, usually more, and then increasing in multiples of six. Mouth fissure-shaped ; œsophagus with two œsophageal grooves and two œsophageal lappets.

Ehrenberg had the Hexactiniæ and the Corals connected with them in view when he separated his *Zoocorallia polyactinia* with more than twelve radii from the eight-rayed Octactiniæ. In the same way only they can lay claim to the name Hexacorallia bestowed on them by Hæckel (Generelle Morphologie, Bd. ii., 1866). As they form the principal part of the Actiniæ, they have long been taken as types for the remainder. After Hæckel had detached *Cerianthus* by reason of the observations on its development made by Jules Haime, my brother and I pointed out the varying position of the Zoanatheæ and

Edwardsiæ. The examination of the Challenger material has further confirmed the correctness of this view, but shows at the same time that the number of the varying types is by no means exhausted.

Most corals will doubtless be placed later on with the Hexactiniæ; perhaps a natural division into forms having a skeleton and forms without skeleton may not be possible, as even the closer limitation of the Hexactiniæ given here does not exclude the possibility of many of their families having more affinity to single families of corals than to other Hexactiniæ. At all events it is advisable to keep this possibility in view in investigating corals.

I shall discuss the families in an ascending series, according to the grade of their organisation, and shall define the latter from two points of view. An Actinia is placed lower down in the scale (1) the more uniformly the parts of the body are developed, (2) the smaller the degree of histological differentiation. The first point requires us to consider how far the septa resemble one another, how far the reproductive organs are uniformly distributed, and so forth. From the second point we must keep in view the nature of the muscular system ; is it preponderately ectodermal, endodermal, or mesodermal, is there a circular muscle present and to what degree is it developed ? Further, I consider the presence of the acontia, the cinclides, and the "bourses marginales" as tokens of a higher organisation. Taken from this point of view, the Corallimorphidæ are the lowest in every respect, the Sagartidæ and Amphianthidæ the highest.

Family, CORALLIMORPHIDÆ, R. Hertwig.

Hexamerous Actiniæ with a double corona of tentacles, a corona of marginal principal tentacles, and a corona of intermediate accessory tentacles. Septa slightly differentiated, all furnished with reproductive organs. Muscular system weak in all parts of the body. No circular muscle.

Corallimorphus, Moseley.

Corallimorphus, Moseley, 1877, Trans. Linn. Soc., ser ii., Zool., vol. i. p. 299.

Marginal and intermediate tentacles knobbed and distinguished from one another by their size. The largest tentacles correspond to the first cycle of septa, the smallest to the last cycle of septa and to the interseptal spaces ; no terminal tentacle-openings (perforations through the extremities of the tentacles, see p. 8).

The family Corallimorphidæ is at present represented only by a single genus, *Corallimorphus*, which was founded by Moseley for deep-sea Actiniæ shortly after the conclusion of the voyage of the Challenger, and divided into two species, *Corallimorphus rigidus* and *Corallimorphus profundus*. It was considered most closely allied to Leuckart's genus *Discosoma* (Rüppell, Reise im nordl. Africa, 1828), and characterised as follows :— " Body rigid, smooth, gelatinous, not contractile, without pores, but with an adherent base ; disk circular and large ; tentacles non-retractile, elongate, conical, with a rounded terminal knob, of several sizes, disposed in regular series at the margin of the disk, and in two circlets on its surface."

Setting aside such characters in this definition as are common to many Actiniæ, and are therefore only of secondary value for differential diagnosis, the following points remain :—(1) The stiffness and slight contractility of the body, (2) the knobbed nature of the tentacles, (3) their distribution in several series. I attach special importance to the second and third characters, but the third requires to be more clearly defined, for it often happens in the Actiniæ that some of the tentacles have migrated inwards, far on to the disk, and are separated by a broad interspace from the marginal tentacles ; Moseley has not taken into account a characteristic in the position of the tentacles which distinguishes the Corallimorphidæ from nearly all true Actiniæ, viz., that two tentacles, a marginal and an intermediate, communicate with the same intraseptal space. The intermediate tentacles thus acquire special value, as they have not merely been pushed by growth from the margin towards the centre, but may be considered as new formations of independent origin. They are therefore distinctly opposed to the marginal tentacles, have no homology with anything in most other Hexactiniæ, and consequently deserve the special designation of " accessory" tentacles.

In considering the tentacles we must not forget their varying size, especially as it reveals at the first glance the whole arrangement of the body of the Actinia. Of the marginal tentacles six are the largest, and are distributed at equal distances, then follow six more the next in size, which halve the interspaces between the first six, then twelve which come in the interspaces between the first six and the second six, and so on. This also holds good for the intermediate accessory tentacles, so that we can speak of tentacle cycles of the first, second, and third orders which completely correspond to the cycles of septa. The equalisation of the tentacles, which is elsewhere met with, has not made its appearance, and the arrangement according to cycles, which must be regarded as a primitive condition, still predominates.

An equally primitive condition is shown in the distribution of the reproductive elements over all the septa, in the indistinctness of the œsophageal grooves on the œsophagus, and in the slight differentiation of the muscular system in all parts of the body. The transverse and the longitudinal muscles form a uniform, hardly even slightly pleated layer on the septa, so that both the strong retractor and the parietobasilar muscle are still wanting ; the muscular layers on the oral disk and the tentacles are smooth, and there is not the least indication of a special circular muscle. All this explains the small capacity for movement in our animal, which is, moreover, due to the nature of the supporting substance, which by its toughness reminds us of cartilage, and is richly developed in the septa, the oral disk, and the wall.

The close relationship of the Corallimorphidæ to *Discosoma*, which Moseley declared probable, undeniably exists. Verrill was the first to point out (Proceedings Elliot Soc., vi., Communications, p. 69) what was corroborated by Klunzinger (Korallthiere des rothen Meeres, Heft i. p. 82, 1877), that the numerous tentacles, which in *Discosoma* (Verrill and Klunzinger) and in the allied *Homactis* and *Stephanactis* (Verrill) are always united in a radial series or a group, are connected with the same radial chamber. The circular muscle seems also wanting in *Discosoma*, as the animal is not able to draw the wall over the oral disk. We might therefore incorporate the genus *Corallimorphus* with Verrill's sub-family the Discostominæ, were it not for the difference that the secondary tentacles in *Corallimorphus* are limited to a single corona, whilst in the Discostominæ they appear in larger and variable numbers. This greater regularity indicates an essentially higher grade of organisation in the Corallimorphidæ.

We must likewise bear in mind an affinity between the Corallimorphidæ and Allmann's genus *Corynactis* (Ann. Mag. Nat. Hist., ser. i., vol. xvii. p. 417), as in the latter the tentacles end in a roundish head and are partly intermediate, partly marginal. Many might also consider as points of affinity the facts that in both genera the nematocysts attain an extraordinary size, that both genera recall the skeleton-forming Zoantharia, and that the nature of the mesoderm is the same in both. The cardinal point only remains open to discussion. Are the intermediate tentacles secondary tentacles, which share the intraseptal parts with the marginal tentacles, or have they merely been forced by growth from the periphery towards the centre? This question cannot be settled by studying either the drawings or the descriptions given by Allmann, Gosse, Klunzinger, and others. Verrill also, who placed the genus *Corynactis* among the Discosomidæ, considered it as probable, but certainly not proved by actual observation that several tentacles are evaginated from each radial chamber.

Finally, it may not be superfluous to lay stress on this fact, that the double corona of tentacles does not justify us in assuming any connection between the Corallimorphidæ and the Cerianthidæ, which also have a circle of accessory tentacles in the periphery of the mouth; for what turns the scale in the definition of the grade of relationship is that the Cerianthidæ have not yet attained to the characteristic paired arrangement of the septa.

As at present there is only one genus in the whole family, it depends upon the degree of importance assigned to the special characters, whether we consider them to be characteristic of the genus merely or of the whole family. The most important undeniably are the double corona of tentacles, the equal distribution of the reproductive elements, and the absence of the circular muscle, and for this reason I have included these points in the diagnosis of the family.

Corallimorphus rigidus (Pl. II. figs. 1 and 4–6; Pl. IX. 11, 12; Pl. XII. 1–7).

Corallimorphus rigidus, Moseley, 1877, Trans. Linn. Soc., ser. ii., Zool., vol. i. p. 301.

Number of the intermediate tentacles twenty-four, of the marginal forty-eight. Origins of the septa, in the lower third of the wall and outer third of the pedal disk, shown by swollen thickenings of the supporting plate.

Habitat.—(*a*) Station 146. December 29, 1873. Lat. 46° 46' S., long. 45° 31' E. Depth, 1375 fathoms. Three specimens. (*b*) Station 157. March 3, 1874. Lat. 53° 55' S., long. 108° 35' E. Depth 1950 fathoms. One specimen. (*c*) Station 195. October 3, 1874. Lat. 4° 21' S., long. 129° 7' E. Depth, 1425 fathoms. One specimen.

Colour.—Not recognisable in *a*; blue-violet in *b* (determined from a spirit specimen); pale reddish-yellow in *c* (determined by Moseley in the fresh condition).

Dimensions.—Height, 1–2 cm.; breadth of the oral disk, 2·5–6 cm.; of the pedal disk, 1·5–6 cm.

The specimen on which Moseley founded his characteristics of the species *Corallimorphus rigidus* was not among the material handed over to me for investigation. He states that it came from a depth of 1425 fathoms, and was taken between the Banda Islands and Amboyna on October 3, 1874. On the other hand, two other bottles contained Corallimorphidæ, which answered, on the whole, to Moseley's description. The differences were merely those of colour and form, which might be easily caused by preservation and by difference of age, so that I considered it best to determine these specimens as *Corallimorphus rigidus*. I found one specimen in a bottle marked "Station 157; March 3, 1874; 1950 fathoms," which also contained a *Cereus spinosus*, and in another bottle—"Station 146; December 29, 1873; 1375 fathoms,"—there were three specimens, along with a number of other Actiniæ. The first specimen was admirably preserved, and therefore formed the principal object of my investigation. I shall deal with it exclusively in what follows, recurring at the conclusion to the variations in the three other specimens.

The body of the animal is discoid, as the pedal disk and oral disk are of equal size (6 cm.), and lie exactly parallel, whilst the height does not amount to more than 2 cm. The tentacles are deep blue-violet, the remainder of the body paler and even whitish in some parts.

The pedal disk (fig. 5) is furnished with forty-eight equally distinct radial furrows, which are limited to the outer third, and gradually become shallower as they run inwards; they do not correspond to the insertions of the septa, but to the interseptal spaces between them. The margin of the pedal disk and lower part of the wall is slightly inverted and indented, in such a way that an indentation comes in the interspace between each two radial furrows.

The points at which the septa are inserted in the wall (fig. 4) are recognisable by longitudinal furrows only half-way up the middle part; they are otherwise covered by pad-like thickenings, which are placed near the base in such a way that the furrow between each two pads occupies the middle between the insertions of two septa. Moseley also describes these pads, but gives them a different position, as he terms them "smooth, slightly projecting, rounded ridges or costæ, corresponding in position to the intervals between the attachments of the mesenteries." The conditions differ somewhat near the oral disk. Here there is a broad circular swelling, which is traversed by a number of longitudinal furrows. All the swellings of the wall and of the pedal disk are caused by thickenings of the supporting substance.

The oral disk is smooth and very firm. Moseley has given a perfectly correct account of the manner in which the tentacles are distributed on the oral disk. The principal tentacles are placed on the margin, exactly where the oral disk and the wall meet at right angles. Among these are six tentacles, recognisable on closer observation as the largest, which are disposed at equal distances, two of them, occupying the ends of the sagittal diameter, running through the corners of the mouth. The next six tentacles stand in the middle of the interspaces between the first six, which they nearly equal in size. On the other hand, there is a noticeable difference of size between the last-named six tentacles and the twelve following, and further between these twelve and the twenty-four tentacles composing the last cycle. Whilst, therefore, there are in all forty-eight marginal tentacles, the number of the intermediate tentacles only amounts to twenty-four, which are distributed in three circles. Six tentacles, furthest in and nearest the oral opening, are placed upon the same radii with the six marginal tentacles of the first order; six others follow a little further out, and twelve others still further out, the former of which correspond to the marginal tentacles of the second, the latter to those of the third order. The first-named six are the largest, but even they are hardly so large as the smallest among the marginal tentacles.

All the tentacles are knobbed, and therefore consist of a stalk and an expanded vesicular end. The stalk is stiff and thick-walled, and bears a very thin layer of ectodermal longitudinal and endodermal circular muscular fibres. The head is thin-walled, without muscles, and not pierced by a terminal opening.

The oral opening and the œsophagus are very small. The fissure-like form, usually so distinct, is hardly recognisable, and has therefore been overlooked by Moseley. On closer examination, however, we find even here the two oral angles and œsophageal grooves, which differ very little from the numerous indentations of the oral margin and the longitudinal furrows running out from them. The corners of the mouth and of the œsophagus are more closely defined anatomically by the insertions of the directive septa.

There are altogether twenty-four pairs of septa : the first six, the principal septa, and the following six, secondary septa, are fastened to the œsophagus, even though the latter do not reach so far down as the former ; the remaining twelve are imperfect. All the septa are plates of equal strength, which is essentially due to the thickness of the supporting lamella. The muscular system is extremely weak and simply arranged, as transverse fibres run on the one side and longitudinal fibres on the other in what is hardly even a slightly pleated layer. Septal stomata are wanting also in the complete septa (fig. 6).

The ovary, an oval body consisting merely of few broad transverse folds, lies in the middle of each septum, not excepting the directive septa. The excellent state of preservation allowed of a detailed histological examination, which on the one hand confirmed the view already put forward as to the endodermal origin of the reproductive organs, and on the other threw new light on the nature of the filamental apparatus.

The youngest ovicells are placed on the margins of the ovary, especially on the lower and upper; they were unmistakably recognisable as ova from the size of 9 μ upwards, and then consisted almost entirely of the nucleus, surrounded by a thin mantle of protoplasm. They lie between the bases of the epithelial cells, distinctly still outside the supporting lamella, often united in small groups. So far *Corallimorphus* confirmed what had already been observed in *Calliactis* (*Sagartia*) *parasitica* (Actinien, p. 88); but, on the other hand, it was a new condition, that relatively large ova, measuring from 40–50 μ in longitudinal diameter, were still found in the endoderm; since they were almost as long as the epithelial cells, one end reached nearly as far as the surface. Twice I observed one of these larger cells, which was clearly in the act of migrating into the mesoderm (figs. 2 and 3). It had an amœboid, hour-glass-shaped, constricted body, of which one end lay in the epithelium, the other in the mesoderm; the nucleus was mostly in the latter, but the point of it projected into the former.

The ovicells enclosed in the mesoderm all appeared to me to have, from the first, the filamental apparatus, though in different stages of development. In the largest, almost mature ovicells (fig. 7), it is a conical body, whose base rests on the surface of the ovum. It likewise lies in the mesoderm, and its extreme point only reaches to the base of the epithelium: in this way it is distinguished from the formation of the same name in *Calliactis*, which belongs to the epithelium itself, and even projects as far as its upper surface. The distinction is of no importance, and is clearly owing to the different development of the connective tissue, which is very visible in *Corallimorphus*, whilst in *Calliactis* it is so scanty that the ovicells lie close to one another, and only a delicate supporting framework remains when they are taken away.

A second difference is of greater importance. In *Calliactis* it was not possible to distinguish nuclei in the filamental apparatus, which thus showed itself to be a differentiation of the ovum itself, whilst its cellular structure is very distinct in *Corallimorphus*. The apparatus consists of filament-shaped cells, carrying their nuclei on the base resting on the ovicell. Preparations stained with carmine showed us here a corona of oval bodies coloured red. It is possible that, in spite of all trouble taken, I did not succeed in finding out the nuclei in *Calliactis*, because I was working with osmium preparations, in which the nuclei often are difficult to colour. I might, however, have had to deal with different stages of differentiation of the structure, and this is corroborated by the following observations on the development of the apparatus in *Corallimorphus*.

Young ovicells have a single finely striated process, piercing the supporting lamella, by which they are fastened on the base of the epithelium. The epithelium is modified in a peculiar fashion at the point in question; whilst it is elsewhere overloaded with roundish granules and shows an irregular distribution of its nuclei, its cells here become fine filaments, reminding us of sense cells, which are thickest in the middle where they bear their nucleus. They form a body which may be best compared in shape to a gustatory bulb of the mammalia ; it is broad in the middle, but pointed above towards the surface of the epithelium and below towards the junction with the process of the ovum. This constitution of the filamental apparatus is rather a transition to *Calliactis*; it seems to me to indicate that the process of the ovicell only corresponds to the fibrous cord in *Calliactis*, whilst the modified epithelial cells compose a newly added constituent.

The transition into the final condition can be followed in different ovicells, step by step, through all the stages (fig. 6). Whilst the process of the ovicell is contracted, the epithelial cells penetrate the supporting substance. Their body, therefore, still lies with the nucleus in the epithelium. The nuclei gradually migrate ; we first see only a few on the surface of the ovicell, later on the number increases till we have the appearance described above.

The peripheral part of the gastric cavity is divided by the twenty-four pairs of septa into twenty-four intraseptal and twenty-four interseptal spaces. Twenty-four intermediate tentacles and twenty-four marginal tentacles are connected with the former, but only twenty-four marginal tentacles, and these the smallest, with the latter. Two tentacles, an intermediate and a marginal, consequently belong to each intra-space. (Pl. II. fig. 6, shows an open intraseptal space with the two tentacles belonging to it.)

The three other specimens of *Corallimorphus rigidus* were taken at another date (29th December 1873), and in a different place, at a depth of 1375 fathoms ; and as the animal observed by Moseley belonged to a third locality, it appears that these Actiniæ are very widely distributed in the great depths.

There was little indication of the natural colouring in any of the three animals, as their yellowish-brown hue was certainly referable to the change caused by the spirit. They were all distinctly smaller ; one, plainly a very young specimen, was only 1 cm. high, 2·5 cm. broad at the oral disk, and 1·5 cm. at the pedal disk. It had forty-eight marginal tentacles arranged in the order already described ; on the other hand, there were only twelve intermediate tentacles, the remaining twelve belonging to the third cycle being still wanting. There were eight intermediate tentacles of the third cycle in the specimen next in size, and ten in the third specimen. The last showed also most striking irregularities in the number of the marginal tentacles, of which forty-two only were observable.

The pad-like thickenings were wanting on the wall, and the insertion lines of the septa were consequently plainly indicated externally only by longitudinal furrows ; in this respect the three specimens deviate from the typical *Corallimorphus rigidus* and approach *Corallimorphus profundus*. The histological character of the supporting substance also varies. In *Corallimorphus* the cartilage-like consistency is caused by a homogeneous matrix, which is richly excreted, and within which traces of a fibrous tissue may still be recognised. In the specimen first described from Station 157 the fibrous mass is indistinct (Pl. IX. fig. 11); on the other hand, in the last-named three specimens (fig. 12) it is very distinct and sharply separated from the homogeneous fundamental substance, so that the latter forms a special layer contiguous to the endoderm.

Numerous small, ramified cells are scattered in the supporting lamella; some of these contained vacuoles and a single space, filled with fluid, and surrounded by a thin protoplasmic layer containing the nucleus. The vesicles of the cells were large and numerous in the first specimen, but easily overlooked in the others, as they were rarely met with and small in diameter.

The last-named diversity may be explained by admitting that the specimens are of different ages, an admission which is supported by the difference in size, and which may also explain differences in the muscular system, viz., that the ectodermal muscular layer is a smooth lamella in the three smaller specimens, whilst in the larger one it is finely folded. It is, however, advisable, under existing circumstances, to include all the four individuals under the same name.

Finally, the specimen described by Moseley had a somewhat different shape, inasmuch as the pedal disk was only half as large as the oral disk, so that the side walls of the body diverged as in an inverted cone. But as it had the longitudinal swellings on the wall described above, and the number and arrangement of the tentacles were exactly the same as in the specimen on which my description is founded, I did not consider it to the purpose to divide the material into two species.

Corallimorphus profundus, Moseley (Pl. II. figs. 2 and 3).

Corallimorphus profundus, Moseley, 1877, Trans. Linn. Soc., ser. ii., Zool., vol. i. p. 300.

Number of the intermediate tentacles limited to twelve, number of the marginal tentacles, forty-eight. Mural membrane marked by longitudinal furrows corresponding to the insertions of the septa.

Habitat.—(*a*) Station 293. November 1, 1875. Lat. 39° 4' S., long. 105° 5' W. Depth, 2025 fathoms. One specimen. (*b*) Station 300. December 17, 1875. Lat. 33° 42' S., long. 78° 18' W. Depth, 1375 fathoms. One specimen.

Colour.—(Described from life by Moseley) in *b*, ochre-yellow, with dark radial madder-coloured streaks, which are wanting in *a*.

Dimensions.—Height, 0·8 and 2·5 cm.; breadth of the oral disk, 3·2 and 7·0 cm.; of the pedal disk, 1·7 and 4·5 cm.

The characteristics by which *Corallimorphus profundus* is distinguished from *Corallimorphus rigidus* are of a subordinate nature, so that I can include them in a short description. Moreover, I had before me only the two specimens upon which Moseley has founded the species.

According to Moseley, the colour is ochre-yellow, the large specimen having darker madder-coloured radial streaks, of which traces were still visible. The base of the animal was hollowed into a cavity, and enclosed a stone to which it was attached. The insertions of the septa shone through it as white lines. The margin by which the base passes into the mural membrane is indented, the wall itself furrowed longitudinally; the number of furrows and indentations amounted to fifty. The oral disk is also furrowed, though irregularly, in a radial direction, and has the small but distinctly fissure-shaped opening in the centre.

Whilst the septa and reproductive organs show nothing new, the tentacles furnish an important characteristic by which to distinguish *Corallimorphus profundus* from *Corallimorphus rigidus*. This does not apply to the marginal principal tentacles, which are likewise present to the number of forty-eight, and are also distinguished by their different sizes, but to the intermediate accessory tentacles ; these are limited to twelve, and clearly never go normally beyond this number, as one of the specimens examined was larger than the largest specimen of *Corallimorphus rigidus*. In that one of the two animals which furnished the drawing fig. 3 there was a small variation from what I have laid down as typical, which, however, may be regarded as abnormal. As Moseley observed, the number of the marginal tentacles has been increased by four, and amounts to fifty-two ; instead of six secondary tentacles, halving the interspaces of the primary, there are seven secondary tentacles, one more than usual in one of the interspaces. It therefore follows that the twelve tertiary tentacles are increased by one, and the twenty-four quaternary by two, making on the whole four tentacles more. An increased growth has taken place in one of the sextants, which is shown also by the intermediate secondary tentacles ; the sextant in question likewise contains two secondary tentacles of the second order, of which one, the supernumerary tentacle, is so small that Moseley has quite overlooked it.

Moseley describes the reproductive organs, of which he draws twelve, as brownish bodies showing visibly behind the thin wall. As there are twenty-four pairs of septa, all of which bear reproductive organs, the number of the latter amounts to forty-eight.

Family, ANTHEOMORPHIDÆ, Hertwig.

Hexactiniæ, with slightly developed muscular system, and long, slightly contractile tentacles, without any circular muscles (tentacles consequently non-retractile) ; reproductive organs present on all the septa ; numerous complete septa ; accessory tentacles wanting.

I have associated under the name Antheomorphidæ Actiniæ, which resemble in many respects the following family, the Antheadæ. Like the latter they have long tentacles, of which the muscles are but slightly developed, and which are consequently capable of a small amount of contraction, and they are also unable to draw the upper margin of the wall over the oral disk. The most important difference between the two families is, that in the Antheomorphidæ incapacity for protecting the oral disk is caused by complete want of the circular muscle, whilst in the Antheadæ it is owing to the muscle being only slightly developed.

The Antheomorphidæ are easily distinguished from the Corallimorphidæ by the absence of the intermediate secondary tentacles; in other respects the grade of development is the same in both families. The principal tentacles form a single corona, which exactly occupies the point of junction of the oral disk and the mural membrane. The muscular layers of the oral disk and of the septa are hardly pleated at all. The reproductive organs are developed on all the septa.

Besides the species described two other species should perhaps be added to this family, but these were unfortunately not sufficiently well preserved to allow of detailed examination. I have therefore inscribed them on the roll of doubtful forms under the names of *Porponia elongata* and *Porponia robusta*.

Antheomorphe, n. gen.

Antheomorphidæ with a corona of tentacles placed in a single row; tentacles of different sizes decreasing according to the orders; wall smooth.

Antheomorphe elegans, n. sp. (Pl. I. fig. 8).

Twenty-four extremely long marginal tentacles of different sizes, the six largest corresponding to the six pairs of principal septa, the six middle to the six pairs of septa of the second order, the twelve last to the interseptal spaces.

Habitat.—Station 244. June 28, 1875. Lat. 35° 22′ N., long. 169° 53′ E. Depth, 2900 fathoms. Three specimens.

Dimensions.—Height, 1·5–2·0 cm.; breadth, 1·5–3·0 cm.

The three specimens upon which I founded the erection of the new genus and new species were unfortunately not well preserved, so that I had almost to desist from any examination of the inner parts, such as the septa with their muscular system. On the other hand, the general form of the body was very well preserved.

The animals had been dredged from the depth of 2900 fathoms, and were attached to stones by their extended bases. In the largest specimen the diameter of the base amounted to 3 cm., whilst the height of the cylindrical body was only 2 cm., and the diameter of the oral disk again 3 cm. The lines of origin of the septa shone distinctly through the wall as twenty-four streaks; these passed on to the oral disk, which was somewhat raised and thickened in the periphery of the mouth. In one specimen the mouth even rose like a proboscis above the upper surface of the peristome.

The twenty-four tentacles are of extraordinary length compared with the size of the animal; the largest of them are 3-5 cm. long, whilst the smallest are only 1·5-2·0 cm., the six others being of medium length. The tentacles have precisely the same arrangement as in the Corallimorphidæ, so that the largest of them correspond to the intraseptal spaces of the primary septa, the six following to the intraseptal spaces of the secondary septa, and the twelve smallest communicate with the remaining interseptal spaces in the periphery of the œsophagus.

We may therefore assuredly assume, from this distribution of the tentacles, that the septa are arranged exactly on the same principle as in the other Hexactiniæ. This is corroborated by the distinct presence of two oral angles in the mouth, and two œsophageal furrows on the œsophagus. I was, however, only able, from personal observation, to ascertain that the septa are arranged in pairs, and that all the twenty-four bore reproductive organs.

The muscular system is nowhere mesodermal, the muscular lamellæ are, moreover, nowhere thickly pleated, either in the septa or in the tentacles and oral disk. The circular muscle is consequently entirely wanting.

Family, ANTHEADÆ, Gosse.

Hexactiniæ with long marginal tentacles and slightly developed endodermal circular muscle (so that the oral disk cannot be covered at all, or only incompletely); numerous septa, reaching for the most part up to the œsophagus, distinguished only by their size, and all (?) furnished with reproductive organs.

The family of the Antheadæ, of which the well-known *Anthea cereus* is the typical representative, was erected by Gosse. Owing, however, to my having limited it here on the basis of a more exact anatomical definition, it differs in extent from that given in Gosse's well-known work. On the one hand, I have separated from it the genus *Aiptasia*, which has acontia and cinclides, following Verrill, who was the first to declare this necessary (Comm. Essex Inst., vol. v. p. 322, 1866-7), whilst, on the other hand, I have no hesitation in incorporating in this family the Actiniæ with rough surface of the body, inasmuch as they fulfil the above-mentioned conditions, whilst Gosse considers the smooth surface of the wall as the most important characteristic.

According to my own observations, *Anthea cereus* has marginal spherules, though these do not strike the eye by their bright colours, so that we cannot separate the Antheadæ from the Actinidæ furnished with marginal spherules, on account of absence of these formations; it therefore becomes a question whether it would not be more to the purpose to follow Verrill and unite the two families (Trans. Connect. Acad., vol. i. p. 491, 1867-71). As my own experience has shown that the nature of the circular muscle in *Actinia mesembryanthemum* approaches that in *Anthea cereus,* I am inclined to answer the question in the affirmative. In the meantime, however, we have no accurate anatomical studies of this most abundant Anthozoon.

All Antheadæ are easily recognised by their habit of body. As Verrill has already specially remarked, the first thing which strikes the eye is the numerous, extremely long tentacles, which spring from the junction of the wall and the oral disk. Their longitudinal muscles are slightly pleated, and lie in the ectoderm, as they do also in the oral disk. The circular muscle may easily be overlooked, as it is very small, and merely consists of a few folds of the circular muscular layer of the wall; hence the Antheadæ are either incapable of drawing the wall over the oral disk, or can only do so slightly, and then very slowly. The septa are very uniform, and the majority reach the œsophagus, so that only the youngest and smallest are imperfect. Whether, as I presume, they are all furnished with reproductive organs or not remains to be proved by further investigations, as I have hitherto only examined immature animals.

Comactis, Milne-Edwards.

Antheadæ with smooth body surface, with marginal spherules, which lie on a fold running outside the corona of tentacles.

Comactis flagellifera, Milne-Edwards (Pl. III. fig. 5; Pl. VI. fig. 6; Pl. VIII. fig. 9)

Actinia flagellifera, Drayton, in Dana Explor. Exped., Zooph., p. 126, pl. i. fig. 1, 1846.
Comactis flagellifera, Milne-Edwards, Hist. d. Corall., tom. i. p. 236, 1857.
Comactis flagellifera, Verrill, Comm. Essex. Inst., vol. v. p. 323, 1867.

Marginal spherules on a fold, which is separated from the tentacles by a circular depression. Tentacles moderately long, with distinct terminal opening, placed in two to three rows. Body discoid.

Habitat.—Simon's Bay, Cape of Good Hope. Depth, 25 fathoms. One specimen.

Dimensions.—Height, 0·5 cm.; breadth, 1·5–2·0 cm.

The small Actinia, which I define with some reserve as *Comactis flagellifera*, came from Simon's Bay, Cape of Good Hope, where it was dredged at the insignificant depth of 25 fathoms. As no trace of reproductive organs could be found even on minute investigation, it was, at all events, an immature animal, so that the above assertion as to size cannot be considered as the standard for characterising the species.

The wall is smooth, for although the surface in the specimen before me was repeatedly wrinkled, both transversely and longitudinally, this was plainly owing merely to the high degree of contraction of the animal. There are, moreover, two very distinct circular constrictions, a lower one caused by the action of the parietobasilar muscle, which divides the body into two equal parts, and an upper one lying close under the tentacles, and caused by the circular muscle which runs there. Outside the latter the wall-membrane forms a circular fold, with numerous small evaginations on its edge. These correspond to the intraseptal and interseptal spaces, and must be compared to the marginal spherules, which are found in the same situation in *Actinia mesembryanthemum*, and are conspicuous by their splendid colour ; they are, however, not so richly furnished as in the above-named Actinia with the strongly refractive nematocysts, which Rötteken, Schneider, and Duncan (Proc. Roy. Soc., London, vol. xxii. p. 263) held to be retinal rods, and were thus led to regard the marginal spherules as eyes.

The circular muscle (Pl. VI. fig. 6) is not visible to the naked eye, as it is very weak, and may be easily overlooked even under the microscope. The endodermal circular muscular layer is only folded a little more thickly than at other points, and shows three to four larger and a few smaller dendritic figures in transverse section. The folded muscular lamellæ, which are supported by relatively strong connective substance, project towards the gastric space, and are not enclosed in the connective substance of the wall, and in this way an insignificant circular swelling is formed. The nature of the circular muscle as described above furnishes a further point of comparison with *Anthea cereus*, in which the organ is only slightly stronger.

The tentacles are over a hundred in number, and lie in three circles close to the peripheral margin of the oral disk ; the largest of them, belonging to the innermost circle, are only 0·5 cm. long ; they are all thick-walled, and as thick at the rounded end as at the base. They are pierced by a small terminal opening, which is usually perceptible to the naked eye, especially in tentacles from which the epithelium has been stripped off.

The longitudinal muscles in the ectoderm, which pass on to the oral disk as radial fibres, recall in many respects the ectodermal muscular fibres in the wall of *Cerianthus* ; they are borne by very thin supporting lamellæ, which are slightly branched and lie close together, though they never attain the same extraordinary length as in *Cerianthus* (Pl. VIII. fig. 9). Here and there we find isolated mesodermal bundles of muscles, whose fibres correspond in their extreme fineness to the longitudinal ectodermal muscles. As the wide œsophagus protrudes outwards the numerous longitudinal streaks on it are almost obliterated. The œsophageal grooves are also somewhat indistinct, as the tube is folded irregularly here and there. There is no reason, however, to question their existence, as I observed the directive septa in transverse sections.

All the septa appeared to be perfect, though the youngest did not reach far down the œsophagus. I could not settle their number accurately : the portion which I cut off, and which I took to be about one-fourth of the entire animal, contained six pairs of two different sizes, the smaller alternating regularly with the larger. This would give forty-eight septa for the whole animal, which are distributed in three cycles, taking for granted that this Actinia follows the hexamerous type. This view is so far warranted by the undeniable approximation of *Comactis flagellifera* to the hexamerous *Anthea cereus*.

I must finally justify my determination of the animal as *Comactis flagellifera*. The much shrunken specimen before me had at first sight but little resemblance to the first and only drawing of *Comactis flagellifera*, given by Dana in the account of his voyage, the contrast being especially marked in the shortness of the tentacles, which Dana has drawn and described as very long. This, however, becomes of less importance if we consider that we have before us a young specimen preserved in spirits. Verrill, who was able to examine spirit specimens of this species, also lays stress on the fact that their very numerous tentacles, which are of nearly equal length and placed closely together, are contracted into a compact, conical form, that they then measure only 0·25 of an inch in length, and have a very distinct terminal opening. The last characteristic becomes more important, from the circumstance that I have never met with any other Actinia in which the existence of the terminal openings could be recognised with the naked eye. (Those forms, of course, being naturally excepted in which the tentacular apparatus has undergone retrograde metamorphosis.)

Verrill's description continues thus : " The column is very short, with a fold below the margin and separated from it by a " fosse." On the outer edge of the fold the tubercles form a simple row. They are prominent, smooth, round, and nearly equal.' All this applies equally to the Actinia examined by me.

Family, TEALIDÆ, Hertwig.

Hexactiniæ with numerous perfect septa, and very contractile, moderately long or short tentacles, which can be completely covered. Circular muscle very strong, endo-dermal, projecting as a thick swelling into the gastric cavity.

The systematic descriptions of former naturalists, such as Gosse, Verrill, Klunzinger, &c., included the *Tealiæ* along with the species of *Bunodes*, as " *actinines verruqueuses* " in the family of Bunodidæ, which I do not consider a happy combination. In the course of this memoir I shall have occasion to describe an Actinia, which must be placed in the genus *Bunodes*, if we keep the definition given by Gosse and others, but whose structure approaches that of *Sagartia* more closely than that of *Tealia*. If it be assumed that this single species, the only one examined in detail till now, may be taken as the paradigm for the other forms of the genus *Bunodes*, there can be no doubt that the genera *Bunodes* and *Tealia* must be widely separated systematically.

Having the possibility just mentioned in view, I considered it to the purpose to introduce the family name Tealidæ, and I took the structure of *Tealia crassicornis* as the paradigm for its definition. Two other Actiniæ, *Tealia bunodiformis* and *Leiotealia nymphæa*, of which I am about to give a detailed description, are allied to this wide-spread form, which, however, was not represented in the Challenger material.

The most important feature of the family is, I consider, the extremely characteristic circular muscle, which can be recognised with the naked eye, as a thick swelling on the inner side of the wall. In transverse section it shows a circular or oval figure, fastened on one side to the wall; it is formed by extremely strong pleating of the endodermal circular muscular layer.

The large number of perfect septa is also of importance; on the other hand, I have entirely disregarded the nature of the surface of the body, so that forms both with smooth and with warty wall may find their place in the family.

Tealia, Gosse.

Wall covered with numerous, irregularly scattered warts; body broader than high, tentacles numerous, retractile, all of equal size.

Tealia bunodiformis, n. sp. (Pl. VI. fig. 4, Pl. VIII. figs. 3–5).

Warts very numerous, small, densely crowded together, with a tendency to arrangement in longitudinal rows. Surface of the body encrusted with foreign substances.

Habitat.—Shore of Tristan da Cunha. October 15, 1873. Three specimens.

Dimensions.—Breadth, 1·5–2·0 cm.; height, 1·0 cm.

Three small forms, collected as shore inhabitants on the coast of Tristan da Cunha, belonged to this Actinia, which, in consequence of the strong contraction of the body and the influence of the alcohol, had lost in great measure the marked characteristics of its external habit of body. They had been partially injured by being detached, and were otherwise so much contracted, that the oral disk and tentacles were covered by the margin of the mural membrane, and the body formed a shapeless mass, from 1·5–2 cm. in diameter.

The wall is encrusted in some parts with sand granules and covered with numerous papillæ, which are simply small elevations of the supporting substance covered with the usual epithelium. As they are of unequal size and irregularly and thickly distributed over the surface, the animals must be referred to the genus *Tealia* (Gosse). The constitution of the circular muscle, which is intermediate between that of *Tealia crassicornis* and of *Leiotealia nymphæa*, also favours this view.

The circular muscle (Pl. VI. fig. 4) is chiefly endodermal, and projects into the gastric cavity as a thick swelling on the upper margin of the wall. It shows an oval figure in transverse section. The margin of the muscle, where it is attached to the wall by a very narrow base, is pierced by a cord of connective substance, which soon divides into two smaller cords only running a little way. The supporting lamellæ covered with muscular fibrillæ run out from the latter; they are extremely long in the middle of the swelling and only slightly ramified, whilst they are shorter towards the sides, and form numerous lateral branches.

The trunk, from which these ramifications proceed, being divided into two main branches, two systems of supporting lamellæ are present, radiating respectively one from each of these ; the two systems are contiguous in the median plane of the muscle, thus giving rise to repeated fusion of their respective supporting plates. The muscular layers become consequently detached into bundles of muscles, and the endodermal muscles partially transformed into mesodermal. The pleatings of the same system rarely become connected with one another by lateral lamellæ, though this is more frequent at the point where the circular muscle passes transversely through a septum ; indeed here they are often connected to such an extent that a great part of the muscular fibrillæ runs for some time entirely in the mesoderm.

In the upper half of the wall we find small endodermal evaginations, which grow like glands into the underlying connective substance (Pl. VIII. fig. 4), and show a streak of blackish colouring in transverse section. Their cæcal end nearly reaches the ectodermal epithelium, but is always separated from it by a thin partition of connective substance, so that we never find small openings comparable to cinclides. The colouring is caused by the accumulation of black pigment granules in the endodermal epithelium. The endodermal muscular layer is not so thickly pleated throughout the region of evagination as in other parts of the wall. The evaginations seemed to me to be present only in the intraseptal spaces, but they were so frequent there that many intraseptal spaces showed three of them in radial section.

The oral disk and tentacles did not admit of detailed examination ; enough that both parts possess an ectodermal, richly-pleated muscular lamella. The septa, on the contrary, are of special interest, firstly, from the constitution of the muscular system, and, secondly, from their arrangement (Pl. VIII. figs. 3 and 5).

The longitudinal muscles of the septa are developed to an extent which I have never met with in any other Actinia ; they form thick swellings, showing an extremely delicate figure in transverse section. The pleatings of the supporting substance, which are covered with muscular fibres, are thickly branched, lie closely together, and pass one between the other in such a way as to form in transverse section what one might almost call a "meandrous complication," although the supporting layers never absolutely become fused. The mass of the muscle actually projects above the surface of the septum, and presents a mushroom-shaped appearance, caused by the constriction at its base.

The muscular swellings lie on the septa till within a short distance from the wall and from the oesophagus ; there the muscular fibrillæ extend in a smooth layer, and only become again more closely pleated when still nearer the wall. A slight parietobasilar muscle on the side of the transverse muscular layer corresponds to this second longitudinal cord.

All the septa are grouped in pairs in such a way that, with the exception of the two pairs of directive septa, the faces provided with longitudinal muscles are turned to one another. The directive septa on both sides (fig. 5, *rh*) are formed very irregularly; in each pair one septum is very strong, whilst the other is rudimentary; the latter never reaches as far as the œsophagus, and was so small in one case that it was not possible to perceive the manner in which the muscles were arranged.

The other pairs of septa vary in size, though they could not be divided into different orders, as a series of strong, large septa, which have almost all attained to an equal degree of development, is followed by a number of smaller septa; the former reach to the œsophagus, whilst the latter are imperfect. There were, on the whole, probably from thirty to forty pairs of septa. This difference of size in the septa, and especially the disproportion between the directive septa, is so unusual that it comes to be a question whether the specimen examined was normally developed.

Tealia bunodiformis belongs to those species in which I have observed that two adjacent septa may be connected by their free margins. In such cases it is two septa of different adjacent pairs which pass continuously into one another inside the strong longitudinal swellings.

The reproductive organs of the animal examined were ovaries, and were found on all the septa, except on those which were behindhand in their development. Two of the directive septa were consequently sterile, whilst the other two were furnished with reproductive organs.

Tealia bunodiformis differs very markedly from *Tealia crassicornis*. In *Tealia bunodiformis* the muscular fibres of the tentacles and oral disk are ectodermal, whilst in *Tealia crassicornis* they have passed into the mesoderm; in the former, reproductive organs are present on the septa of the first and second order, whilst in the latter they are absent. It may, therefore, perhaps be well at some future time to make *Tealia bunodiformis* represent a new genus distinct from *Tealia crassicornis*. I have chosen the name "*bunodiformis*," because in some parts the warts are grouped in longitudinal rows, and therefore have the same arrangement which characterises the genus *Bunodes*.

Leiotealia, Hertwig.

Tealidæ with smooth body surface, without warts, and without spherules, but with longitudinal furrows corresponding to the insertions of the septa; tentacles of equal size, arranged in several rows.

Leiotealia, as the name shows, is a *Tealia* with smooth body surface, and therefore bears the same relation to the true *Tealia* as *Paractis* does to *Tealidium*. According to Milne-Edwards they belong to the genus *Paractis*, from which I have separated them on account of the endodermal position of the circular muscle.

Leiotealia nymphœa (Pl. VII. figs. 1 5).

> *Actinia nymphœa*, Drayton, in Dana. Expl. Exp., Zooph., p. 146, pl. iv. fig. 33 (Synopsis, p. 10), 1846.
> *Paractis* (?) *nymphœa*, Milne-Edwards, Hist. des Corall., tom. i. p. 252, 1857.
> *Sagartia* (?) *nymphœa*, Verrill, Trans. Connect. Acad., vol. i. p. 486, 1871.

Tentacles short, in three rows, body constricted half-way up by a special circular muscle, insertions of the septa shining through the wall as longitudinal lines.

Habitat.—Station 149.   Christmas Harbour, Kerguelen.   January 29, 1874. Depth, 120 fathoms.   One specimen.

Dimensions.—Height, 1 cm. ; breadth of the base, 2 cm.

This small Actinia, of which there was only a single specimen, was examined in a strongly contracted condition. The oral disk was completely inverted, and the margin of the peristome drawn over it, so that only a narrow passage was left ; at two-thirds of the height the body showed a circular constriction, caused, as we shall see, by a special muscle, which is wanting in most Actiniæ.

The surface of the body in *Leiotealia nymphœa* is perfectly smooth, and so thin that the origins of the septa, which number more than a hundred, shine distinctly through it, in the form of white lines.   Muscular fibres are present only on the endodermal side, and form a smooth layer, which, from the contraction of the animal, was only slightly pleated, though it was thickened at two places into distinct sphincters. The upper sphincter is the more powerful, and corresponds to the sphincters of other Actiniæ in its position, immediately under the margin of the peristome, and in its action, for like them it draws the wall together like a bag ; it is a circumscribed muscle, and projects into the stomach as a circular swelling, which is only fastened to the wall by a narrow base, and pierces the origins of the septa. Seen in transverse section (Pl. VII. figs. 2 and 4) a process of the supporting lamella of the wall makes its way into the inside of the swelling, and traverses it nearly to the opposite end ; it thus divides the swelling into two parts, the upper being about three times as broad as the lower, which pass into one another at the free end of the process. Unless the section passes through the precise point where the sphincter pierces the septum, each part shows on the surface a layer of epithelium, and inside the repeatedly folded muscular lamella, supported by very fine folds of connective tissue. The folds of connective tissue spring from the axis of connective tissue, and throw out irregularly several lateral branches, all equally covered with muscular fibrillæ. The spaces between the folds of connective tissue are open towards the epithelium, so that the latter passes in between them. The lower ends of the pleatings of the muscle are rarely detached, so as to form flat mesodermal bundles of fibrillæ ; this takes place more frequently at the free end of the axis of connective tissue.

The lower circular muscle (figs. 2 and 5, *ms'*) is less highly developed ; to the naked eye it shows as a narrow palish-yellow tract, running upwards and downwards ; seen under the microscope, it consists of a muscular lamella pleated into unbranched folds, which lie closely together like the leaves of a book, are highest in the middle of the tract, and gradually decrease in size on either side till they pass into the smooth fibrillar layer of the wall.

The constitution of the oral disk of the specimen examined could not accurately be determined, as it was closely folded in consequence of the extreme contraction. Its peripheral margin bore three alternating rows of tiny tentacles, which only projected like small buttons, and corresponded in number to the individual septa. On transverse section, the tentacles of the inner circle proved to be evaginations of the intraseptal, whilst those of the outer circles belonged to the interseptal spaces.

The radial muscular fibres of the oral disk (Pl. VII. fig. 1) are mesodermal, but otherwise only slightly developed. Sparse thin bundles are separated from the ectoderm by a narrow layer of connective substance, and connected like a net with one another by an interchange of fibres. They enter the bases of the tentacles and extend to their points. There were apparently no openings in the tentacles.

The pedal disk is of no great interest. A small circular ridge, caused by a thickening of the supporting lamella, ran on its inner side between the septa, at a little distance from and parallel to the margin. As I only examined a single specimen of this Actinia, it is impossible to determine whether this structure is constant or not.

The species before us is chiefly characterised by the size and disposition of the septa, of which I therefore give a more detailed description. It is difficult, on the whole, to recognise in their arrangement the regularity shown by the Hexactiniæ. The six pairs of principal septa, of which two lie as directive septa in the sagittal axis, are certainly distinguished at once by their size, but the six pairs of the second order are very small, and in this respect fall short of the twelve pairs of the third order. All the septa already mentioned reach to the œsophagus, whilst those following are imperfect. Of these the twenty-four pairs of septa of the fourth order are always present, but unequally developed, being larger in the neighbourhood of the principal septa, smaller in the neighbourhood of the septa of the second order. This latter region is, therefore, plainly retarded in growth, and this becomes still more conspicuous in the following septa. In the interseptal spaces, which are contiguous to the septa of the second order, the septa of the fifth order are extremely small, and those of the sixth order are still completely wanting. On the other hand, in the neighbourhood of the principal septa, the septa of the sixth order are already as large as those of the fifth order. It is, however, quite possible that the irregularities just described become equalised in the course of growth, as the specimen examined was a young animal without any indication at all of reproductive organs.

The muscles of the septa show peculiar conditions, especially the longitudinal and parietobasilar muscles. The former is only distinctly present on the septa of the first three orders, and except in the directive septa projects into the intraseptal space ; it is a powerful muscular protuberance, which begins at nearly equal distances from the middle point and the periphery of the pedal disk, becomes distended half-way up, and then gradually becomes narrower till it is inserted at the oral disk inside the tentacles (Pl. VII. fig. 5). The muscular protuberance lies almost freely on the surface of the septum, and is only fastened to it near its adaxial margin by a kind of mesentery. In transverse section, it therefore shows (fig. 3) a figure resembling a mushroom-shaped excrescence, a broad mass from which a stalk thrust to one side passes up to the septum. The connective substance of the septum enters through the stalk into the longitudinal muscle, where, seen in transverse section, it becomes dendritically branched. The ramified lamellæ of connective tissue, which produce the dendritic figure in transverse section, are covered by a continuous layer of muscular fibrillæ ; the whole is covered with epithelium, which reaches to the bottom of the interstices between the layers of connective tissue, so that the endodermal muscular fibres never become transformed into mesodermal fibres.

The longitudinal muscle described above is part of the layer of longitudinal fibres, which is slightly folded in other places, and shows in transverse section a second smaller dendritic figure at the base of the septum only. Opposite it, on the other side of the septum, we reach the site of the transverse muscular fibres, which are directed transversely from the wall towards the axis of the body of the Actinia, and as usual are strongest in the upper third. The parietobasilar muscle is found on the same side, where it can be distinctly recognised as originating by a pleating of the transverse muscular layer. It is, in fact, simply a crescentic fold lying loosely on the septum, so that a pouch-shaped space opening into the stomach, into which one can thrust the point of a needle, always runs in between the two parts. The fold is covered on both sides with an ample muscular layer running parallel to the margin of the fold. The parietobasilar muscle springs from the pedal disk, from its margin nearly to its middle, after which it is attached to the wall as far up as the lower circular muscle. When the animal is contracted it draws the pedal disk and the wall nearer one another, and as the former is the part which is more easily moved, it becomes arched upwards, and so forms a slightly depressed sucker ; the muscle therefore plays an important part in attaching the body of the Actinia to the ground beneath. As regards septal stomata, the inner or peristomial appear to be present, whilst the outer or marginal are certainly wanting.

I consider the small Actinia described above as identical with a small form found by Dana, near Valparaiso, in the American expedition under Captain Wilkes. According to Dana's description, the whole animal is whitish, with a touch of yellowish-brown, the oral disk pale flesh-colour, and the tentacles yellow. Drayton gave it the name of *Actinia nymphæa*, which was afterwards changed by Milne-Edwards into *Paractis nymphæa* ; finally, Verrill included the species with a mark of interrogation in the genus *Sagartia*, for which, however, there is no sufficient ground.

Family, PARACTIDÆ, Hertwig.

Hexactiniæ, with numerous perfect septa, and with very contractile, moderately long tentacles, which can be completely covered ; circular muscle very strong, mesodermal.

The Paractidæ form a family parallel to the Tealidæ; they agree with the latter in the nature of the septa and the tentacles, but differ from them in the nature of the circular muscle. The latter is enclosed in the mesoderm, and either lies close under the endoderm or is forcibly separated from the epithelium by the secretion of abundant connective tissue. In this family, as in the Tealidæ, I include not merely the animals with smooth body (genera *Paractis* and *Dysactis*), but also the papillose forms of the genera *Tealidium* and *Antholoba*.

Paractis, Milne-Edwards.

Paractidæ with smooth body surface, without papillæ and without marginal spherules ; tentacles nearly equal in length and in strength ; numerous longitudinal furrows of the wall.

The genus *Paractis* was founded by Milne-Edwards for Actiniæ, of which the wall has neither papillæ nor marginal spherules, but can be drawn completely over the oral disk and tentacles ; the tentacles are said, moreover, to be nearly equal in length.

Two forms of the Challenger material fulfilled these requirements ; they differed, however, in one very important point, as the circular muscle was endodermal in the one, mesodermal in the other. The former consequently belongs to the family of the Tealidæ, and for it I have composed the new name *Leiotealia*, whilst for the latter I have retained the name *Paractis*.

Paractis excavata, n. sp. (Pl. I. fig. 6, Pl. XI. figs 13, 14).

Wall with more than fifty longitudinal furrows, corresponding to the septa, oral disk hollowed like a dish, with two rows of tentacles, the outer somewhat larger than the inner ; tentacles thick walled, with strong mesodermal muscles, which are present only on the adaxial side at the base, but surround the tentacles on all sides towards the point.

Habitat.—Station 300. December 17, 1875. Lat. 33° 42′ S., long 78° 18′ W. Depth, 1375 fathoms. One specimen.

Dimensions.—Diameter of the pedal disk, 2·5 cm., of the extended oral disk, 6 cm. Height of the wall in the contracted animal 2·5 cm., from the pedal disk to the margin of the mouth 1 cm.

Paractis excavata, which I describe as a new species, founded by me upon a single specimen, is one of the most characteristic forms of the Challenger material, both as to the shape of the body, and as to its finer structure.

In the strongly contracted condition, shown by the specimen, the body appears to be as high as broad, and also of equal breadth in the region of the pedal and of the oral disks. On dissecting the animal, however, it becomes evident that if the height of the animal is to be determined by the distance of the oral margin, from the pedal disk, it will fall far short of the breadth, and, moreover, that the diameter of the contracted oral disk is considerably greater than that of the pedal disk, which it must have exceeded twice at least. When fully extended, our Actinia must have been shaped like a dish, the wall diverging from the narrow base towards the broad oral disk.

The wall rises from the margin of the moderately firm pedal disk, which measures about 2·5 cm. in diameter, and is irregularly wrinkled and furrowed, to a height of about 3·0 cm. ; it is covered with fifty-four longitudinal furrows, which are separated from one another by equal intervals, and reach from the lower to the upper margin of the wall. These longitudinal furrows are crossed in the lower part of the wall, by irregular transverse furrows, which become more indistinct towards the upper part. The wrinkled and knobby appearance of the lower part of the wall thus produced I consider to be the consequence of the high grade of contraction of the animal.

The wall is firm like leather, but of no great thickness ; only that portion of it contiguous to the oral disk is distended about 0·5 cm. by the contained mesodermal circular muscle. The bundles of the latter are small, and composed merely of a few fibrillæ ; they run irregularly, either singly or united in groups in the fibrous connective substance. They are separated from the ectoderm by a broad interspace, but extend nearly to the circular muscular layer of the endoderm, and are even connected with it in some parts, so that steady growth of the circular muscle undeniably takes place by the transformation of endodermal elements into mesodermal. The principal mass of the circular muscle still extends downwards a little way, in a layer of mesodermal bundles of fibres, lying close under the endoderm.

The oral disk bears fifty marginal tentacles, and is covered with an equal number of radial furrows, which begin at the oral margin and end between each two tentacles. The radial swellings lying between the furrows are flattest near the mouth, and become more distinct in proportion as we approach the tentacles. This proceeds from the distribution of the muscles, which are very weak near the oral margin, and become stronger towards the periphery till they swell out into the powerful muscular masses of the tentacles. The muscular fibrillæ are remarkably strong, partly perhaps in consequence of having swollen from the unsatisfactory state of preservation. Their principal mass lies united in thick bundles in the mesoderm ; where the muscular system is weak the bundles are scanty, and the separating tracts of connective tissue broad, whilst towards the corona of tentacles the bundles lie close to one another, and the fundamental substance becomes a slender framework. As muscular fibres still remain in the ectoderm the oral disk, if well preserved, would furnish an admirable subject for studying the different stages by which the ectodermal muscles are transformed into mesodermal. As far as I could observe the supporting substance rises on the surface of the disk in numerous folds covered with muscular fibrillæ.

The tentacles are placed in two alternating rows, those of the inner row being rather shorter and weaker than those of the outer row, whose length in a contracted condition was 1·0-1·3 cm. They are thick-walled at the base, and run out into a fine point, without any terminal opening. They are all strongly bent inwards, and have a hook-like shape, which is caused by the distribution of the muscles. In most Actiniæ, as we know, the muscles surround the tentacles uniformly, but in *Paractis excavata* they are crowded together towards the adaxial side where they form a muscular pad, which I have never found equalled in strength in any other Actinia. In the tranverse sections (Pl. XI. fig. 14) the muscular fibrillæ lie close together, and the framework of connective tissue is completely hidden, and only becomes distinct by appropriate staining; it forms a network whose meshes are small near the supporting lamella, but large and longish towards the epithelium, enclosing spaces lying perpendicular to the surface of the tentacle. The surface of the tentacles was not well preserved, so that I could not determine whether these spaces were completely closed, or whether they communicate here and there with the epithelium, which appears to me more probable.

Over one half the circumference of the tentacle the muscular layer is of uniform thickness, but thins out over the remaining half into a delicate membrane, which seemed to me to be wanting at the base of the tentacle, unless perhaps it had been rubbed off. In spite of the varying strength of muscular layer, the thickness of the tentacle wall is essentially the same all through in transverse section, as the connective tissue substance becomes thinner in proportion as the muscular layer becomes thicker.

It is, however, only the lower third of the tentacle which comports itself in the manner above described, a transverse section through the point presents an essentially different figure. The muscular layer is weaker indeed but present on all sides, it merely becomes a little smaller for a short space on the abaxial side than on other parts of the transverse section. A series of transverse sections rising from the base to the point shows all the transitions between the two extremes, and we can follow step by step the process by which the muscular layer, which originally lies only on one side of the tentacle, gradually surrounds it entirely. I have only figured three transverse sections of such a series, of which one is taken at the base (fig. 13, *c*), the second (fig. 13, *b*) from the middle, and the third (fig. 13, *a*) from the point. In all of these the thickness of the muscular layer is indicated by hatching.

The œsophagus is very short, corresponding to the height of the animal; it is furnished with two œsophageal grooves, and eighteen longitudinal swellings. Six pairs of septa of the first order, and six pairs of the second order, are inserted in the œsophagus, besides which there are twelve pairs of imperfect septa of the third order. Septal stomata are wanting throughout. The parietobasilar muscle reaches to about one-fourth of the height of the wall, where it gives rise to a circular constriction.

All the septa bore reproductive organs. As the animal examined was a female, I was able to prove the existence of the filamental apparatus, which most resembles that of *Calliactis parasitica*. A conical process rises on the surface of the ovum, the point of which pierces the supporting lamella, and reaches to the free surface of the epithelium. The specimen was, unfortunately, not sufficiently well preserved to determine whether the process is formed of special cells, or is part of the ovicell itself.

Paractis excavata is perhaps allied to the *Actinia peruviana* of Lesson (Voyage de la Coquille, Zoologie, tom. ii. part ii., 2, p. 75 ; Zoophytes, pl. ii. fig. 3) ; the number, form, and arrangement of the tentacles, and the expansion of the body at the upper end is common to both. The longitudinal furrows on the outside of the wall, which are so distinct in *Paractis excavata*, are however wanting in the *Actinia* (*Paractis*) *peruviana*; there are said to be merely " quelques plissures brunâtres " present on the lowest section of the wall.

Dysactis, Milne-Edwards.

Paractidæ with smooth body surface, without papillæ, and without marginal spherules ; tentacles very unequal in size, the inner essentially larger than the outer, completely retractile.

I have kept essentially to the definition of the genus *Dysactis*, as given by Milne-Edwards ; differing from him only in one subordinate point, for while he limits the number of the rows of tentacles unnecessarily to two, I make no definite assertion on this point. I differ more decidedly from Verrill (Mem. Boston Soc., vol. i. p. 26, 1866-69), who has placed the genus *Dysactis* among the Antheadæ, and consequently makes it the most important character of the genus, that the wall cannot be drawn over the oral disk and tentacles. I do not understand why Verrill should differ in opinion from Milne-Edwards, who has placed the genus *Dysactis* among the forms with retractile tentacles.

Dysactis crassicornis, n. sp. (Pl. VII. figs. 6–12).

Height of the body rather greater than the breadth ; tentacles short, thick-walled and conical, arranged in four to five rows, and decreasing in size from within outwards, 24 tentacles in the first row, 24 in the second, 48 in the third, &c.

Habitat—(a) Station 312. January 13, 1876. Lat. 53° 38′ S., long. 70° 56′ W. Depth, 10 to 15 fathoms. One specimen. (b) Station 313. January 20, 1876. Lat. 52° 20′ S. long., 68° 0′ W. Depth, 55 fathoms. Four specimens.

Dimensions.—Height, 4–7 cm. ; diameter of the pedal disk, 3–7 cm.

I made *Dysactis crassicornis* the subject of detailed examination, as there were several points about it which seemed to indicate it as a suitable object for such a purpose. In the first place the unusual size of the body is favourable to dissection by means of knives and scissors, and in the second place, it was represented in the Challenger material by a large number of tolerably well preserved specimens. Two of the individuals were in a state of intense contraction, whilst in the other three the tentacles still projected through the opening formed by the upper margin of the half-contracted wall.

The pedal disk is moderately thick, irregularly warted on the surface, otherwise flat. It passes at right angles into the wall, of which the surface is perfectly smooth, except in the upper part, which is folded longitudinally in consequence of the contraction of the circular muscle. Most of the animals are distended like a drum, as sometimes happens in the Actiniæ, so that the wall has become a thin membrane with the origins of the septa shining through it. At its upper margin only, where it is connected with the oral disk, the wall becomes thickened to from four to five times its usual strength (fig. 12), and shows in transverse section a yellowish tract, lying in whitish fundamental tissue close under the endoderm, which is caused by the circular muscle running in this part.

The bundles of fibrillæ appear in transverse section (Pl. VII. fig. 7) as roundish or repeatedly indented figures, whose periphery consists of a corona of fine fibres, but whose centre appears in the spirit material almost empty, whilst in the living animal it is filled with protoplasm and the nuclei of the muscular corpuscles. The bundles of fibrillæ lie so closely together in the fibrous fundamental tissue of the mesoderm that it is hardly possible to determine distinctly whether or not they are united into smaller and larger groups. As the section shows, they become divided and united by anastomoses into an annular plexus, lying parallel to the course of the fibrillæ, i.e., parallel to the pedal disk (fig. 9).

Different points in the distribution of the bundles of fibrillæ favour the view that the mesodermal bundles originate in the endoderm, and only become deposited secondarily by detachment in the mesoderm, where they increase still more by division and separation. The bundles of fibrillæ lie usually in layers parallel to the endodermal surface, as a few more compact layers of supporting substance extend through the mass of the bundles parallel to the endoderm. The largest bundles are placed nearer the ectoderm, where they are separated from one another by broader layers of connective substance, whilst the smallest bundles (fig. 8) lie close under the endoderm, and—what is the most important point—are connected here and there with the circular layer of fibres which run on the endodermal surface of the mesoderm.

The oral disk is covered with numerous shallow furrows, running from the oral margin towards the tentacles. Their radial muscles form a tolerably broad stratum in the mesoderm, and this is separated from the ectoderm by a thin, and from the endoderm by a thick, layer of connective substance (Pl. VII. figs. 10 and 11). This stratum is again composed of bundles of fibrillæ, which are chiefly flattened in a lateral direction, so that the stratum seems to consist merely of apposed bands of muscles. As each band is repeatedly indented laterally, and can be dissected into separate pieces lying one below the other, they give rise to the very complicated formation shown in fig. 10, which is specially striking from the close apposition of the bundles of fibrillæ.

The bundles of fibrillæ are more scattered in the younger animals; smaller bundles of fibrillæ are also found here lying towards the ectoderm in the intermediate layer of connective tissue. It is quite conceivable that these smaller bundles may have migrated from the ectoderm into the mesoderm, in order to supplement the mesodermal muscular layer. The state of preservation of the material did not allow me to confirm this supposition, as I could not make out whether or not radial muscular fibres were persistent in the ectoderm. In the peripheral part of the oral disk the bundles of fibrillæ pass into the tentacles, where they preserve exactly the same arrangement and position in the mesoderm.

The corona of tentacles is immediately contiguous to the wall, whilst in *Tealia crassicornis*, which in other respects is not unlike *Dysactis* in its general habit of body, it is separated from the wall by a portion of the oral disk capable of becoming pleated. The corona consists of several hundred tentacles, which are distributed in four to five rows, and decrease distinctly in size from within outwards. If we examine an animal which is developed uniformly in all sextants, we find twenty-four tentacles in the first or innermost row, and twenty-four tentacles also in the second row, which alternate with the preceding twenty-four. In the third row the number rises at once to forty-eight, which are placed in such a way that they alternate both with the twenty-four tentacles of the first row, and the twenty-four of the second row. In the fourth row the number is again doubled, so that it consists altogether of ninety-six tentacles, which still alternate with all the preceding tentacles. The last row is always irregularly developed; the number of tentacles ought to amount to 192, but only came to some 90.

It will be seen at once from this mode of arrangement that all the tentacles of *Dysactis*—and this applies to almost all Actiniæ—lie in different radii, and must therefore belong to different radial chambers; they are merely parts of a single circle which have become distributed in different rows, from being displaced in the course of growth. It follows necessarily, from the whole mode of arrangement, that the separate rows of tentacles stand in regular relation to the radial chambers, as the same principle of arrangement, viz., that each cycle contains the same number of units as all the preceding taken together, applies to both. From my own observation in making preparations, I am convinced that the twenty-four tentacles of the first series belong to the twenty-four intraseptal spaces of the septa of the first to the third orders, the next twenty-four tentacles to the twenty-four intraseptal spaces of the fourth order, and so on.

Exceptions occur to the conditions which I have laid down as regular, but these can be easily explained by the fact that growth is not equally rapid in different sextants, or even in the separate parts of the same sextant. For example, in one sextant of a *Dysactis*, in which the first circle consisted of only eighteen tentacles, I found that the tentacles really corresponding to the septa of the third order were still in the second row, and that all the following tentacles were correspondingly a row in arrears; the first row in the said sextant only contained two tentacles instead of four.

Terminal openings are wanting in all the tentacles. In consequence of the strongly developed mesodermal muscles they are unusually thick-walled, on account of which I have named the species "*crassicornis*." The largest of them, the tentacles of the first row, are not 1 cm. long in a contracted condition, whilst they spring from a base of considerable size whose diameter in a radial direction nearly equals the height of the tentacle. The tentacles have therefore the form of short cones, flattened in a tangential direction; seen from the side of the radial chambers they extend like wide-mouthed pouches, running to a point.

The tentacles lying towards the outside not only become smaller but, above all, narrower at the base, and consequently more slender. The outermost tentacles are so small that they merely project like small knobs above the surface of the oral disk.

The oral fissure is bordered by twelve broad, swelling papillæ, of which two at either end enclose the entrance to the œsophageal grooves. They are stronger than the others, and are, moreover, divided by a horizontal furrow into two swellings lying one above the other. Whilst the œsophagus itself is short, its sagittal prolongations, the œsophageal lappets are very long, and extend nearly as far as the pedal disk.

The number of the septa is very large, and in the oldest animal amounted to ninety-six pairs, which were distributed in five cycles. In many places there were additional indications of the ninety-six septa of the sixth cycle, which however merely projected as thin folds between the wall and the pedal disk, and as yet had no mesenteric filaments.

We can generally distinguish two parts in the septa, one thick walled and muscular, the other delicate and veil-like (fig. 12). The former lies on the wall; its longitudinal fibres spring not only from the pedal disk but also from the lower part of the wall, and converge towards the oral disk and the œsophagus, especially towards the base of the tentacles. We cannot precisely talk of a special longitudinal muscle, but still the fibres are more thickly compacted in the middle of the lamella and united into thick cords, showing the following figure in transverse section (Pl. VII. fig. 6). Underneath each cord lies a thickening of the supporting substance of the septa, which sends out bushily branched folds of connective tissue in all directions, and these again bear the richly pleated muscular lamella. The whole is covered with epithelium, which also has hollows corresponding to the depressions between the ridges of connective tissue, so that the inequalities caused by the distribution of the muscles also become visible externally.

The transverse muscles, which run from the wall principally towards the stomach, but also towards the oral disk and pedal disk, are weak in the lower parts, but very strong at the upper end. The upper portion draws the oral disk very energetically towards the wall, and is assisted in this by part of the longitudinal fibres. The interspace between the oral disk and wall is here reduced to a minimum, which renders the separation of detached single septa more difficult. The parietobasilar muscle is moderately strong in most septa, and does not even extend up to the third of the height of the animal ; it is not merely connected with the septum by epithelial adhesion, but by coalescence, as the supporting lamellæ of both parts are fused to a great extent. The epithelial lamellæ and the muscular fibres of the surfaces of the parietobasilar fold and the septum which are turned towards one another still remain, however, here and there between the fused streaks of the supporting lamellæ, and in transverse section originate circular figures which are enclosed in the connective substance, and indicate by their serial arrangement the boundary between the septum and the fold.

Two kinds of stomata are found in the muscular part of the septa ; the peristomial are very large, whilst the marginal, which lie close to the wall, are small, and, in fact, so small in the oldest septa that they are almost entirely obliterated.

The thin-membraned veil-like part of the septum is only furnished with a weak layer of muscles, and bears both the mesenteric filament, which is fastened to its free margin, and the reproductive elements, which in *Dysactis* are not rolled up into compact masses as they are in most Actiniæ. The follicles of the testes in the male, the ova in the female are scattered over the supporting lamella, which, consequently, has the look of being strewed with isolated star-like points. The filamental apparatus appeared to be present in the ova.

A remarkable diversity usually prevails in the development of the septa. The directive septa are very small, but, on the other hand, they are connected to a great extent with the œsophagus, as the latter, in correspondence with them, is produced into the long œsophageal lappets, which reach nearly to the pedal disk. The thin-membraned part is small ; all the muscles, especially the parietobasilar muscle, stronger than on any other septa ; reproductive organs wanting throughout. The directive septa agree in the last respect with the other principal septa, and also with the six pairs of septa of the second order, which are chiefly distinguishable from the principal septa by not extending so far on the œsophagus. We first find the reproductive elements richly developed on the twelve pairs of septa of the third order ; they are present on all other septa, with the exception of the unimportant rudiments of those of the sixth order ; on the other hand, the muscular parts of the septa become almost imperceptible, and they themselves no longer project so distinctly into the gastric space. Only the septa of the third and fourth orders still reach the œsophagus, though their insertion occupies no great space ; the septa of the fifth order end on the oral disk.

It is remarkable that from the third cycle of septa onwards, the septa of one and the same pair are never of the same size, so that for example half of the septa of the fifth cycle are inserted at a considerable distance on the oral disk, whilst the other half run only to two-thirds of the height of the wall. Closer investigation shows that this difference of size is governed by fixed laws. From the moment when the septa of the first two cycles are developed onwards, we find that after these all the interseptal spaces are bounded by septa of different grades, i.e., by a septum of a higher and a septum of a lower order. The propinquity of the former causes a stronger development, e.g., in the newly-formed pairs of the third order, the septum turned towards the older pair is always stronger than the other. In the following pair of the fourth order, the septum which adjoins the septum of the third order is always the smaller. These differences cannot, of course, arise in the second cycle, as the interseptal space lies between septa of the first order which are of equal value.

As *Dysactis crassicornis* is not found at any great depth, and was dredged up by the Challenger at several places, the probability that the animal may have come under the observation of former naturalists deserves special consideration. Let me draw attention to two forms which are perhaps identical with it. In the Annals and Magazine of Natural History, 1872 (series iv., vol. ix. p. 304), Kyle describes an Actinia which he procured by means of the hooks on fishermen's deep-sea lines. Like the form under discussion, this Actinia reminds us of *Tealia crassicornis*, but differs from it in having a smooth body surface which brings it nearer our *Dysactis*. The second Actinia is the *Rhodactinia davisii*, minutely described by Verrill (Mem. Boston Soc., vol. i. p. 18, 1866–69), in which the papillæ on the wall are so indistinct that the surface appears almost smooth. The tentacles also appear to be similar, and, according to Verrill, are numerous, and arranged in several indistinct rows; they are conical or cylindrical, thick, rather short, rounded obtusely at the end or even club-shaped. There is, however, some doubt about this second form, as Verrill himself identifies it with *Tealia crassicornis* or rather *Urticina crassicornis*, as he terms the species (Transactions Connecticut Acad., vol. i. p. 469).

Dysactis rhodora.

> *Actinia rhodora*, Couthouy, in Dana,[1] Explor. Exped., Zooph., p. 148, pl. iv. fig. 37, 1846 (Synopsis, p. 11).
> *Dysactis rhodora*, Milne-Edwards, Hist. des. Corall., tom. i. p. 263, 1857.

Tentacles tolerably long and slender, arranged in three rows; the tentacles of the inner row essentially longer and stronger than those of the middle and outer rows.

Habitat.—Station 313. January 20, 1876. Lat. 52° 20′ S., long. 68° 0′ W. Depth 55 fathoms. Two strongly-contracted specimens.

---

[1] The edition of Dana's chief work, Report on the Zoophytes of the U.S. Exploring Expedition, which appeared in 1846, was very limited, and was soon out of print; the author therefore subsequently (1859) published a synopsis. I was only able to refer to the synopsis and the atlas, for the loan of which I am indebted to the kindness of Prof. Hæckel. The quotations referring to the large work are taken from Milne-Edward's Histoire des Coralliaires, whilst I have myself looked over the synopsis and the atlas.

All the quotations have been verified in the Challenger Office by reference to the original work.—J. M.

Dimensions.—Pedal disk, 2·5 and 1·5 cm. ; height, 1·2 and 0·5 cm.

The two Actiniæ, which I shall now briefly describe, belong to that class of specimens in which the shape of the body has been so decidedly modified by the high grade of contraction, and the colour is so completely gone from the action of the alcohol, that we must observe very great caution in referring them to any species hitherto figured and described. We must also bear in mind that in the case before us, even the larger specimen under examination is not yet mature, and we must therefore consider that the structure may undergo considerable changes in the course of growth.

The pedal disk and wall are tough-walled ; they seem to have been perfectly smooth in a fresh condition, and only to have become irregularly wrinkled and pleated in consequence of being preserved. The wall is thickened two or three-fold for a short space at the upper end by the circular muscle. The latter is separated from the endoderm by a narrow layer of connective substance, and greatly resembles in form the circular muscle of *Tealidium cingulatum* figured in Plate VI. fig. 2. Seen in transverse section, it widens towards the upper end like a club, though not so strikingly ; towards the lower end it runs out into a fine point, by which it nearly reaches the endoderm. The bundles of fibrillæ are formed of a few very strong fibrillæ, which are apposed one to the other in form of a ring in transverse section ; they are separated by a sparse layer of interstitial substance, and are only indistinctly arranged in larger and smaller groups. The smallest bundles are found towards the lower pointed end, where they often merely consist of from three to four fibrillæ.

The tentacles, whose number may be roughly estimated at about a hundred, are placed in three circles, the innermost are the longest and decidedly the strongest ; they measure more than 0·6 cm., even in the contracted animal, whilst the outermost present very thin filaments only 0·3 cm. in length. I could not perceive any terminal openings. The muscular system on the surface is a repeatedly folded layer of ectodermal fibres, which also pass uniformly on to the oral disk. By this difference, and also by the varying character of the circular muscle, *Dysactis rhodora* can be at once distinguished from *Dysactis crassicornis*, in which the muscles of the oral disk and the tentacles have passed into the mesoderm, whilst the circular muscle lies close under the endoderm.

Any description of the œsophagus would be of little interest. I shall therefore pass this over, and proceed at once to discuss briefly the septa, the regularity of whose arrangement is remarkably clear in section. There are in all four orders ; the six pairs of principal septa and the six pairs of secondary septa are perfect, and only distinguishable from one another by the former being more muscular than the latter. The septa of the third order are imperfect and essentially smaller, whilst the last septa are narrow, thin lamellæ. In the quadrant, used for investigation, the septa of a cycle were of equal size throughout, and showed a very unusual regularity of development. Directive septa are present, as I have proved from direct observation.

The longitudinal lamella is not very strong, but pleated in a large part of the septa. The parietobasilar muscle reaches half-way up the wall; it is partly fused with the septum, partly laid on it in loose folds.

Finally, the two kinds of openings, already known in various other Actiniæ, are found in the perfect septa; from their small size they might easily be overlooked, though I have observed them in dissected septa, both seen from the surface and in transverse section.

Tealidium, Hertwig.

Paractidæ, having the tentacles placed in several rows and of uniform size in the same row, and having the wall covered with fine papillæ.

As I limited the genus *Tealia* (see p. 34) to animals with an endodermal sphincter, projecting in the form of a swelling into the stomach, it became necessary to form a new genus, which I have named *Tealidium*, for all forms which agree with the Tealidæ in the papillose nature of the wall, but which differ from them in the mesodermal position of the sphincter. I consider it of no importance whether the papillæ are regular or irregular, compacted or scattered, or whether the wall is incrusted with foreign bodies or not. On the other hand, I have included the uniform character of the tentacles in the diagnosis, for I regard *Tealidium* as a genus parallel to *Paractis*, which it resembles except in one distinguishing point, viz., the warty nature of the body surface.

Tealidium cingulatum, Hertwig (Pl. III. fig. 3; Pl. VI. fig. 2; Pl. VIII. figs. 7, 8).

Tentacles small, placed in two rows; the mesodermal circular muscle projecting as a circular swelling from the outer surface of the wall; the wall covered with numerous longitudinal furrows, corresponding to the origins of the septa.

Habitat.—Station 158. March 7, 1874. Lat. 50° 1′ S., long. 123° 4′ E. Depth, 1800 fathoms. One specimen.

Colour.—(Determined from the spirit specimen) pale saffron yellow.

Dimensions.—Diameter of the pedal disk, 1 cm.; height, a few millimetres.

The single specimen of *Tealidium cingulatum*, which was taken attached to a stone from a depth of 1800 fathoms, belongs to the smallest forms among the Challenger material. It is so strongly contracted that the wall closes over the entrance to the oral disk till only a small opening is left. I could therefore neither determine the extent of the oral disk nor the height of the body, and the only means of determining its size was the diameter of the pedal disk, which amounted to about 1 cm. The colour of the body, if it has not been changed by the influence of the alcohol, is a delicate saffron-yellow.

Twenty-seven sharply-defined longitudinal furrows can be counted on the wall; they begin at a little distance from the margin of the pedal disk, become less distinct as they run upwards, and disappear towards the margin of the peristome. Besides the furrows the body is covered with numerous small papillæ, which can only be distinctly recognised with the magnifying glass, and which show a pattern like shagreen on the wall, as they are all of the same size and closely compacted. The entrance to the oral disk is surrounded by a circular swelling projecting above the surface, which belongs to the upper end of the wall; a shallow circular furrow runs near the lower end at a short distance from the margin of the pedal disk.

Nothing further could be observed in the uninjured animal, and on account of its smallness and strong contraction no further results could be expected from a dissection with scissors and knife. I therefore cut out a piece about the size of a quadrant, in which I examined the circular muscle, the oral disk, the tentacles, the œsophagus, and the septa in transverse sections, changing the plane of the section as occasion required.

The circular muscle, which lies in the mesoderm, is so powerful in *Tealidium* that the bulk of it has not room enough in the thickness of the wall. Just as a purely endodermal circular muscle causes a circular swelling on the inside, so this strong mesodermal muscle causes a similar swelling on the outside, as the surface of the wall is arched out to nearly four times the usual thickness; it can be recognised by simply looking at the animal, and has already been briefly mentioned. It probably becomes still more apparent when the *Tealidium* is extended, and then produces a girdle under the origins of the tentacles, on account of which I have named the form *Tealidium cingulatum* (Pl. VI. fig. 2). The entire mass of the muscle is club-shaped in transverse section. The smaller end, which is turned downwards, runs out into a fine point, which extends nearly to the endoderm, through the broad intermediate layer of connective substance.

The separate muscular fibres are fine, and so are the primitive bundles formed by them; from the manner in which the latter are grouped, it seems probable that they arise from division of larger bundles, of which a few still remain (Pl. VIII. fig. 8). The process of division seems to go on very rapidly in the peripheral parts, as we there find not only groups of two, three, and four fibrillæ enclosed in the fibrous connective substance, but very frequently completely isolated single fibrillæ (Pl. VIII. fig. 7).

There was nothing remarkable about the oral disk and the tentacles; their radial longitudinal muscular fibres are ectodermal, and extend in an almost smooth layer, which is only distinctly pleated at the bases of the tentacles. The number of the tentacles which are distributed in two circles amounts to twenty-four; they are of no great length, so that they are completely hidden under the contracting circular muscle.

The number of the septa in the quadrant examined amounted to seven; as they usually correspond to the longitudinal furrows already mentioned, their number in the entire animal must be reckoned at more than twenty. Their paired arrangement is shown by the course of the muscles; two directive septa were present in the quadrant, so that there is no reason why we should not regard the animal as conforming to the common plan of the Actiniæ. The result would therefore be that the animal has altogether two cycles or twelve pairs of septa. All the pairs of septa are quite uniform, all reach the stomach, and all bear reproductive organs. In the case before us, the latter are mature testes, closely filled with separate follicles of spermatozoa. As usual the tails of the spermatozoa lie inwards, the heads outwards, the former converge at the same time towards a point in the surface where the follicle projects into the epithelium, and where it probably bursts later on, in order to empty out its contents.

Antholoba, Hertwig.

Metridium, Milne-Edwards, *pro parte.*   Hist. des Corall., tom. i. p. 252.

Paractidæ with innumerable small tentacles, which lie on a swollen thickening of the margin of the disk ; margin of the disk lobed as in *Metridium*.

After Oken had erected the genus *Metridium* for the beautiful *Actinia Plumosa s. dianthus* (Lehrbuch d. Naturgeschichte, Th. III. Abth. 1, p. 349, 1815), Milne-Edwards included in it all the forms which agreed with the typical representatives in the peculiar arrangement of the tentacles and in the beautiful wave-like form of the lobes which border the oral disk. The probability that animals which resemble each other externally may differ essentially in their internal organisation was quite overlooked.

This is, in fact, the case, as I have proved from my own observation. It is quite correct to place *Metridium dianthus* among the Sagartidæ, since, in it as in them, only the six pairs of principal septa reach the œsophagus, and, according to Gosse (Actinologia Britannica, p. 20), are also furnished with acontia. *Metridium dianthus* differs in both these points from an Actinia, which was first observed by Dana, and was erroneously added to the genus *Metridium* by Milne-Edwards (Histoire des Coralliaires, tom. i. p. 253) and Verrill (Trans. Connect. Acad., vol. i. p. 479). In this Actinia the acontia are wanting, and the septa for the most part perfect as in the Paractidæ. Other conditions, such as the presence of a mesodermal sphincter, also show that this Actinia is a true Paractid. I therefore propose to form the new genus *Antholoba* for these forms which externally recall *Metridium*, but which, on the other hand, have no acontia, and are furnished with numerous perfect septa as well as with a mesodermal sphincter.

Antholoba reticulata (Pl. I. fig. 9 ; Pl. X. figs. 11, 12 ; Pl. XIII. fig. 9).

Actinia reticulata, Couthouy, in Dana, Explor. Exped. Zooph., p. 144, pl. iv. fig. 31, 1846 (Synopsis, p. 10).
Metridium reticulatum, Milne-Edwards, Hist. des Corall., tom. i. p. 255, 1857.
Actinoloba reticulata, Gosse, Actinologia Britannica, p. 24, 1860.
Metridium reticulatum, Verrill, Trans. Connecticut Acad., vol. i. p. 479, 1871.

Margin of the disk five-lobed, with several thousand small tentacles, the twelve tentacles of the first and second cycles larger than the others, and placed towards the centre at a little distance from them ; the thirty-six following still easily recognisable ; the wall traversed by reticulated furrows ; mesodermal muscle developed throughout the entire length of the wall.

Habitat.—Station 313. January 20, 1876. Lat. 52° 20' S., long. 68° 0' W. Depth, 55 fathoms. Three specimens.

Dimensions.—Diameter of the oral disk, 3·5-6·0 cm. ; height of the body column, 2·0-2·5 cm.

The three specimens of *Antholoba reticulata* included in the Challenger material were admirably adapted for examination, as the body was only slightly contracted. This applied especially to the largest specimen, which was 6 cm. broad and 2·5 cm. in height, and upon which the following observations have been principally made.

The pedal disk is very thin walled, so that the insertions of the septa shine through it as innumerable clear lines ; the margin is indistinctly lobed, probably five-lobed like the margin of the oral disk. The firm compact wall of the Actinia rises in a curve at an acute angle from the pedal disk, and is constricted more or less distinctly at a third of its height. The lower part of the wall is traversed by circular furrows, which are perhaps merely caused by the contraction of the muscles of the body, its upper part is covered with soft papillæ, about 0·5-1·5 mm. broad, which are not sharply separated, lie close together, and are very much flattened. Shallow furrows, which give the surface of the body its reticulate appearance, and which Couthouy had in view in naming the species, remain between the papillæ.

The mesodermal circular muscle is never very strong, but, on the other hand, it extends from the upper to the lower end of the wall, a formation which I have never found in any other Actinia. In longitudinal section it can be distinguished by the naked eye as a yellowish layer, situated close under the endoderm, which is 0·5 mm. broad in its upper third, but diminishes as it runs downward (Pl. XIII. fig. 9). Its bundles of fibrillæ (Pl. X. fig. 11) are all very small but thickly compacted, and only separated by a little connective substance ; they are all strongly flattened in the same direction in such a way that their edges lie perpendicular to the endodermal epithelium. They have an inclination to lie one behind the other in rows, which run outwards from the epithelium, and in this way they have the appearance of being produced by the breaking up of long thin muscular plates. The large bundles of fibrillæ are found on the outside, but the smaller ones inside, close under the endodermal layer of circular fibres, which is repeatedly pleated over them. From all this it seems probable that small bundles of fibrillæ are continuously detached by pleating from the endodermal layer, and are transformed by growth into larger bundles in the depth of the layer.

At the upper end the wall passes gradually into the oral disk, the margin of which is swollen like a pad. The limits of the disk are indicated by the appearance of the tentacles and the disappearance of the circular muscle.

The oral disk is five-lobed, its periphery being delicately sinuated; its upper third is so thickly strewn with small tentacles that it is impossible to determine their number, though we may estimate them at from two to three thousand; they are all very slender, thin-walled, and cœcal; they are largest towards the centre of the disk, and become smaller towards the periphery. Twelve tentacles, which are particularly conspicuous from their size, lie somewhat apart from the rest, nearer the centre of the oral disk, so that they are isolated from the others. They are distributed at equal distances round the oral fissure in such a way that two of them correspond to the corners of the mouth; this mode of distribution leads us to conclude that they belong to the intraseptal spaces of the six pairs of principal septa and the first six pairs of accessory septa. Outside these come thirty-six other tentacles, which make up a circle; twelve of these alternate with the first twelve, the other twenty-four falling between the latter and the former. The thirty-six tentacles can hardly be defined from the peripheral principal mass, because, in the first place, there is hardly any interspace between them, and, in the second place, because they are but slightly superior in size. They belong to the tertiary and quaternary intraseptal spaces. By dissecting the septa, the peripheral mass of small tentacles may also undergo examination, the result of which is to show that they all lie in different radii of the body. We never find more than one tentacle in communication with the same intraseptal space, though such a result seems highly probable on mere superficial examination. All the tentacles belong primarily to a single circle, and have only been forced into different circles by want of space.

The radial muscular system, which in this case also lies in the mesoderm, shows the same characters as those which we have already observed in the circular muscle. The mesoderm is pleated in transverse section, and, in well preserved animals at least, is covered with a layer of radial fibres; the mesodermal bundles of fibrillæ are flattened and placed in rows which begin in the pleating on the surface of the mesoderm and run straight towards the inside. We may say that we have before us deep laterally compressed folds, which fall asunder into numerous bundles of fibrillæ placed one below the other (Pl. X. fig. 12).

The layer of muscle is strongest between two septal insertions, and the mesoderm consequently slightly thickened. In this way radial swellings are formed on the oral disk, which, however, become more perceptible in transverse section than when looked at from the surface of the oral disk, and more perceptible near the tentacles than in the periphery of the mouth.

The oral opening rises slightly like a proboscis above the surface of the oral disk, and forms an oval fissure, one end of which is directed towards one of the points where the margin of the oral disk arches inwards, and the other end to a point where it arches outwards. The two œsophageal grooves are remarkably distinct on the œsophagus, as they are enclosed by high lips, which project like combs, corresponding to which the œsophageal lappets extend downwards, far into the stomach. The upper half of the œsophagus shows about twenty longitudinal ridges which are prolonged lower down into a larger number of smaller ridges. The boundary between the oral disk and the œsophagus is defined by a sharp line.

The septa (Pl. XIII. fig. 9) are very simple in construction, as specially differentiated muscles (retractor and parietobasilar muscle) are wanting, and the two primitive layers of muscles only are present. Transverse muscles, which run obliquely between the wall on the one hand and the oral disk, œsophagus, and free margin of the septa on the other, extend on one side, and are strongest in the upper and lower third, where their lamellæ are repeatedly folded; on the other side run parallel longitudinal muscles also in a repeatedly folded layer from the pedal disk to the oral disk and the œsophagus. In the perfect septa a small peristomial opening lies hidden in the angle formed by the junction of the proboscis-like part of the oral disk with the œsophagus.

As may be concluded from the large number of the tentacles, the number of the septa is something quite unusual, even though many of them have stopped growing at a very early stage. The septa of the second and third cycles are perfect as well as the principal septa, and are easily distinguished from one another by the difference in size and by the extent to which they descend on the œsophagus. Of the imperfect septa, those belonging to the fourth and fifth orders are still well developed; after that they decrease rapidly in size, so that the other septa almost come to be mere folds projecting more or less in the angles on the upper and lower end of the wall. This recalls the comportment of the tentacles in which the first four to five cycles are the most easily distinguished.

In order to obtain a general idea of the aggregate number of the septa, I prepared an intraseptal space of the third order as completely as possible, and made a transverse section through it, which passed through the upper part of the wall and the peripheral part of the oral disk. In this section I found more than sixty separate septa. This would give over 1500 septa, or over 700 pairs of septa for the entire animal. There appear, therefore, on the whole, to be eight cycles or 768 pairs of septa. There may perhaps be traces of a ninth cycle, as each interseptal space of the eighth order is furnished with at least three tentacles.

I can say nothing as to the distribution of the reproductive elements on the septa, as their thin-membraned parts had stuck together and were badly preserved. Some figures which I got in the sections lead me to believe that *Antholoba* may possibly be hermaphrodite. This would be very unusual, as I have as yet only observed hermaphroditism in *Cerianthus* and *Scytophorus*.

Ophiodiscus, n. gen.

Paractidæ with a single corona of long tentacles, which project at the margin of the wall and oral disk, and are only furnished with muscles on the upper side; wall smooth, with longitudinal furrows, indicating the insertions of the septa; septa differentiated into muscular septa and reproductive septa. The animals do not appear to draw the oral disk over the mouth, though a mesodermal muscle is present.

The external appearance of the Actiniæ, for which I have formed the new genus *Ophiodiscus*, recalls that of *Anthea cereus*, as the tentacles are of great length, project in a single row on the outer margin of the oral disk, where it is turned over into the wall, and hang down like flowing hair over the side walls of the body. The margin of the wall was also not drawn over the oral disk as in the Paractidæ. It would, however, be rash to conclude from the form presented by the animals before me that they are quite incapable of concealing the oral disk, and the more so as I succeeded in finding a mesodermal sphincter. It is possible, however, that, considering the size of the body, the sphincter is not very strongly developed, so that the contraction caused by it is a slow process.

A further point which distinguishes *Ophiodiscus* from the other Paractidæ is the constitution of the tentacles. As one wall of the tentacles is formed by the prolongation of the body wall, the other by the prolongation of the oral disk, they show the same differences in the distribution of the muscles which characterise the said sections of the body wall. The former only has longitudinal muscles, the latter is without muscles and is correspondingly thinner walled.

The differentiation of the septa into sterile septa with muscles and reproductive septa with weak muscles is still more important. The latter are extremely rudimentary, and have even lost the mesenteric filaments ; whilst in other Actiniæ a distinct graduation in size prevails in the separate cycles of septa, there is a pronounced distinction between the smallest muscular septa and the reproductive septa. It may be advisable at some future time to erect this form into a special family.

Ophiodiscus annulatus, n. sp. (Pl. X. figs. 1–10).

Wall surrounded close below the tentacles by numerous circular furrows, caused by the sphincter, which become less distinct towards the lower part of the wall.

Habitat.—Station 299. December 14, 1875. Lat. 33° 31' S., long. 74° 43' W. Depth, 2160 fathoms. Four specimens.

Dimensions.—Height, 0·5–1·8 cm. ; breadth of the oral disk, 2·0–4·5 cm.; breadth of the pedal disk, 1·0–3·5 cm.

Before proceeding to describe *Ophiodiscus annulatus*, I wish to make a few preliminary remarks as to the state of preservation in which I found the animals in question. It was unfortunately extremely unsatisfactory, which I regret the more as they are a particularly interesting form. In all the specimens the tentacles were tattered and frayed out at the end, and there were rents here and there in the wall between the insertions of the septa. The largest specimen was so much destroyed that I could not take any measurements from it. All this must be ascribed to the fact that the animals came from a great depth, and had been injured in hauling up the dredging apparatus. The animals have, moreover, suffered from having been pressed closely one against the other in the same bottle, so that they are flattened, and the relief of the body surface rendered indistinct. The dimensions given above and the following description of the form of the body are therefore merely of hypothetic value; the unfavourable state of preservation also explains why I have omitted to give exact numbers in describing the different parts of the body.

The height of the body in the living animal seems to have been small, its breadth essentially greater in the region of the oral disk than at the base, so that the whole form of the body may be termed "dish-shaped." It is divided into an upper broader and a lower narrower section by a deep circular constriction. Nearly one hundred tentacles, probably of astonishing length, hang down from the margin of the oral disk. In the smallest specimen there was still one tentacle which extended into a thin filament, 8 cm. long. I grant that this measurement may have resulted from the tentacle having been forcibly stretched, but considering that the diameter of the animal itself only amounts to 1·0 cm., we may safely assume that the length of the tentacles exceeds the former several times. This is also perhaps the reason why the tentacles are nearly all torn away. Whether the tentacles of each different order are of equal size or not, can only be determined by examination of other specimens.

The surface of the wall (fig. 1) is marked by about one hundred longitudinal furrows, which lie at equal distances from one another, correspond to the origins of the septa, and pass as radial streaks on to the pedal disk. Besides these longitudinal furrows, horizontal furrows run in the upper fourth close under the corona of tentacles, parallel to the margin of the oral disk; the swellings between the circular furrows are broadest above, whilst they become narrower and flatter below. The swellings and furrows are more pronounced on the endodermal side than on the ectodermal; at the same time we see in longitudinal section (fig. 6), that the internal furrows correspond to the external swellings and *vice versa*, so that the wall is pleated transversely. Its substance is, moreover, partially thickened, and it is on account of these partial thickenings that the swellings project more towards the inside than towards the outside.

The thickening and pleating of the wall are caused by the mesodermal circular muscle, whose bundles of fibrillæ are arranged close under the endoderm in layers, which run parallel to the surface and follow all its pleatings. There are from nine to ten such layers inside the uppermost and broadest swelling (fig. 6, a); they gradually decrease in number, in the middle (fig. 6, β) there are only about four, and later (fig. 6, γ) only two, till finally the circular muscle extends a little way in the now flat part of the wall as a single layer of small bundles which continue to become more sparse (fig. 6, δ). The separate muscular fibrillæ are remarkably thick, whilst the bundles formed by them are small, and as usual compressed in the direction of the longitudinal axis of the animal. The smallest bundles lie immediately below the epithelium, from which they appear to be formed, as shown in figs. 7, a, β.

The surface of the oral disk is smooth, or only indistinctly furrowed radially ; if examined in transverse section (fig. 5) it shows a set of strong mesodermal muscles, a broad band, separated both from the endoderm and the ectoderm by a layer of supporting substance. This band is broken by a separating bar of connecting substance, corresponding to the insertion of every septum. It is further a law of its development that the supporting substance grows out strongly into the muscular band from the endodermal and ectodermal sides alternately, and forms ridges from which ramified supporting layers stretch towards the opposite side. In this way smaller and larger elongated compartments are formed, which are filled with muscular fibres. These muscular fibres, like those of the wall, are extremely thick, and the manner in which they pass on to the tentacles distinguishes the *Ophiodisci* sharply from other Actiniæ.

Although the tentacles were badly preserved, it was perfectly clear that they are thin-membraned on one side but thickened on the other (fig. 2). This thickening is caused by a muscular cord which can be followed even with the naked eye as a broad fibrous streak running from the oral disk to the tentacle. It occupies that side of the tentacle which is turned upwards in a state of rest, and projects at its base right and left a little above the surface. It thus forms two wing-like expansions which pass a little way on to the oral disk. The structure of this cord is the same as that of the muscular band of the oral disk ; it is composed of strong, thickly compacted muscular fibres, divided by thin layers of connective substance into compartments of muscular fibres.

Muscular fibres are wanting in the thin membraned parts of the tentacles, unless they be present in the ectoderm, which could not be determined, as the ectoderm was completely macerated away. Whilst the muscular cord passes into the oral disk, the thin membraned parts of the tentacles, on the other hand, are prolongations of the wall. This is brought about by the fact that the tentacles lie exactly on the border line at which wall and oral disk are united.

Before passing into the œsophagus, the oral disk is raised in the periphery of the mouth into a proboscis-like projecting lip. The proboscis is marked on either side with about ten longitudinal furrows, and is likewise furnished with two œsophageal grooves, which are enclosed by two strong longitudinal folds, hard as cartilage, and pass downwards on to the long œsophageal lappets. In one specimen the lower part of the œsophageal grooves appeared closed into a tube by fusion of the margins of the folds.

The number of the septa amounted in all to forty-eight pairs, which are distributed in four cycles. The first three cycles, that is, the first twenty-four pairs, are formed exclusively of muscular septa which do not bear reproductive organs ; of these the septa of the first two cycles only reach the œsophagus, the remaining twelve pairs are imperfect. Septal stomata are wanting. The muscles are slightly developed, for I could not even find a parietobasilar muscle. In consequence of insufficient preservation, the free margins of the septa had become frayed out, and only part of the mesenteric filaments remained (fig. 4).

In contrast to the sterile muscular septa, it is the last twenty-four pairs of septa which alone bear the reproductive organs (fig. 4, *g*), but, on the other hand, have neither muscles nor mesenteric filaments; they have, moreover, undergone retrograde formation, for they merely project as small folds in the angle between the wall and the pedal disk, and only extend up the wall as far as the circular constriction described above. We can distinguish two parts on each septum, the free margin, which is thickened by the layers of reproductive elements and much folded, and a thin veil-like membranous part which, like a mesentery, fastens the reproductive organ to the pedal disk and wall.

The septa of a reproductive pair are always unequal in size, and that one of them is always the largest which stands next the muscular septum of the higher order.

Enveloped in the same bit of cloth as the four specimens of *Ophiodiscus*, there was a peculiar, dendritically branched body, which may possibly have belonged to one of the animals as an appendage of the wall from which it had been torn away; I shall therefore give a supplementary description of it.

The pseudo-tentacle—as I shall term it in what follows, though I do not wish to settle its signification—is a very dainty, delicately-walled formation (fig. 8); a short basal stem is almost immediately divided into numerous branches, and these, undergoing repeated dichotomy, finally form a terminal bush of club-like twigs. The principal branches frequently anastomose, so that it is difficult to subdivide the brush of tentacles according to its principal ramifications, which, moreover, form here and there small vesicular swellings.

By the help of weak magnifying power we can make out accurately the nature of the ramification and the form of the twigs (fig. 9). Each new branch is separated from the preceding by a circular constriction, and begins and ends with a small swelling. One of the twigs formed by dichotomy is usually behind hand in becoming branched, and this is specially apparent at the ends. These present three points, as one of the twigs caused by the last bifurcation only is redivided, whilst the other remains simple.

Like the tentacles, the pseudo-tentacle contains a hollow space, which is without doubt an evagination of the gastrovascular system; we can also distinguish three layers, an inner layer, probably endodermal, an outer, ectodermal, and the intermediate supporting lamella. Within the latter small fusiform cells are enclosed in a perfectly homogenous fundamental substance (fig. 10). Strong, circular muscular fibres run in the ectoderm; seen from the surface these caused an annulation of the branches which becomes less distinct at the ends. Transverse and longitudinal sections are necessary in order to make out the position of these fibres. In these sections I also observed fine fibres on the endodermal side; they were arranged longitudinally, and consequently crossed the course of the others. They also seemed to be of a muscular nature.

The epithelial layers were badly preserved, the ectodermal layer all but wanting, and the endodermal merely showed a thin layer of protoplasm with scattered nuclei.

What grounds have we for assuming that the structure described above is a component part of an *Ophiodiscus?* From the structure of the organ we may assume one thing, that it belongs to a Cœlenterate, as it shows the three body layers which characterise these animals ; the presence of cells in the supporting lamella makes it still more probable that it belongs to an Actinia. There is therefore nothing in the structure which goes against this view, but what is greatly in favour of it is the fact that the pseudo-tentacle and the Actinia were found in the same envelope, not accidentally, but because they belong to one another.

In fact there are descriptions published of Actiniæ which bear richly branched bush-shaped appendages as well as tentacles. Such, for example, is *Lebrunia,* found by Duchassaing and Michelotti in the Antilles (Memoire sur les Coralliaires des Antilles, Memorie della R. Accademia di Torino, ser. ii. t. xix. p. 324, pl. vii. fig. 8). The only species of the genus, *Lebrunia neglecta,* bears outside the corona of long simple tentacles five composite tentacles, which spring from the wall, and dichotomise till they run out into numerous terminal branches. The general habit of body of the four Actiniæ examined by me also recalled *Lebrunia,* inasmuch, as appears from Duchassaing's plates, the tentacles also spring from the outermost margin of the disk and hang down like hair over the wall.

I endeavoured to find remains of pseudo-tentacular appendages on the walls of the four specimens, but my attempts were unsuccessful, which is not to be wondered at considering the injuries which the animals have suffered, and that if these occasioned the loss of the stronger tentacles, it is likely that the very delicate pseudo-tentacles have been completely destroyed. Whether *Ophiodiscus* be related to *Lebrunia,* and might even be placed with it in a common genus, or whether they have absolutely nothing in common, remains therefore an open question. If the drawing given by Duchassaing of the branched pseudo-tentacles be true to nature, they differ so widely from the pseudo-tentacle described above, that it would be advisable at least to separate the species.

Ophiodiscus sulcatus, n. sp. (Pl. III. fig. 8).

Wall smooth ; oral disk covered with numerous radial, deeply sunk furrows ; body discoid.

Habitat.—Station 300. December 17, 1875. Lat. 33° 42′ S., long. 78° 18′ W. Depth, 1375 fathoms. One specimen.

Dimensions.—Diameter of the oral disk, 9 cm.

In fig. 8 of Plate III. I have endeavoured to reconstruct an Actinia, which was so completely tattered that a superficial examination could hardly recognise an Actinia in the whitish mass. I succeeded by careful apposition of the parts in restoring the whole of one half and the greater part of the other half ; I also discovered the œsophageal grooves, and in this way, determined the sagittal plane, so that I believe the drawing accurately reproduces the essential points of the animal's habit of body. In preparing the drawing I copied the one half, extending from one œsophageal groove to the other, as accurately as possible, and filled up the other half which was still more torn. I have only given the bases of the tentacles, as they were either only preserved in short pieces or were torn away close to the body of the animal.

The pedal disk is much smaller than the oral disk, and is covered with numerous radial ridges, somewhat in the same way as in *Polysiphonia tuberosa* (Pl. IX. fig. 5). The wall is smooth and tolerably thick-walled; its upper part contains a mesodermal circular muscle, which is very weak in proportion to the size of the animal, both in extent and in the number of its bundles of fibrillæ and the strength of the single fibres. On the other hand, powerful masses of muscle are accumulated in the oral disk. The latter is covered with deeply sunk furrows, which begin between the bases of the tentacles and run in a radial direction towards the oral opening. The furrows end in the periphery of the mouth, which is somewhat swollen, and at which two adjacent furrows are sometimes united. The swellings between the furrows, which are sometimes narrow sometimes broad, are caused by the deposition of strong mesodermal muscles. Their structure resembles that already described in *Ophiodiscus annulatus*, except that the bundles of fibrillæ are much more numerous, and form a layer which is at least twice as strong. The number of the radial swellings in the well-preserved half amounts to twenty-four, therefore to forty-eight in all.

There are likewise forty-eight tentacles which spring exactly from the junction of the wall and the oral disk, one of their walls representing a prolongation of the former, the other a prolongation of the latter. The thick muscular cords therefore only pass on to one side of the tentacle walls, whilst the other consists merely of supporting substance.

Though only a few of the septa were preserved, these were sufficient to show that they are distributed in alternate pairs of muscular and genital septa. The genital septa are thin-walled, whilst the muscular are strengthened by a thick supporting lamella. As there are in all forty-eight tentacles, the number of the muscular septa also amounts to forty-eight or twenty-four pairs.

The above statement suffices to prove that *Ophiodiscus sulcatus* is very closely allied to *Ophiodiscus annulatus*, but distinguished from it by the absence of annulation of the wall and by the strong formation of furrows in the oral disk. The two forms may even represent one and the same species, and the differences merely arise from difference of age. At any rate they were both taken at a great depth in two localities, geographically not far apart.

It is also well worthy of our consideration that in no other Actinia did I find the tentacles so shattered as in the two species before me, not even in specimens dredged from still greater depths. This may perhaps have to do with the fact that the animals attach themselves to foreign bodies by their muscular tentacles. I have already specially remarked that the tentacles are probably of great length in the living animal, so that they would be especially adapted for holding on to other objects.

LIPONEMIDÆ, Hertwig.

Hexactiniæ with numerous perfect septa and with marginal tentacles transformed by retrograde formation into short tubes or into stomidia.

Among the Actiniæ of the Challenger material there were some forms in which the tentacles had undergone a greater or less degree of retrograde formation. One part of these, *i.e.*, all the true hexamerous Actiniæ, I have united in the family of the Liponemidæ. I shall discuss the others afterwards in the tribe of the Paractiniæ, as they are distinguished from the Liponemidæ by the principle of arrangement of the septa, and I attach more importance to this characteristic than even to the peculiar constitution of the tentacles.

If this retrograde formation of the tentacles is therefore to be regarded as a process which is carried on repeatedly and independently, the question may justly be raised if it would not be advisable to distribute the Actiniæ without tentacles among the other families. In this case the genus *Polysiphonia* ought to be placed among the Paractidæ, the genus *Polystomidium* among the Antheadæ, as the former has a mesodermal circular muscle, and the latter a weak endodermal circular muscle.

Polysiphonia. n. gen.

Liponemidæ with tentacles, transformed by retrograde formation into short tubes with wide terminal mouths ; circular muscle mesodermal, slightly developed.

In the genus *Polysiphonia* we find the first stage of the retrograde formation of the tentacles ; they have become short, stiff-walled tubes, which have only a weak set of muscles, are, at any rate, only capable of a small amount of contraction, and are therefore of no great value, either for groping about or for seizing upon prey. But as the terminal opening is very much enlarged and appears to remain permanently open, they have become inhaling tubes, through which the animal can draw in water and the nourishment suspended in it.

Polysiphonia tuberosa, n. sp. (Pl. II. figs. 7–9 ; Pl. VI. fig. 3 ; Pl. IX. figs. 1–10).

Body stiff and thick-walled, shaped like a stemless chalice, the surface beset with roundish knobs ; oral disk, twelve lobed ; tentacle tubes thickened to a swelling at the base, of different sizes, placed in two alternating rows ; the larger tentacles correspond to the archings inwards, the smaller to the archings outwards of the oral disk.

Habitat.—Station 235. June 4, 1875. Lat. 34° 7′ N., long. 138° 0′ E. Depth, 565 fathoms. Twenty specimens.

Dimensions.—Diameter of the pedal disk, 3–4 cm. ; diameter of the oral disk, 8–10 cm. ; height, 5–8 cm.

Numerous specimens of a beautiful large Actinia, *Polysiphonia tuberosa*, were all dredged on the same spot from the bottom of the sea, at a depth of 565 fathoms. To judge from the nature of the material, part of them had been placed at once in spirit, part previously treated with chromic acid. The former were unfortunately of absolutely no use, their tissues were macerated, and the form of the body disfigured by pressure almost past recognition, whilst the latter permitted a detailed description of the body form and of many anatomical conditions; the septa had, however, suffered severely in preservation, which, as I have noticed, is usually the case in material prepared by means of chromic acid.

Making allowance for changes caused by pressure, the form (Pl. II. fig. 7) is the same in all the specimens. The body begins with a relatively small, firmly attached base, rises to a considerable height, and gradually expands like a stemless chalice up to the oral disk, which unfolds like a flower. This form is rare among the Actiniæ, especially in contracted animals, since, on the other hand, the inversion of the margins of the oral disk usually causes the body to diminish in size upwards like a cone.

The ectodermal side of the pedal disk (Pl. IX. fig. 5) is covered with numerous (more than a hundred) radial ridges, which begin at the margin, and, partly at least, extend as far as the centre. They form a very dainty figure, as they have a vandyked, wavy course, and project with unusual sharpness above the level of the disk. On the endodermal side there are strong muscular cords, piercing the bases of the septa in bundles (fig. 4); they are crossed by other muscular cords, which pass transversely through the pedal disk from the endodermal to the ectodermal side. These perforating muscular fibres originate from the two muscular layers of the septa; this is best shown in transverse sections taken perpendicularly to the direction of the septa (fig. 1). Some of the longitudinal and of the transverse fibrillæ diverge and reach the mesoderm in bundles; their fibrillæ become intermixed, as they become interwoven with one another and with the layer of the basal circular muscles. The bundles then run towards the depressions which separate the ridges on the ectodermal side, and become fastened at the bottom of them; here they split up into the fibrillæ of which they are composed (fig. 7), so that their ends appear to be dendritically branched, and remind us of the ends of the muscular fibres of the Ctenophora.

As the perforating bundles originate from the muscles of the septa, it naturally follows that they are arranged regularly in radial rows. Each septum has two hardly separate corresponding rows, one of which is derived principally from the transverse muscles, the other principally from the longitudinal muscles. This is seen in the section which I have given in fig. 3, and which was taken parallel to the boundary surfaces of the pedal disk. As the section has fallen somewhat obliquely, we see at one end the bases of the septa cut through obliquely, then the circular muscles intersected by the bundles of perforating muscles, and, finally, the bundles running in two rows through the supporting substance.

Both the intersecting bundles of muscles and the depressions on the surface of the pedal disk (fig. 1) are wanting below the beginnings of young septa. This shows that the muscular layers of the septa only grow secondarily into the supporting substance, and that the depressions on the surface are occasioned by their becoming fastened to its ectodermal side.

The function of the muscular bundles is easily seen ; they tend to raise the pedal disk at certain points from the underlying substance, and by thus forming a vacuum, cause the pedal disk to act like a sucker and secure the firm attachment of the animal.

The wall is 1 cm. thick, and is, moreover, remarkably firm, so that it furnishes a very effectual protection ; it feels like cartilage or like the cellulose mantle of *Phallusia mammillata*, and, like the latter, easily separates into shreds on division. Under the microscope it shows a homogeneous fundamental substance in which fine filaments cross in all directions, and form a thickly tangled layer. Each filament runs separately, and can be followed some little way. From these the processes of the numerous minute cells are to be distinguished by their greater thickness and fine granulation.

The surface of the wall rises in numerous knobs 0·5 cm. across, which often have a small dark spot on the highest point ; they are commonly arranged, though irregularly, in transverse and longitudinal rows. The wall feels otherwise quite smooth.

A special mesodermal circular muscle is present, even though in all the specimens the oral disk was widely extended, and the wall only slightly or not at all contracted. The circular muscle is of some breadth, as it measures nearly 2 cm., but its thickness can hardly be measured without the microscope ; it lies close under the endoderm as a thin layer of bundles of muscular fibres (Pl. VI. fig. 3). If we consider that the body wall of the animal is not only very thick, but of cartilage-like consistency, we can easily understand that the contraction of the muscle is unable to effect rapid closure of the oral disk.

The bundles vary in strength, according as they consist of a smaller or greater number of fine muscular fibres; in their lower third they form a single layer, in which there is no perceptible further grouping ; farther up, the bundles become arranged in rows, and then, as a larger quantity of connecting substance passes in between the rows, the latter radiate to the number of nine or ten into the gelatinous substance.

The wide oral disk, whose surface is covered with indistinct radial furrows, is not so strong as the wall, but, in comparison with other Actiniæ, equally rich in cartilage-like supporting substance. The radial muscles, whose bundles are compacted into a tolerably thick and firm layer, lie in the oral disk, separated from the ectoderm by a broad intermediate layer of supporting substance ; some of the bundles become detached from the principal mass, and run through the fundamental connective tissue towards the endoderm, where they terminate. As they cross each other on the way they form an irregular network.

The tentacles are undeniably the most interesting portion of the oral disk, and their odd form attracts attention even on a superficial glance. They consist of two parts, a basal tuberous swelling, or bulb, and a hollow process, or tentacle tube (Pl. 11. fig. 9 ; Pl. IX. figs. 8 and 9). The bulb is formed by a strong thickening of the supporting substance; and since this is most extensive on the peripheral side of the tentacle, the canal, which is not enlarged in other respects, runs eccentrically near the adaxial side.

Another consequence of this peripheral thickening is the eccentric position of the tentacle tube, which is thrust towards the adaxial side, where it rises in the form of a short process bent slightly outwards. It is furnished at the end with a wide opening, visible to the naked eye; its surface is wrinkled in consequence of muscular contraction, and its walls are brittle like those of other parts of the body.

The longitudinal bundles of the tentacles being prolongations of the radial muscles of the oral disk are likewise mesodermal, though forced apart and into an irregular course by the abundant connective substance (Pl. IX. fig. 2); it is only near the point of the tentacle that the muscular bundles are collected into a layer close under the endoderm (Pl. IX. fig. 6); they are consequently separated from their place of origin, the ectoderm, by a wider interspace than in any other Actinia. The bundles, which are still strong in the bulb, are, in the tentacle tubes, resolved by repeated division into very small groups of fibrillæ, if they have not ended previously as many of them do. In short, the tentacles are, both from the extreme weakness of their muscles and from the stiffness of their walls, very ill adapted for seizing upon prey, whilst, on the other hand, the wide lumen of the terminal opening indicates their function as inhalent canals and tubes. We have therefore plainly before us a process of transformation, which is further advanced in *Sicyonis* and still more so in *Polyopis* and *Polystomidium*, and which consists in the walls of the tentacle, its muscles, and its supporting lamella becoming reduced, whilst the terminal opening becomes widened. The tentacles are first transformed into tubes, and later into simple openings in the oral disk. As this is plainly the most important characteristic of our Actinia, I have named the animal *Polysiphonia* on account of the tubular nature of the tentacles.

The number of the tentacles amounts to nearly two hundred, perhaps to even more. They are distributed in two alternating rows, which do not, however, describe a simple circle, but are twelve times arched outwards at equal distances, so that the periphery of the oral disk becomes twelve lobed. At each of the twelve points which project inwards and separate the twelve lobes there is a remarkably large tentacle, which can easily be recognised by the thickness of its bulb; outside it, and belonging to the outer row, there are two equally large tentacles, whose bulbs are fused together; the other tentacles become smaller the further they lie right and left from these fused tentacles, so that the smallest are found on the outermost portions of the lobes.

The arrangement just described is still more plainly seen if we cut away the tentacles and their basal swellings by a horizontal section; this gives the figure shown in Plate II. fig. 8, in which the position of the tentacles is shown by the transected triangular canals. The mode in which the size of the tentacles gradually diminishes in the two alternating rows is very characteristic of *Polysiphonia tuberosa*, and distinguishes it from the majority of Actiniæ. In the Introduction I laid down the following rules:—(1) that the tentacles of one circle are commonly of the same size; (2) that the tentacles, if they are not of the same size, become smaller in proportion as they belong to the more lately formed intraseptal spaces. Neither of these rules applies to *Polysiphonia tuberosa*. A glance at fig. 9 (Pl. II.) shows at once the differences which take place in one and the same circle, and if we go into the relations with the intraseptal spaces, we find that the twelve largest tentacles open into the twelve primary and secondary intraseptal spaces, whilst the smallest of all the tentacles belong to the twelve tertiary intraseptal spaces. In *Polysiphonia* the principle which regulates the size of the tentacles may be included in the proposition, that the tentacles become smaller the further they are removed from the twelve large tentacles of the first and second orders.

The œsophagus is tough and thick walled like the oral disk, whilst the septa are thin like veils ; the œsophageal grooves and longitudinal furrows require no special description. Of the forty-eight pairs of septa twenty-four are perfect, but the state of preservation of all the internal organs of the species was such that I can say nothing as to the structure and arrangement of the reproductive organs.

Polystomidium, n. gen.

Liponemidæ, with longitudinal furrows and marginal spherules on the wall ; tentacles transformed by retrograde formation into stomidia ; circular muscle endodermal.

In the *Polystomidia*, the tentacles have undergone retrograde formation to an extent which has hitherto been observed only in the genus *Polyopis;* the only traces of them are the terminal openings, which lead directly into the radial chambers and are surrounded by swollen margins, the remains of the tentacle wall. In their habit of body, in the endodermal position of the circular muscle, and in the presence of the marginal spherules, these animals are allied to the Antheadæ.

Polystomidium patens, n. sp. (Pl. V.).

Body dish-shaped, widening from the small pedal disk to the wide oral disk ; stomidia in two alternating rows.

Habitat.—Station 296. November 9, 1875. Lat. 38° 6' S., long. 88° 2' W. Depth, 1825 fathoms. One specimen.

Dimensions.—Diameter of the oral disk, 6 cm.; diameter of the pedal disk, 1·5 cm. ; height of the wall, 2·7 cm.

Colour.—(Determined from the spirit specimen) brownish-grey, the endodermal parts brown-violet, except the filaments which were coloured white.

Of this interesting deep-sea Actinia, which I have placed here under the name *Polystomidium patens* as the representative of a new genus and new species, I had unfortunately only one specimen at my disposal, and it had been so severely injured in being dredged from the depth of 1825 fathoms, that it was in a condition but little adapted for minute examination. The body was flattened into a cake, of which one side was completely covered with parts of the thin-membraned lamellæ of the septa, hanging in tatters, and with the reproductive organs and mesenteric filaments. The latter protruded partly from the œsophagus, partly from rents and fissures in the oral disk and wall, and partly from the openings, which replace the tentacles and represent them morphologically.

After the tattered fragments had been partially removed, it was found that one side of the Actinia was formed by the œsophagus and oral disk, the other by the wall and the pedal disk (fig. 3). The pedal disk is only slightly distinguished from the wall as a shallow depression 1·5 cm. in diameter, the bottom of which forms a convex projection into the interior of the gastric space of the Actinia. The wall, which is about 2·7 cm. long, shows distinct longitudinal furrows, which run from the margin of the pedal disk to the margin of the oral disk, and indicate externally the origins of the septa. As they amount to more than seventy in number, they correspond to thirty-six pairs of septa, which were also visible on dissection. Small knobs, which may perhaps be compared to the " bourses marginales" of other Actiniæ, lie one in each of the interspaces between these longitudinal lines, at a little distance from the margin of the oral disk. The surface of the wall is otherwise quite smooth.

The endodermal circular layer of fibres is pleated as far as the wall extends, and rises in muscular folds, which usually remain simple or are only slightly branched (fig. 10). The folds are more extensively branched only in the uppermost section of the body, where they form a sphincter which lies between the marginal spherules and the corona of stomidia, somewhat below the latter, and causes the wall to project outwardly (fig. 8). A longitudinal section through the wall, therefore, shows us two evaginations lying at the upper end, the one above the other, in which the supporting lamella becomes very much thinner. The lower one is caused by the marginal spherule, the upper by the circular muscle; the former contains a hollow space and is lined by a weak muscular layer, the interior of the latter is almost completely filled by the deep muscular folds, whose arrangement is more minutely given in fig. 9. The ramification of the separate folds decreases both above and below, so that the circular muscle is gradually transformed into the usual muscular layer.

The entire absence of the tentacles is a striking feature of the oral disk; they are replaced by openings like buttonholes (fig. 6), which I shall term "stomidia," and on account of which I have named the genus *Polystomidium*. Their exact number could not be directly determined, as the oral disk was greatly injured in many places, but, bearing in mind their relation to the septa, it may be estimated at about seventy-two. In dissecting the septa we find that one stomidium opens into each radial chamber. The stomidia belonging to the intraseptal spaces are usually smaller, and form an inner circle by themselves; the stomidia of the interseptal spaces alternate with them, and are placed in an outer circle; their longitudinal diameter runs in a radial direction, and amounts to about 0·5 cm.

The constitution of the margins is the standard by which I have determined that the stomidia may be normal phenomena and not merely rents in the oral disk. The outer stomidia leading into the interseptal spaces are separated from one another by narrow ridges, which have arisen from the septa belonging to a pair converging upwards and becoming directly united. The roof of an intraseptal space furnished by the oral disk, which is usually of considerable breadth, has consequently undergone almost complete retrograde formation. Towards the oral opening the stomidia are surrounded by swollen lips, folded like frills; these are still more perceptible on the inner stomidia, round which they form a border.

As the arrangement of the stomidia follows that of the tentacles in other Actiniæ, there seems no doubt that they represent the latter morphologically. I have already shown in the Introduction that they may be derived in the most simple way from the tentacles if we assume that the wall of the tentacle has become contracted into the encircling lip-swelling, whilst the terminal opening has become proportionably widened.

The oral disk is thickly pleated inwards from the stomidia, and covered with radial swellings, which lie between the insertions of the septa and gradually disappear towards the oral opening. The radial muscular fibres do not pass into the mesoderm, but remain in the ectoderm; like all muscular fibres of *Polystomidium*, they are very powerful, and are united into a thickly-pleated lamella. The muscular folds are specially high in the peripheral parts of the oral disk, where they lie thickly compacted and repeatedly branched (figs. 4 and 7).

On the œsophagus there is a remarkable circular fold, which runs at a little distance below the labial margin, and marks off in this way a small upper section of the œsophagus. Openings, equal in number to the stomidia on the oral disk, lie in this section, and lead directly into the radial chambers (fig. 1). I have only observed similar formations in *Polyopis striata*, another Actinia in which the tentacles have undergone retrograde formation. The lower section of the œsophagus is covered with numerous longitudinal furrows. Besides these there are two well-marked œsophageal grooves, and two long œsophageal lappets, by which the directive septa can be easily determined.

The number of the septa is smaller than in most of the larger Actiniæ. Calculating the number in the entire animal from the quadrant in which I dissected the septa, and from the longitudinal lines on the surface of the body, there are altogether thirty-six pairs of septa; six pairs of principal septa of the first order, six pairs of the second order, and twenty-four pairs of the third. The last number is very remarkable, as there are usually only twelve pairs of septa of the third order. In consequence of this the interseptal spaces of the second order are divided, not as usual into two, but into three interspaces, because of the duplication of the septa of the third order. In this way *Polystomidium patens* shows a variation from the regular conditions of the hexamerous Actiniæ.

The muscular part of the septa is very thick and powerful, and uniformly strong throughout; their longitudinal muscular fibres are developed into a repeatedly folded muscular lamella, whilst their transverse fibres are weak. The parietobasilar muscle, which springs from the small pedal disk, and reaches half-way up the wall, is also weak (fig. 2).

The greater part of the thin-membraned portions of the septa had been torn away; where they still remained they lay in the interseptal and intraseptal chambers, from which they protruded through the stomidia. They contained the reproductive organs, the specimen examined by me being a male. The follicles, filled with spermatoblasts and spermatozoa, are not so thickly compacted as in most other Actiniæ, but rather isolated and of considerable size, so that they can be separately recognised with the naked eye placed beside one another like paving-stones.

All the septa reach the œsophagus; the upper part only of the forty-eight septa of the third order is connected with the œsophagus, whilst the others extend much farther downwards; they are all pierced by peristomial openings, forming a circular canal in the aggregate. The only difference between the septa—apart from size—seems to be that the principal septa are without reproductive organs. I must, however, remark that in consequence of the numerous injuries, it is impossible to make any positive statements as to the distribution of the reproductive elements upon the septa.

All the surfaces of the wall and of the septa covered with endoderm are brownish-violet, as numerous pigment granules are deposited in the epithelium. The mesenteric filaments, which I have figured in transverse section in fig. 5, form the only exception; they are whitish like the ectodermal parts, and are distinguished in this way from the dark ground of the septa on which they run in numerous meandrous curves.

Family, SAGARTIDÆ, Gosse.

Sagartinæ = *Phellinæ*, Verrill.

Hexactiniæ with acontia, a strong mesodermal circular muscle and numerous very contractile tentacles; the principal septa, or septa of the first order, only are perfect and at the same time sterile; all the remaining septa are imperfect.

In my researches on the Actiniæ, which have already extended over a very large amount of material, I have almost always found two characters combined. (1) The presence of filaments known as acontia near the lower end of the mesenteric filaments; they float freely in the gastric cavity, are thickly covered with nematocysts, and if danger threatens can be protruded quickly as weapons of defence. (2) The six pairs of principal septa only reach the œsophagus, all the others being imperfect. Reproductive organs are found only on the secondary septa, of which, however, the older are often permanently sterile.

My brother and I first observed these facts in *Adamsia diaphana*, *Metridium dianthus*, and *Calliactis* (*Sagartia*) *parasitica*; I have been able to corroborate them in five different species of the Challenger material, and found, moreover, that in no instance, where the acontia were present, was the differentiation of the septa wanting, and that the Amphianthidæ were the only Actiniæ in which the acontia were absent, though the septa showed the Sagartid type. I therefore feel justified in making use of both characters to limit a family of Actiniæ, which I still term Sagartidæ, as most of the forms belonging to it have been determined as such by former authors.

A third characteristic is common to all Sagartidæ, viz., the presence of a strong mesodermal circular muscle, but this is only of subordinate value, as it occurs in other families.

Nearly all the descriptions published of the *Sagartiæ* and the closely allied forms are unfortunately so imperfect that it is impossible to determine how far the forms hitherto described come under the above diagnosis. As yet, we can only assume this to be definitely the case in *Sagartia schilleriana*, discovered by Stoliczka (Journ. Asiat. Soc. Bengal, vol. xxxviii. part ii. p. 28–63, 1869). Another form, *Sagartia troglodytes*, may, on the other hand, be considered as an exception; v. Heider states (Sitzungsber. der Wiener Akad., Math. Naturw. Cl., Bd. lxxv. Abth. 1, p. 367, 1877) that in it forty-eight pairs of septa reach the œsophagus, and at the same time describes formations in it, which undeniably are acontia, though the author does not distinguish them from the mesenteric filaments. However, as I have already specially remarked, I am doubtful whether v. Heider has not confused sections through the oral disk with sections through the œsophagus, and consequently over-estimated the number of the perfect septa. Such a mistake might easily occur in highly contracted animals like those which he examined.

As far as we can judge at present, the family of the Sagartidæ, as I have now defined it, would coincide on the whole with Gosse's Sagartidæ. The most essential difference is that I have included the genus *Bunodes* in it. In so doing I relied upon the examination of a single species, which showed externally the arrangement of papillæ characteristic of the *Bunodes*, but which must be placed among the Sagartidæ, from its anatomical constitution. It remains for future observers to determine whether the structure is the same in the other species as in our *Bunodes minuta*; at present it is quite possible that perfectly heterogeneous species have been included under the same generic name. It must, however, be borne in mind that Verrill (Transact. Connect. Acad., vol. i. p. 467) and Jourdan do not attribute any acontia to the genus *Bunodes*, and Gosse (Actinologia Britannica, p. 204) only to a single species.

Verrill has separated the sub-family of the Phellinæ from the Sagartidæ, an innovation of which I do not approve, as there are transition forms between *Sagartia* and *Phellia*. The cuticular secretion, the "epidermis" of the said authors, which covers the wall of *Phellia* as far as a ring close under the tentacles, is present, though less highly developed, in *Cereus spinosus*, but is not so sharply confined to definite parts as in *Phellia*.

After what has been said in the preface, no further explanation is required as to my reasons for omitting the cinclides in the general character of the family. I shall henceforward mention the cinclides only in cases where they can be observed anatomically by transverse and horizontal sections, or by observation with the naked eye. This is possible in a number of species belonging to the genus *Calliactis*. In *Calliactis parasitica* there are openings at certain points, having swollen margins, which project somewhat above the surface of the wall; they can be easily observed even in the dead animal, but they are so distinct in the living Calliactis that they have been already described and figured by earlier naturalists, such as Forskål (Descriptiones animalium, &c., 1775), Ehrenberg, and Dana. This is not the case in the majority of the Sagartidæ.

Sagartia, Gosse, *pro parte.*
Sagartia, Verrill.

Sagartidæ with smooth wall and numerous powerful tentacles arranged in several rows; with circular oral disk; without anatomically perceptible cinclides.

Though I agree as far as possible with Verrill in the limitation of the genera, I restrict the genus *Sagartia* to forms in which it can be shown at most that the acontia pass out through the wall, but in which, however, no openings can be pointed out, either because they are not preformed or because they are so small and indistinct as to be easily overlooked even with most careful observation. The genus *Sagartia* is distinguished in this point from *Calliactis*; it is, moreover, distinguished from *Cereus*, *Bunodes*, and *Phellia* by the smooth nature of the wall, arising from the absence of papillæ and cuticular excretions, and finally from *Metridium* by the circular shape of the oral disk, and by the powerful development of the tentacles.

Sagartia, sp. ?

Body flattened like a cake in the contracted condition; tentacles nearly two hundred in number, placed in five rows, and decreasing in size from within outwards; muscles of the tentacles and of the oral disk ectodermal, hardly at all pleated.

Habitat.—Station 194. September 29, 1874. Lat. 4° 33′ S., long. 129° 58′ E. Depth, 360 fathoms. One specimen.

Dimensions.—Diameter of the pedal disk, 4 cm.

Colour.—(Determined from the spirit specimen) whitish on the whole, the middle third of the wall yellowish-red.

There was only a single specimen of a true *Sagartia* in the Challenger material. It was attached to a very porous stone of volcanic origin, but it was so strongly contracted, and its external appearance presented so little that was characteristic, that I gave up the idea of determining the species more closely, and only decided to give a description of it in order that the important genus might not be left unrepresented.

The animal was so strongly contracted that its body formed a cone, nearly flattened into a disk, the base of which measured 4 cm., whilst its height measured little more than 0·5 cm. The surface of the animal is extremely smooth ; it is whitish at the base, then assumes a yellowish-reddish colour, which again passes gradually into white. The coloured part appears longitudinally striated, because the red and yellow alternately predominate in the ground-tint.

The wall is on the whole thin-membraned, and becomes about six times as thick only at the upper margin. This very unusual increase in bulk is explained partly by the high degree of contraction, partly by the great strength of the mesodermal circular muscle. The latter occupies nearly the entire thickness of the wall, and is only separated from the ectoderm by a very thin layer of connective substance, whilst a rather broader layer separates it from the endoderm. Its contour corresponds to the form of the wall, so that it is broad above and drawn out to a point below. We rarely find such beautiful primitive bundles in transverse section as in our *Sagartia ;* they are formed of strong fibrillæ, are regularly oval or rounded circularly, and of medium size. On the other hand, the way in which they run is remarkably irregular. In the same transverse section we find, side by side, bundles, some divided obliquely, and others divided perpendicularly, and we see in the thicker parts of the section how the bundles cross and become interwoven in their course.

Contrasted with the circular muscle, the radial muscular fibres of the oral disk and of the tentacles are only slightly developed, and form a very slightly pleated layer in the ectoderm. The tentacles are limited to the periphery of the oral disk, where they are arranged in five rows, and decrease a little in size from within outwards. They are of medium length, rather slender, and pointed at the end. I counted twenty-five in about an eighth of the animal, so that there are probably one hundred and ninety-six in all.

From transverse sections taken through the œsophagus I estimated the number of septa at forty-eight pairs, of which the six principal pairs only are perfect. There would probably be a much larger number at the base, as small septa reaching only a little way project there, in the angle between the pedal disk and the wall. There were reproductive organs (mature testes) on all the larger secondary septa. Finally, in transverse section, I could perceive wide openings in the septa near the wall.

Calliactis, Verrill.

Sagartidæ with smooth wall and numerous tentacles, with distinct cinclides which pierce the wall not far from the base in one or several transverse rows.

Following Verrill's example (Trans. Connect. Acad., vol. i. p. 481), I have separated the genus *Calliactis* from *Sagartia*, as in it we find distinct cinclides constantly present in a circle above the base. They are easily made out in a fresh state, and often after treatment with reagents as warts, into which a small evagination protrudes from the gastric space, so that the membrane of the wall becomes much thinned away; an opening, which it is more difficult to find, lies in the middle of the knob. If the knobs do not project sufficiently above the surface, it is merely necessary to remove the uppermost layer of the wall by means of a section parallel to the surface in order to make the cinclides which traverse the thickness of the supporting substance distinctly visible; this method answers very well, if we wish to determine the number of cinclides in preserved specimens of *Calliactis*.

The forms belonging to this genus agree so far in their manner of life that they are only found upon Gasteropod shells, the interior of which is occupied by a *Pagurus*. Their best known representative is *Calliactis (Sagartia) parasitica*, in which my brother and I have made out and described the cinclides; other forms are *Calliactis polypus*, *Calliactis decorata*, and *Calliactis variegata*. All these species are difficult to distinguish in a preserved state, as the colour has usually formed an important point in their definition. The forms of *Calliactis* in the Challenger material appear to me identical with *Calliactis polypus*; none of them belong to *Calliactis parasitica*.

Calliactis polypus.

Priapus polypus, Forskål, Descriptiones animalium, p. 102, tab. xxvii. fig. C, 1775.
Cribrina polypus, Ehrenberg, Corallen. d. roth. Meeres, p. 40, 1834.
Adamsia priapus, Milne-Edwards, Hist. des Corall., tom. i. p. 280, 1857.
Calliactis polypus, Klunzinger, Korall. d. roth. Meeres, i. p. 76, taf. v. fig. 1, 1877.

Wall smooth, with a circle of 24 cinclides; tentacles long and slender, above 600 in number, placed in numerous circles, decreasing in size from within outwards; twelve tentacles in the innermost circle, twelve in the next, twenty-four in the third, and so on.

Habitat.—(*a*) Station 208. January 17, 1875. Lat. 11° 37′ N., long. 123° 32′ E. Depth, 18 fathoms. Three specimens on one Gasteropod shell. (*b*) St. Vincent, Cape Verde Islands. Six specimens on one Gasteropod shell.

Dimensions.—Breadth of pedal disk up to 4 cm.; height up to 3 cm.

The specimens of *Calliactis polypus*, taken at two different places, lay, in the one case, in a group of six individuals on the shell of a *Natica*, and in the other in a group of three on the shell of a *Murex*. They were, however, all contracted into a shallow conical mass, at the point of which the tentacles appeared here and there, as Klunzinger has already described in this Actinia.

The pedal disk is very large, and firmly fastened to the shell by means of a brownish mass. The wall is smooth, and only folded longitudinally above in consequence of contraction; it is tough and opaque except in a small portion adjoining the pedal disk,

REPORT ON THE ACTINIARIA.   75

which is thin as paper, and through which the insertions of more than one hundred and fifty septa are visible. The cinclides form a single circle at a little distance from the pedal disk ; they are placed irregularly, sometimes higher, sometimes lower and closer to the disk. Their walls rise above the surface in places like an hour-glass ; where this is not the case they cannot be seen from the surface, and only become visible after the superficial layer of the wall has been removed by a section parallel to the surface in the manner already specified. Their number seemed to amount invariably to twenty-four ; they open into the intraseptal spaces of the first three orders of septa.

The circular muscle at the upper end traverses the entire mass of the wall, which is trebly thickened at this point, but is separated from the endoderm by a narrow layer of connective substance, from the ectoderm by a rather broader layer of connective substance ; it is most powerful in the middle, and becomes weaker above and below ; above, it reaches as far as the origin of the oral disk, where at the same time it most closely approaches the two layers of epithelium.

The bundles of muscular fibrillæ show a tendency to arrangement in parallel layers, placed one above the other as in *Phellia pectinata* (Pl. VI. fig. 5) and *Cereus spinosus* (Pl. VI. fig. 1), though not so distinctly as in the latter species. Each layer again consists of a number of smaller and larger groups of bundles of fibrillæ, placed in a line one behind the other, and each bundle, in transverse section, is divided by constrictions of its surface into lobes which are sometimes more, sometimes less distinctly separated from one another. The muscular fibres which occupy the periphery and enclose the protoplasmic axis in an undulating layer, are of medium strength.

The arrangement of the bundles of fibrillæ in layers becomes less distinct above and below ; above, because the bundles are so pressed together that only a scanty framework of the separating connective tissue trabeculæ remains ; and below, because, on the other hand, the bundles become very small and are isolated from one another. Finally, the bundles of fibrillæ become flatter from the outside towards the inside, but this is merely in consequence of the contraction of the animal.

The circular muscle of *Calliactis polypus* described above, is chiefly distinguished from the circular muscle of *Calliactis parasitica*, which we have already investigated (Actinien, p. 180), by not being divided into two distinct parts. There are also differences in the muscular system, which enable us to distinguish the two species in a preserved condition. I refer to the radial muscles of the oral disk, and to the similarly constructed longitudinal muscles of the tentacles.

The radial muscular fibres in *Calliactis polypus* form a thick layer which is always thinned away above the insertions of the larger septa, and so divided into broader and narrower radial bands. Their figure in transverse section is difficult to make out ; at first sight it gives the impression that masses of compacted muscular fibres, placed in repeated layers the one above the other, have been deposited between the supporting lamella and the layer of nerve fibres of the ectoderm. It is necessary to employ a staining fluid (picro-carmine), which impregnates the supporting substance strongly, in order to distinguish a framework of connective tissue between the muscular fibres ; and as this gives rise to extremely fine-walled meshes, it divides the muscular fibres into mesodermal bundles of fibrillæ. Numerous supporting layers run out from the surfaces of the supporting lamellæ, and these ramify and anastomose with one another. The anastomoses are wanting towards the ectoderm, so that the meshes open towards the layer of nerve fibres ; the muscles are consequently partly mesodermal, partly ectodermal.

In *Calliactis parasitica* the boundary line between the mesodermal muscles and the ectoderm is also indistinct, but the bulk of the former is much smaller, so that sparse bundles only are enclosed in an abundant fundamental substance.

The tentacles of *Calliactis polypus* are long, slender, and end in a fine point. I made out about seventy in a twelfth part of the animal, so that altogether they amount in number to several hundreds, which decrease in size. from within outwards, and are arranged in about ten circles. The first and second circles, beginning at the inside, each contain twelve tentacles placed somewhat apart, the third twenty-four tentacles, the fourth forty-eight, and so on.

If we take the well-developed septa only into consideration, there are altogether our cycles or forty-eight pairs, the first six pairs of which are perfect. The following six pairs are imperfect and sterile like the first six, so that the reproductive organs are confined to the septa of the third and fourth orders. The specimen examined by me was a male, and contained ripe testes.

Cereus, Oken.

Sagartidæ, with numerous tentacles and circular oral disk, without cinclides which can be anatomically demonstrated ; wall rough, and covered with knobs.

Milne-Edwards (Hist. des Corall., tom. i. p. 263) included all the more typical representatives of his "Actinines verruqueuses" in Oken's genus *Cereus*. After it had been shown that acontia existed in *Cereus bellis*, which had been taken by Oken as the typical representative of the genus (Lehrbuch d. Naturgeschichte, Th. III. Abth. 1, p. 349, 1815), Verrill limited the name to forms of the family Sagartidæ. I agree with Verrill on this point, but wish to attach more importance in the diagnosis to the papillose nature of the wall, in order to establish a sharp distinction between this genus and *Sagartia*. I have therefore altered the description of the wall, which runs thus in Verrill : "upper part with small, inconspicuous contractile suckers ; walls nearly smooth."

Cereus spinosus, n. sp. (Pl. I. figs. 3–5; Pl. VI. fig. 1; Pl. VIII. fig. 6; Pl. XII. fig. 10).

Papillæ of the wall unequal in size, with a tendency to arrangement in transverse and longitudinal rows ; each papilla runs out into a fine point, which is placed on a hemispheroidal base ; surface of the wall rough and bark-like ; tentacles tolerably long, placed in three rows decreasing in size from within outwards.

Habitat.—(*a*) Station 157. March 3, 1874. Lat. 53° 55′ S., long. 108° 35′ E. Depth, 1950 fathoms. One specimen. (*b*) Station 237. June 17, 1875. Lat. 34° 37′ N., long. 140° 32′ E. Depth, 1875 fathoms. Four specimens.

Dimensions.—Diameter of the pedal disk, 5 cm. ; height, 7 cm.

Colour.—(Determined from the spirit specimen) a dirty violet.

The new species, which I have named *Cereus spinosus*, was found at two different places. The first time there were several specimens, which were unfortunately preserved in chromic acid, and thus rendered of no practical use. The second time there was only a single specimen, which was very well preserved in spirit, and from which the following description was exclusively taken.

The colour of the body was a dirty violet in all parts to which the spirit had easy access, whilst in other parts it had become discoloured into a greyish-yellow. For example, the outer tentacles were violet, and so were the points of the inner tentacles, whilst the bases of the latter were yellowish. This was caused from the animal being in a semi-contracted condition, in which portions of the tentacles project freely.

It was plain that the pedal disk had been attached to a very narrow underlying substance, and had consequently acquired a very irregular shape. Part of the disk surrounded the stalk of a *Hyalonema*, which was consequently enclosed in a canal, so that the edges of the disk are not only placed firmly one against the other, but have actually become fused. The pedal disk is otherwise opaque, tough, and knobbed, and thus presents a bark-like appearance.

The surface of the wall is likewise very rough. Its lower third is covered with circular furrows, which are placed at a little distance from one another, and run parallel to the margin of the pedal disk. At the upper end the furrows lie further apart and become irregular, whilst at the same time they are crossed here and there by longitudinal furrows. The numerous knobs with their pointed ends, on account of which I have named the species *Cereus spinosus*, deserve special attention ; they show a tendency to arrangement in transverse and longitudinal lines, but are wanting in some places, whilst they are thickly compacted in others. In the upper third of the wall they are of considerable size, begin with a broad hemispheroidal base and end in a thorn-like point, marked off by its dark brown colour from its surroundings. Lower down the knobs become smaller, and are finally merely minute pointed knobs, which are very firm, and coloured an intense brown.

The bark-like appearance of the pedal disk and wall is owing to a cuticular deposit (the "epidermis" of former authors), in which we can distinguish two layers (Pl. VIII. fig. 6). The surface of the epithelium is covered first of all by a yellowish, irregularly fibrous border, which is torn in some places, and raised here and there in tube-shaped processes, of which one is shown in fig. 6, *b*. Outside the fibrous border comes a granular mass traversed by foreign bodies. The epithelium lying below this deposit is without cilia, and varies very much in height; the epithelial stratum sometimes shrinks to an almost invisible layer, and sometimes rises into long, filamentous cylindrical cells.

The wall in *Cereus spinosus* is very thick (as much as 3 mm. in transverse section), tough, and leathery as in the majority of Sagartidæ. It is constricted at the upper end by a circular muscle, which, in spite of its strength, is entirely concealed in the mesoderm of the wall. The muscle is nearly 1·5 cm. long and nearly 2 mm. broad in section at its upper end, whilst it becomes narrow below as usual. It is separated both from the ectoderm and the endoderm by a layer of connective tissue, 0·5 mm. broad, and without muscles. Seen in transverse section (Pl. VI. fig. 1), the muscular fibrillæ in the upper half of the muscle form rows rising from within and below, obliquely upwards and outwards; they are separated by broad bands of connective tissue, and placed in tiers one above the other. Here and there a row consists of a single flattened primitive bundle, the indentations of whose surface indicate its tendency to split up into a series of smaller bundles. This process has, however, usually taken place, so that each single tier is composed of a series of smaller roundish bundles and larger flattened bundles. Two successive tiers of bundles are not completely separated, but connected by a network of thin branched anastomosing cords; the bundles of each tier are connected with one another in the same way. The former is visible in sections taken parallel to the surface of the wall, the latter in sections parallel to the base of the animal.

The character of the muscle changes in the lower half as the bundles of fibrillæ are scattered at considerable distances from one another. The larger bundles are lobed in transverse section, or resolved into a group of smaller bundles of fibrillæ.

The radial striation is distinctly marked on the oral disk, and is caused by the manner in which the muscles are arranged, while this again is correlated with the distribution of the tentacles. The radial muscular layer is ectodermal and pleated very uniformly, so that the single folds of muscles are only slightly branched, and lie beside one another like the leaves of a book. Besides this uniform pleating, the enlargement of the muscular layer is due to the fact that the supporting layer is thinner at the insertions of the septa, but becomes thickened above the middle of each interseptal space, where it forms a sharp, roof-like ridge. The ridges formed in this way produce the radial striation of the oral disk already mentioned ; seen from the surface, they do not project very sharply so long as they are covered by epithelium, which in a measure reduces their inequalities. The ridges begin near the margin of the mouth (Pl. I. figs. 4 and 5) ; they are forty-eight in number, twenty-four corresponding to the intraseptal spaces of the first, second, and third orders, and the other twenty-four to the intermediate interseptal spaces. The first twenty-four are broadest near the margin of the mouth, become narrower towards the periphery, and end on the twenty-four tentacles of the innermost row, where they run a little way divided into two by a shallow furrow. The second twenty-four ridges differ, inasmuch as they are broadest towards the periphery, where they are each divided by two long radial furrows into three ridges, a middle ridge belonging to one of the twenty-four tentacles of the second cycle, and two lateral ridges which pass on to two of the forty-eight tentacles of the third cycle. This division corresponds at the same time to the arrangement of the septa, the twenty-four interseptal spaces are divided in the periphery by the twenty-four pairs of septa of the fourth order into three compartments, an intraspace and two interspaces.

The number and mode of arrangement of the tentacles may be deduced from what has been said. We find altogether ninety-six tentacles distributed in three rows, twenty-four in the first or innermost row, twenty-four alternating with them in the second row, and forty-eight in the third row. This is best seen if we cut away the tentacles, leaving only the short basal stumps (Pl. I. fig. 4). The tentacles have a slender shape, diminishing uniformly from the base towards the point; they are distinctly striated longitudinally and perforated at the end by a fine opening; they are largest in the innermost row, where they attain a length of 2 cm. The longitudinal striation is caused by elevations of the supporting lamella, which are covered moreover with small folds bearing the muscles.

The boundary between the oral disk and the œsophagus is only indicated by a slightly swollen lip. The œsophagus has tolerably broad œsophageal grooves and short œsophageal lappets; it also shows eleven powerful longitudinal swellings on either side (fig. 5).

The arrangement of the septa is governed by the same principle, which has been already laid down as applicable to most *Sagartiæ*. Its characteristic is, that only the six pairs of principal septa, of which again two pairs are directive septa, reach the œsophagus. The principal septa are, at the same time, exclusively muscular septa, i.e., they do not develop reproductive organs. Their muscular systems are not very strong; for example, the parietobasilar muscle is merely a slight fold; the most distinct among them are the longitudinal fibres, which rise obliquely from the wall and the base to the oral disk. An internal septal stoma is certainly present, but so small as to be easily overlooked; an external septal stoma is wanting.

The principal septa are followed by three cycles of imperfect septa; the development of their muscular system is far behind that of the principal septa, but, on the other hand, they are furnished with reproductive organs (in the present case with ovaries). In each cycle they become smaller, and project less into the gastric space and towards the pedal disk and oral disk. The last forty-eight pairs are hardly recognisable as longitudinal lines on the wall, and merely project as folds in the angles formed by the wall on one side and the oral disk or pedal disk on the other (figs. 4 and 5, h^4). The reproductive organs lie highest up, and quite hidden by the œsophagus on the septa of the second order (figs. 4 and 5, h^2); in the septa of the third order they are visible under the lower margin of the œsophagus (figs. 4 and 5, h^3), while in the septa of the fourth order they are insignificant bodies, confined to the lowest section.

The free margin of each septum is occupied by the mesenteric filament. The upper section is tripartite, the lateral ciliated streaks still lying beside the median glandular streak, whilst the lower section is simple, and formed merely of the glandular streak. This last comports itself differently on the different septa; in the septa of the first and second orders it is disposed in meandrous curves and coiled into a thick mass, which, in the septa of the first order, is visible beneath the margin of the œsophagus, whilst it is covered by the latter in the septa of the second order; in the other septa it appears as a slightly waved border. The acontia common to all *Sagartiæ*, and of which one at least is found in each septum—even in the small septa of the fourth order—arise at a little distance from the lower end of the mesenteric filaments. In transverse section the acontium shows a roundish figure flattened somewhat to an oblong (Pl. XII. fig. 10). On one of the longer sides there is an indentation, the expression of a groove which runs on the acontium as far as its point of attachment to the septum. Histologically we can distinguish an axis of connective tissue and a cylindrical epithelium, containing numerous nematocysts, especially on the side of the acontium remote from the groove. In *Calliactis parasitica*, we had previously distinguished fine muscular fibres and a layer of nerve fibres; these doubtless exist in *Cereus spinosus*, but the specimen was not well enough preserved to admit of their being made out plainly.

If we open a *Cereus spinosus* by a longitudinal incision we can distinguish the different pairs of septa, without further dissection, by the constitution of the reproductive organs and of the mesenteric filaments (fig. 5). The pairs of septa of the first order (h^1) are recognisable by the thick coils of mesenteric filaments, which spring from them below the œsophagus, whilst the pairs of septa of the second order (h^2), the reproductive organs and mesenteric filaments of which are usually completely covered by the œsophagus, appear only as sharply defined lamellæ with smooth margins; in the septa of the third order (h^3), in which the coils of filaments are wanting, the ends of the reproductive organs project from beneath the lower margin of the œsophagus, whilst the pairs of septa of the fourth order are so small as to be quite out of sight.

Phellia, Gosse.

Sagartidæ with a rough, cuticular sheath, which is firmly attached to the epithelium, and leaves the upper part of the wall free; the latter is smooth and becomes inverted during contraction; cinclides not demonstrable anatomically; tentacles small, and few in number.

The cuticular sheath, which we have already found in *Cereus spinosus*, is still more strongly developed in a number of Actiniæ, but is here confined at the same time to one part of the wall, leaving the other part free. Close underneath the corona of tentacles, the free part of the wall forms a broader or narrower ring, which is soft-membraned and smooth walled, is pretty sharply defined from the bark-like section of the wall, and, like the oral disk, is inverted during contraction. Gosse formed the genus *Phellia* for these Actiniæ, which are easily recognised even by a superficial observer (Ann. and Mag. of Nat. Hist., ser. iii. vol. ii. p. 192); Verrill went a step further, and erected them into a special sub-family, though in so doing he attached undue value to the character.

Jourdan was the first to explain the essential nature of this formation by pointing out that the bark-like layer is merely a deposit on the ectodermal epithelium, and that the latter has undergone retrograde formation under this deposit so as to become an imperceptible layer (Annales des Sciences Nat. Zool., ser. vi. t. x. p. 98).

Verrill has made some statements about the internal structure of the *Phelliæ* (Transact. Connect. Acad., vol. i. p. 490), which refer to *Phellia panamensis*; the ovaries are irregularly distributed on the septa, are wanting on the smaller, and present only on the twelve largest. This so flatly contradicts all observations on the distribution of the reproductive elements in the Actiniæ, that Verrill must somehow have been mistaken. His observations are of no use for another reason, namely, that he says nothing about the relation of the septa to the œsophagus.

Phellia pectinata, n. sp. (Pl. I. fig. 7 ; Pl. VI. fig. 5 ; Pl. VIII. figs. 1, 2, and 10).

The bark-like part of the wall is covered with transverse and longitudinal furrows; terminating above in twelve knobs, which are prolonged on to the inverted soft-membraned section as twelve longitudinal combs ; each comb ends in a very prominent, bifurcated, nose-like projection ; tentacles small, pointed, arranged in four cycles.

Habitat.—Station 307. January 4, 1876. Lat. 49° 24' S., long. 74° 23' W. Depth, 147 fathoms. One specimen.

Dimensions.—Height of the wall (taken as far as the inverted soft-membraned part), 2 cm. ; breadth, 1·5 cm.

This animal, which I have incorporated as a new species in the genus *Phellia*, would hardly be taken for an Actinia by any one who glanced at it in a contracted condition ; its small body, about 2 cm. high and 1·5 cm. broad, rather resembles the body of a *Cynthia*, perhaps *Cynthia canopus* ; it has the same rough, somewhat shaggy surface, the same leather-like consistency, the same oval form having an opening at the one end, whilst a second opening similar to the egestive opening is naturally wanting. This constitution of body is explained by the peculiar fashion in which the animal contracts itself ; during this process not only the oral disk and corona of tentacles, but the upper part of the wall is so deeply invaginated that not the smallest part of the tentacles nor of the oral disk remains externally visible.

As in every *Phellia* we can distinguish two sections in the wall, a lower section which does not, and an upper part which does, become invaginated. The two parts are very differently constituted. The former, which is the only part externally visible, is covered with transverse wrinkles, crossed here and there with longitudinal furrows. It terminates above in twelve knobs which are placed like a corona round the entrance to the orifice of invagination, and lie close together so as to greatly contract the opening.

In order to understand the construction of the upper part, it is necessary to open up the animal longitudinally, then we see that it extends about 1 cm. inside the animal; it is covered with twelve strongly projecting sharp-edged longitudinal ridges, which begin at the twelve knobs, become higher as they run downwards (upwards in the natural position), till each of them ends in a nose-like projection. This projection is again divided by a longitudinal furrow into a larger and a smaller process. The ridges and their bifurcated ends are extremely smooth, very soft, and of a whitish colour. They consist, however, only of connective tissue, like the rest of the wall.

The varied aspect of the surface of the body is caused by the varying character of the epithelium; on the invaginated part of the wall (Pl. VI. fig. 5) it is a ciliated cylindrical epithelium, such as we find in most Actiniæ; in the other parts it is without cilia, but instead of cilia is covered with a deposit, which may be divided into two layers. One of these (Pl. VIII. fig. 1) is an irregular, fibrous cuticle, which is stained an intense red by carmine, the other is a mucous layer permeated by foreign bodies, lying outside the cuticle.

The mesoderm consists of extremely fine fibrillæ which cross one another in all directions, so that it appears as a finely granulated mass in transverse section. It is partially laid in strata parallel to the surface; in it there are small roundish concrements, which are strongly coloured by carmine, and the structure of which recalls that of granules of starch; they are made up of indistinct concentric layers, frequently appear in section like a figure **8**, and are limited to the superficial layer of the mesoderm.

The existence of a strong circular muscle, which is indeed easily discovered, might be inferred merely from the high degree of contraction. It is mesodermal, and the chief bulk of it lies in the invaginated section of the wall, where it begins close to the commencement of the oral disk, or, to speak more accurately, to the origin of the tentacles (Pl. VI. fig. 5); it extends a considerable way into the outer section of the wall, into which it gradually passes. It is separated from the endoderm by a broad layer of connective substance, so that it lies nearer to the ectoderm than to its place of origin, and consists of numerous very small bundles of fibrillæ grouped together into bundles of the second order (Pl. VIII. fig. 10). The latter are usually flattened, and in transverse section show bands lying perpendicular to the surface of the endoderm.

The comportment of the oral disk is the same as that formerly described in *Calliactis parasitica*. The muscular fibres are still chiefly ectodermal, and the lamella is not thickly pleated, though at the same time single fibrillæ and groups of fibrillæ have passed into the mesoderm. The boundary line between the mesoderm and the ectoderm is therefore indistinct as in *Calliactis*.

The tentacles are small, broad at the base, and pointed towards the end ; they are placed in three rows, as they probably alternate in the first and second row, whilst the third row contains double the number. Their longitudinal muscles are ectodermal and only slightly pleated.

The œsophagus and the two œsophageal grooves are of a deep brown-violet colour even in the spirit material ; this is caused by fine pigment granules deposited in the ectodermal epithelium.

There are altogether four cycles of septa. Only the septa of the first order are perfect, all the others are imperfect, but, on the other hand, the latter only bear (male) reproductive organs, whilst the former are sterile.

The muscles of the septa are very strong, as Jourdan already observed in *Phellia elongata* ; in the first three cycles especially the longitudinal muscles form mushroom-shaped projections in the middle of each septum, which show the delicate, dendritic figures of a repeatedly folded muscular lamella in transverse section. The transverse muscular layer is also thickly pleated, so that it is doubly remarkable that I could find no trace of a parietobasilar muscle even in sections.

All the septa seem to bear acontia ; these are extremely fine, and lie coiled in the lowest section of the gastric space. I was able to make them out distinctly in transverse section, but, on the other hand, I could not find any openings in the wall.

The directive septa were fused by the free margins, nearly their entire length below the œsophagus '(Pl. VIII. fig. 2). I only examined one pair of them, as I wished to destroy the single specimen taken by the Challenger as little as possible. The longitudinal muscles of one septum pass continuously into the longitudinal muscles of the other, whilst a mesenteric filament is wanting at the point of junction. The filament is confined to the short space lying between the lower margin of the œsophagus and the beginning of the fusion, where it is coiled in numerous curves. I shall leave it an open question whether it be correct to speak of a fusion of the free margins, as I have done for the sake of simplicity, or whether the union of the two septa does not rather represent a more primitive condition. I wish, however, to draw attention to one fact which seems to favour the latter view, and which I have formerly noticed repeatedly, viz., that in the young Actiniæ we frequently find the newly-formed septa of a pair connected together in the same manner as in the principal septa of *Phellia* and the secondary septa of *Tealia bunodiformis*, figured by me in Plate VIII. From this it would appear that separation takes place later on, as at a later period all the septa have free margins set with mesenteric filaments.

Bunodes, Gosse.

Sagartidæ (?) with numerous papillæ on the wall, which are placed in regular longitudinal rows, corresponding to the intraseptal spaces.

When Gosse erected his genus *Bunodes* (Trans. Linn. Soc., vol. xxi. p. 274, 1855), he included in it all Actiniæ furnished with a knobbed surface. Later, he limited this name to those Actiniæ on the walls of which the papillæ are arranged in regular, longitudinal rows (Ann. and Mag. Nat. Hist., ser. iii. vol. i. p. 417, 1858). In both instances, however, he laid it down as a rule that there should be no acontia, and the same definition of the genus was accepted by Verrill (Trans. Connect. Acad., vol. i. p. 467), by Klunzinger (Korrallthiere, i. p. 77), and by Jourdan (Annales des Scienc. Nat. Zool., ser. vi. t. x. p. 84, 1879–80). Gosse himself, however, changed his views afterwards, for, in his Actinologia Britannica, he described *Bunodes coronata* as a form in which he had once observed acontia.

Among the Challenger material I found one true representative of the Sagartidæ, the external appearance of which justified its being placed in the genus *Bunodes*. I have determined it as *Bunodes minuta*, as I consider it quite possible that the acontia have hitherto been overlooked in the species of the genus *Bunodes*. If this view be erroneous, it would be necessary to erect a new genus for *Bunodes minuta* and *Bunodes coronata*.

Bunodes minuta, n. sp. (Pl. II. fig. 12).

Wall covered with alternate rows of larger and smaller papillæ, which are confined to the upper half of the body ; tentacles long and pointed, arranged in two circles, the outer circle much smaller than the inner.

Habitat.—Station 147. December 30, 1873. Lat. 46° 16′ S., long. 48° 27′ E. Depth, 1600 fathoms. One specimen.

Dimensions.—Height and breadth, 1 cm.

The general appearance of the small new species of *Bunodes*, which I shall describe as *Bunodes minuta* from a single specimen found among the Challenger material, recalls that of *Paractis excavata* At first sight the body seems as broad as high (fig. 12, *a*), but if we cut open the animal (fig. 12, *b*) we see that the oral disk extends deep down into the body, so that there is but a little distance between the pedal disk and the periphery of the mouth. The diameter of the oral disk is therefore essentially greater than the breadth of the body given above.

The upper section of the wall is brownish, the lower part whitish and covered with small papillæ, which are arranged in from thirty to forty rows. Each row begins at the upper margin of the wall, and reaches half-way down the animal ; the papillæ are small at first and increase in size downwards ; they comport themselves differently, however, in the different rows, as rows with large papillæ and rows with small papillæ alternate irregularly. The same conditions therefore recur in *Bunodes minuta*, which exist in *Bunodes coronata*, a fact of special interest, as they are the only two species of *Bunodes* in which acontia have as yet been found (Gosse, Actinologia Britannica, p. 204).

Histologically, I find that the papillæ are formed of connective substance only, and have therefore come to an entirely different conclusion from Jourdan, who declares them to be products of the ectoderm (Annal. des Scienc. Nat., ser. vi. t. x. p. 78, 1879–80). According to Jourdan, the papillœ which he terms "verrues glandulaires" have arisen from the epithelium pushing its way like glands into the supporting substance, and becoming wholly or nearly detached into epithelial islands. The author gives these epithelial cords as the first stage of development in longitudinal section, the detached epithelial islands in transverse section. I have obtained figures exactly similiar to those given by Jourdan, and am justified in the view that the constitution of the wall agrees in both species of *Bunodes*, but am also justified in maintaining that Jourdan's view is erroneous. These epithelial growths are linings of the depressions and furrows running on the surface, of the wall; they become deeply pleated during contraction, and may look like detached epithelial islands in transverse section, whilst in longitudinal section they may be taken for mere epithelial folds. In order to be quite certain, I made sections parallel to the surface and also examined single papillœ in transverse section; in the former we have invariably islands of connective tissue, the transverse sections of the papillœ, surrounded by an epithelial net-work but without glandular ducts; in the latter the papillœ proved to be solid growths of the connective substance. From these observations I have already, in the introduction, declared myself to be against the acceptation of the term "verrues glandulaires."

The circular muscle is entirely enclosed in the mesoderm, which, however, is only slightly thickened by it; the bulk of it extends longitudinally, is almost equal in breadth the whole way along, and is separated from the endoderm by a narrow layer of connective substance, from the ectoderm by a somewhat broader layer. The roundish bundles of fibrillœ, which merely consist of a few strong muscular fibrillœ, are divided by processes of connective substance into larger and smaller groups; this is beautifully seen in the upper part of the muscle, whilst there is a preponderance of small, irregularly distributed bundles in the lower part.

The muscles of the oral disk are divided into radial bands corresponding to the septa; they lie as a thickly folded layer in the ectoderm, like the longitudinal muscles of the tentacles. Seventy relatively long, filamentous tentacles lie on the margin of the oral disk; they run out into a fine point, and project above the surface even in the contracted animal. The outer tentacles are decidedly smaller than the inner.

In order to observe the septa properly I cut out a quadrant of the body which I made into transverse sections. From these it was plain that the directive septa running towards the œsophageal grooves alone were perfect, and did not bear reproductive organs, whilst all the other septa, not even excepting the principal septa, remain imperfect, and are amply furnished with reproductive organs (testes). The differentiation of the septa into muscular septa and reproductive septa, which is present in all Sagartidæ, extends in *Bunodes minuta* to the more limited circle of the principal septa.

If I may draw a conclusion from a small part of a single specimen, the formation of the septa is very irregular, and seems to proceed more quickly near the directive septa. I have found that septa of the sixth and seventh orders are present in the interseptal space contiguous to the directive septa, whilst septa even of the fifth order are wanting in other parts. This assertion must of course be accepted with reserve, as the septa are so irregularly constituted that it is difficult to determine to which order a septum belongs.

I have found the acontia only in transverse section; they are oval filaments, dotted with nematocysts, quite small, and by no means numerous. This confirms my view that the acontia have hitherto been overlooked in the other species of *Bunodes*.

Family, AMPHIANTHIDÆ, Hertwig.

Hexactiniæ, which are attached to the axial skeletons of Gorgonidæ with shortened sagittal and elongated transverse axis; transverse axis lying parallel to the axial skeleton of the *Gorgonia*; circular muscle mesodermal; the principal septa only perfect and sterile.

Under the names *Actinia abyssicola* and *Actinia gelatinosa*, Moseley described two Actiniæ from the Challenger material, which agree in being attached to the stems of *Gorgoniæ* which they clasp with their base. I was only able to examine the *Actinia abyssicola*, as *Actinia gelatinosa* was not among the spirit specimens sent to me; on the other hand, I found two other new forms among the specimens, which resemble the two species determined by Moseley both in their form and mode of life.

All these forms differ so decidedly from *Actinia mesembryanthemum* that I have not only separated them generically but united them into a new family, the Amphianthidæ. Closer examination shows that the mode in which they attach themselves has influenced their organization in a very important and uniform manner. All the Amphianthidæ are elongated, corresponding to the form of the body to which they are attached, and placed in such a way that their transverse axis is greatly prolonged and runs in the same direction as the longitudinal axis of the *Gorgonia*, whilst their sagittal axis is very much shortened, and crosses the skeletal axis at right angles. The œsophagus consequently differs from that of other Actiniæ, as it is either round or even fissure-shaped in a transverse direction (Pl. III. fig. 7, *a*), and its œsophageal grooves lie so near one another that they almost touch (Pl. II. fig. 13).

The internal anatomy recalls that of the Sagartidæ. The six pairs of principal septa are sterile and alone reach the œsophagus; their interlying interseptal spaces have been modified by the elongation of the form in such a way that the four spaces belonging to the broad sides are more extensive than those belonging to the narrow sides. I was not able to make out any acontia. The circular muscle is powerful and lies in the mesoderm.

Two species already described by other naturalists, *Actinia s. catherinæ* and *Gephyra dohrnii* probably belong to the family Amphianthidæ. The former, which was described and figured by Lesson (Voyage de la Coquille, Zool., tome ii. part ii.

2, p. 74; Zoophytes, pl. ii. fig. 2), is certainly attached to a smooth underlying substance, but is, nevertheless, greatly elongated in one direction, so that, if we may judge from the drawing of it, even the corona of tentacles is divided into a right and a left half. On the other hand, *Gephyra dohrnii*, our knowledge of which we owe to G. v. Koch (Zur Phylogenie der Antipatharia. Morphol. Jahrb., Bd. iv., Suppl., p. 78, 1878), settles like a true Amphianthid on the axis of *Isis elongata*. The animals either live singly or are united by basal processes into a colony ; they are fastened to the axis by a cuticular mass secreted by the pedal disk. The author has unfortunately given no details as to the position of the oral fissure with respect to the axis of the *Isis* and the constitution of the septa and œsophageal grooves.

G. v. Koch considers the *Gephyræ* as transition forms between the Actiniaria and the Antipatharia ; he assumes that Actiniæ settled upon cylindrical bodies and secreted a horny mass by which they attached themselves, that later, from want of a foreign axis, they originated a proper axial skeleton by richer secretion of the adhesive mass, and moreover became branched by forming colonies. The correctness of this view is confirmed by the few remarks made by v. Koch on the structure of *Antipathes larix*. The body is elongated in the direction of the skeletal axis, and the transverse axis of the animal thereby appears lengthened, whilst the sagittal axis is shortened. This I conclude from the position of the mouth and the septa ; the former is either circular or fissure-shaped ; if fissure-shaped, it crosses the longitudinal axis of the animal. The different direction of the longitudinal axis of the body, and the oral fissure is very striking, but can be easily understood if we assume that the oral fissure has maintained its original extension in a sagittal direction whilst the body is prolonged in a transverse direction. We must therefore look for the directive septa on the long sides of the body. In fact, we find there two pairs of septa, which correspond to the oral angles, are sterile, and consequently comport themselves like directive septa, whilst the two remaining pairs, lying in the prolonged transverse axis, bear reproductive organs, and are therefore best termed accessory septa.

It is therefore most probable that the Amphianthidæ bring about the transformation of the Actiniaria to the Antipatharia. A more detailed study of the Antipatharia is however necessary before this view can be fully accepted ; above all, it must be determined whether the paired arrangement of the septa and the presence of the directive septa can be demonstrated in the Antipatharia, and whether the sagittal and the transverse axes are directed in the same manner as in the Amphianthidæ.

Stephanactis, n. gen.

Amphiantidæ with firm wall, divided by a circular swelling into an upper and a lower section ; tentacles numerous, arranged in several rows, decreasing in size from within outwards.

Stephanactis tuberculata, n. sp. (Pl. III. fig. 7).

Upper part of the wall covered with larger and smaller knobs, thickly compacted together, lower part smooth ; tentacles in four to five alternating rows.

Habitat.—Station 232. May 12, 1875. Lat. 35° 11′ N., long. 139° 28′ E. Depth, 345 fathoms. One specimen.

Dimensions.—Height, 2 cm. Length of the pedal disk, 10 cm. ; length of the oral disk, 3·5 cm. ; breadth of the oral disk, 2 cm.

The single specimen of *Stephanactis tuberculata*, which I was able to examine, is attached to the axis of a *Virgularia*, from which the soft cortical layer has been completely stripped as far as the Actinia extends ; the pedal disk encloses the axis so completely that the two margins are pressed together, without, however, becoming fused, and so form a sheath about 10 cm. long. The wall first runs about 2 cm. close to the pedal disk, it then forms a body about 2 cm. high, which, being in a contracted condition, becomes much smaller at the upper end ; the body appears fusiform when seen from the oral side (fig. 7, *a*).

A thick circular swelling, running near the upper margin, divides the wall into a smaller upper and a larger lower portion. The former is slightly inverted as in the genus *Phellia*, and may be completely overlooked from the outside. It is covered with numerous knobs, which lie thickly compacted, smaller and larger intermixed. The smaller are usually rounded spheroidally, whilst the larger stand out as nose-like projections above the level of the smaller ; they may be divided into two by shallow furrows.

The lower section of the wall is essentially smooth, as the transverse and oblique wrinkles and furrows are merely caused by contraction. A more pronounced groove extends on either side in a longitudinal direction, downwards from the circular swelling at an equal distance from the two ends of the body (fig. 7). Four small knobs, in the upper surface of which I could make out a little depression with a magnifying glass, lie at the bottom of each groove. As I proved by means of transverse sections, these depressions are the openings of fine canals, which pierce the wall, and form communications between the surrounding medium and the directive intraseptal spaces which lie opposite to them ; they may be fitly compared to the cinclides of the genus *Calliactis*.

The circular muscle lies in the knobbed upper part of the wall, and extends downwards as far as the circular swelling. It occupies nearly the entire thickness of the mesoderm, which however it does not greatly increase ; in transverse section it is elongated, nearly of equal breadth throughout, and is only reduced a little in size towards the lower end. The bundles of fibrillæ are very small, and distributed with tolerable regularity in the fundamental substance, so that we can hardly observe any arrangement into larger or smaller groups.

Though the sphincter is tolerably strongly contracted, we can make a partial survey of the oral disk. It bears more than a hundred tentacles, placed in from four to five indistinctly defined rows. The tentacles of the innermost row are short, but broad at the base, powerful and compressed; towards the outside the tentacles become smaller and more slender. Indistinct radial furrows, caused by the distribution of the muscles, run from the corona of tentacles to the oral opening. The muscles consist of tough, ecto-dermal fibrillæ, the lamella made up of which lies thickly folded both in the oral disk and in the tentacles.

The oral opening is elongated to an oval in the same direction as the whole body of the animal, and from analogy to other Actiniæ we might expect to find the œsophageal grooves at the ends of the oval. In this case, however, they lie exactly in the middle of the two broad sides and in the contracted animal so near that they almost touch. If we cut out the part in question (fig. 7, *b*) we see that the œsophageal grooves are very broad and reach far down, whilst the remaining irregularly pleated part of the œsophagus only hangs down a little way into the stomach.

Except the two pairs of directive septa, which are attached to the œsophageal grooves, the other four pairs of principal septa only are perfect, whilst all the secondary septa terminate on the oral disk. The former are sterile, whilst the latter bear the repro-ductive organs, which were testes in the specimen examined. There are large marginal stomata in the septa, and in addition to these perioral stomata in the perfect principal septa.

I endeavoured to discover the mode of arrangement of the septa by cutting out two sextants contiguous to the directive septa and making them into transverse sections. I found extremely irregular conditions, and in spite of all my trouble I am unable to explain them with any certainty. Five pairs of septa of considerable strength lie in each interseptal space, but as they were equal to one another I was not able to determine their various ages from the difference in size. I am therefore undecided between two opinions; either the pairs of septa of the second order are doubled and three pairs of septa of the third order are present, or else there is only one pair of septa of the second order developed and the pairs of septa of the third order have undergone duplication.

In the interseptal spaces of the third order I found either only a single pair of the fourth order or two pairs of the fourth order; so that duplication seems also to have partially taken place here.

It would be interesting to examine the sextants occupying the narrow side of the body in order to see whether the arrangement of the septa is more regular in them. I refrained from this, however, in order not to injure the single specimen of the species. We may, however, certainly assume that the irregular development of the septa is the consequence of the elongation of the body, and this is shown by the partial duplication of their number. There would be nothing remarkable in such duplication, since the interseptal spaces belonging to the broad sides are abnormally extended.

Stephanactis abyssicola (Pl. II. fig. 13).

Actinia abyssicola, Moseley, Trans. Linn. Soc., ser. ii., Zool., vol. i. p. 297, pl. xlv. fig. 5.

Both parts of the wall smooth; circular swelling distinctly defined; tentacles in two alternating circles.

Habitat.—Station 46. May 6, 1873. Lat. 40° 17′ N., long. 66° 48′ W. Depth, 1350 fathoms. Two specimens.

Dimensions.—Length, 3·5 cm.; height, 0·5 cm.

Colour.—(Determined by Moseley in the fresh condition), the part inside the circular swelling a beautiful rose-red with a few darker radial streaks; the remainder of the wall reddish-yellow and paler, especially the circular swelling; oral disk rose-red with paler tentacles.

Of the two specimens of *Stephanactis abyssicola*, one was so much destroyed as to be of no use for anatomical examination, and I did not wish to cut up the other as it was the only well-preserved specimen of the species. *Stephanactis abyssicola* is clearly so closely allied to *Stephanactis tuberculata* that I deem a more detailed anatomical study unnecessary, and therefore confine myself to the description of its external appearance.

The body is elongated like that of *Stephanactis tuberculata*, but not prolonged into a process at either end. The pedal disk enclosed the stem of a *Mopsea* so completely that its margins were firmly joined on the lower side. The line of union is slightly undulated, and the insertions of from ninety to one hundred septa, which lie more closely compacted at the two ends of the body, shine through beside it. The spaces between the septa are larger towards the broad sides, but become narrower again towards the middle of the broad sides.

The circular swelling, which Moseley erroneously terms the muscular swelling, is, however, distinctly defined on either side. A small depression, in which rises a papilla, lies on either side close under the circular swelling in the middle of the broad side, resembling those which we have met with in the same position, but in larger number, in *Stephanactis tuberculata*. Otherwise, the wall is smooth, both in the portion lying inside the circular furrow and that lying outside. It is incompletely contracted, so that the oral disk, the oral opening, and part of the points of the tentacles are visible. As the œsophageal grooves plainly occupy the middle between the two ends of the oval oral fissure, it may be again safely assumed that the elongation of the body has taken place in the direction of the transverse axis. Numerous small tentacles (sixty according to Moseley) lie in a double row on the margin of the oral disk.

Stephanactis abyssicola is distinguished from *Stephanactis tuberculata* by its smaller size, by the absence of knobs on the upper part of the wall, and by the lesser number of cinclidal papillæ. These are all differences, however, which may possibly arise from difference of age, and it is quite likely that the two species might require to be united, if we were able to examine a larger number of specimens. In this case, the species would keep the older name of *Stephanactis abyssicola*.

Amphianthus, n. gen.

Amphianthidæ with a firm wall, which is covered with fine papillæ but not divided into two sections by a circular swelling.

Amphianthus bathybium (Pl. III. fig 11).

Upper section of the wall furnished with twenty-four longitudinal furrows, which disappear as they run downwards, and covered with very small papillæ, mostly grouped in transverse rows.

Habitat.—Station 241. June 23, 1875. Lat. 35° 41′ N., long. 157° 42′ E. Depth, 2300 fathoms. One specimen.

Dimensions.—Length, 4 cm. ; height, nearly 1 cm.

I have placed here beside the *Stephanactis* a small Actinia of which a single specimen was dredged from a great depth. It agrees with the genus *Stephanactis* in having an elongated form, and in being attached to a cylindrical foreign body. I was unfortunately unable to determine whether or not the internal anatomy also agrees, as the septa were so badly preserved that, in examining the piece, in which, from analogy to the forms in question, I expected to find the directive septa, I was unable to arrive at any definite results, even by transverse sections. In what follows I shall, therefore, merely give a short description of the form and of the surface of the body.

The Actinia was firmly attached by its base round the stem of a *Gorgonia* unknown to me, so that the margins of the pedal disk clasped one another by alternating indentations like the notched margins of many bivalve shells (fig. 11, *b*). The insertions of from ninety to one hundred septa appearing through the disk may be followed as white lines proceeding a little way from the margins. At first sight the upper part of the wall seems smooth, but under a tolerably strong magnifying glass we see that it is covered with numerous very fine knobs, which look like the papules of an exanthema, and are arranged in transverse rows (fig. 11, *a*), which lie at tolerably regular distances from one another, and are separated by shallow furrows. The latter are crossed by twenty-four longitudinal furrows, which are most distinct at the upper margin of the wall, but become shallower before they reach its middle portion.

The wall is so strongly contracted at the upper end, that the oral disk is completely covered ; in correspondence with which we find in longitudinal sections a circular muscle of considerable size, having the same form as the circular muscle of *Stephanactis*. I only observed these differences, viz., that the bundles of muscles are stronger, more numerous, and more thickly compacted.

Family, ILYANTHIDÆ, Gosse, *pro parte*.

Hexactiniæ, having the aboral end of the body rounded ; without pedal disk.

As I include in the family of the Ilyanthidæ only those forms which have the septal arrangement of the Hexactiniæ, I define it in a much more limited sense than Gosse (Actinologia Britannica, p. 227) or even Verrill (Memoirs Boston Soc., vol. i. p. 26). Verrill has detached the Cerianthidæ only, but left the Edwardsiæ in the family, while Allmann (Quart. Jour. Micr. Sci., new ser., vol. xii. p. 394), my brother and myself (Actinien, p. 124), and Angelo Andres (Mittheilungen der Zool. Stat. zu Neapel, Bd. ii. p. 123) have most clearly pointed out that the latter also ought to be separated. I am of the opinion that even excluding the Edwardsiæ does not free the family from foreign elements, for it is not at all likely that *Halcampa albida* and *Halcampa producta* with twenty tentacles, *Halcampa microps* with sixteen tentacles, &c., conform to the hexamerous type of arrangement of the tentacles.

By the absence of the pedal disk the Ilyanthidæ form a transition to the tribe Edwardsiæ, on account of which I have placed them at the end of the Hexactiniæ ; in their internal anatomy they are also allied to the Edwardsiæ. *Halcampa clavus*, especially, which I am now about to describe, is so clearly an intermediate form that I was for long dubious whether I should treat of it under the Edwardsiæ or the Hexactiniæ.

Halcampa, Gosse.

Ilyanthidæ with elongated, vermiform body ; without sharply defined circular muscle ; the posterior end may be distended into a vesicle ; œsophageal grooves indistinct or wanting.

In all systematic descriptions of the Ilyanthidæ published by former authors, the genera *Edwardsia* and *Halcampa* are placed very close together ; according to Gosse, they are only distinguished from one another by the facts, that the middle part of the body in *Edwardsia* is surrounded by a sheath, an "epidermis," which is wanting in *Halcampa*, and that the body is divided into three sections, the "capitulum," the "scapus," and the "physa." Angelo Andres (*l. c.*, p. 137) has recently made use of a much more important anatomical character, viz., the presence of only eight septa ("octoseptazione") in *Edwardsia*, while there are always at least twelve septa in *Halcampa*. I only attach importance to the different arrangement of the septa, and therefore will place forms with tripartite wall in the genus *Halcampa*, provided only that they be true Hexactiniæ.

Halcampa clavus (Pl. III. figs. 1, 4, 10 ; Pl. XII. figs. 8, 9, 11 ; Pl. XIII. figs. 2, 4–7).

Actinia clavus, Quoy et Gaymard, Voyage de l' Astrolabe, Zoologie, iv. p. 150, pl. x. figs. 6–11, 1833.
Iluanthus clavus, Milne-Edwards, Histoire des Corall., tom. i. p. 284.

Wall smooth, with twelve longitudinal furrows, and numerous small openings at the posterior end of the body; twelve tentacles, each with an adaxial and an abaxial longitudinal furrow; six pairs of septa.

Habitat.—Station 149. Off Kerguelen Islands. (*a*) January 9, 1874. Lat. 49° 16′ S., long. 70° 12′ E. Betsy Cove. Depth, 25 fathoms. Two specimens. (*b*) January 29, 1874. Christmas Harbour. Depth, 120 fathoms. One specimen.

Dimensions.—Height, 1·5–2 cm.; breadth, 0·5–1 cm.

The three specimens of *Halcampa clavus* which were sent me for examination varied in size; the two specimens taken in Betsy Cove were smaller than the one dredged up in Christmas Harbour, and differed from it in habit of body. I believe, however, that they should be referred to the same species, as the slight difference in size and form may be the consequence of difference in age and degree of contraction, and their anatomical constitution harmonizes completely. I examined the larger specimen, which was specially well preserved, and one of the smaller ones.

The body is divided by two circular constrictions into three sections lying one behind the other. The middle section, the scapus—if we adopt the nomenclature proposed by Gosse for *Edwardsia*—in the largest individual was rather longer than the other two sections taken together, and about 1 cm. broad (Pl. III. figs. 1 and 4); it passed anteriorly into a short neck-like part bearing the tentacles, the capitulum, and posteriorly into a terminal part, 0·5 cm. long and broad, the physa. A cuticular deposit, like that covering the scapus of the *Edwardsiæ*, did not exist, but on the other hand the wall is regularly divided by twelve longitudinal furrows, which begin at the upper end between the twelve tentacles and reach as far as the lower umbilically depressed end. The longitudinal furrows are crossed by numerous transverse furrows, which, however, may be caused by the strong contraction of the animal.

The wall is transparent and thin-membraned except at the points where the scapus passes into the capitulum and the physa; at the points mentioned it is greatly thickened by increase of the supporting substance on the one hand and by numerous pleatings of its endodermal and ectodermal surfaces on the other. The pleatings are caused by an increase in the lamellæ of the circular muscles, and may therefore be termed the upper and lower sphincters, though they are by no means sharply defined. If we examine the wall closely in longitudinal section we see that all over the inner side there is a layer of circular fibres. The underlying supporting substance is divided into two layers, an inner, narrower, nearly homogeneous layer, which stains a darker red in carmine, and an outer, broad, fibrous layer, the two being separated by a sharp line. The inner layer is pleated at tolerably regular intervals, into supporting folds, which run circularly, and project into the gastric space; they usually remain simple, and are rarely bifurcated at their margins. Their surface is covered with numerous very fine, secondary folds, which bear a layer of muscular fibrillæ, so that each circular fold appears finely pinnated when seen in sections taken longitudinally through the wall. The two sphincters are in fact merely local accumulations of these muscular rings, which are exceedingly strongly developed (Pl. XIII. fig. 2). The muscular rings rise much more than usual above the surface of the wall, and seldom remain simple, but divide in transverse section into two or three processes; they may even divide repeatedly, and in this way give rise in transverse section to the candelabra-like figure shown in Plate XIII. fig. 2. As the upper sphincter lies at a little distance from the margin of the oral disk, it causes a deep constriction of the wall and a corresponding external collar-like fold (Pl. III. fig. 1, a).

The twelve tentacles are placed on the margin of the oral disk where the latter turns over into the wall; they are pointed in the smaller specimens, obtuse and compressed in the larger. They are distinguished in both cases by two longitudinal furrows, one of which runs on the adaxial side (fig. 1, b), the other on the abaxial (fig. 1, a). The muscular system is ectodermal, and tolerably thickly pleated; it has the same character on the oral disk, which is so small that the tentacles appear to be placed immediately on the oral margin.

The oral opening (Pl. III. fig. 1, b) is circular and enclosed by twelve swellings. It leads into a long similarly shaped œsophagus, which hangs down in the middle of the body; the lumen of the œsophagus is narrow above and becomes wider below. I was not able to find out œsophageal grooves, either in surface view after opening the animal (Pl. III. fig. 1), or in transverse section (Pl. XIII. fig. 4); but, on the other hand, it is set with twelve strongly-marked longitudinal ridges, corresponding to the insertions of the septa. As the free margins of the longitudinal swellings are thickened, the intermediate furrows are closed so as almost to form canals.

The septa are thin, veil-like lamellæ, with a thick longitudinal muscle which lies much nearer the œsophagus than the wall. The muscle begins in the lower part, the physa, bulges out in the region of the scapus, becomes narrow again in the upper part of the body, and ends on the oral disk not far from the oral opening (Pl. III. fig. 1). In transverse section it forms a muscular mass of considerable size, which rests like a cushion on the surface of the septum, but is marked off from it by a deep groove which runs beneath its margin on either side (Pl. XIII. fig. 4). As to its structure it is a thickly pleated portion of the longitudinal muscular layer, which, moreover, forms a small longitudinal cord close to the wall. The rudiments of a parietobasilar muscle are also found in a similar position on the side of the weakly developed transverse muscles.

The septa are placed at regular distances from one another, though at the same time they are associated together in pairs. Two opposite pairs of septa have longitudinal muscles on the sides turned from one another, whilst on either side there are two pairs with the longitudinal muscles turned towards one another. This is, therefore, an arrangement of the septa which must be taken as a starting point for all Hexactiniæ. *Halcampa clavus* has only the principal septa, which, as we have already shown, are distinguished by a peculiar mode of development, whilst the accessory septa, which are paired from the beginning, are still wanting.

The constitution of the septa in *Halcampa clavus* shows further peculiarities worthy of notice, which seem to me to indicate its relation to the Edwardsiæ. As I was preparing a series of sections through the one half of the physa of the larger specimen, it struck me that three septa (including the pair of directive septa) were not so strong as the other septa, inasmuch as their longitudinal muscular cords became sooner indistinct (Pl. XIII. fig. 7). In the second smaller *Halcampa*, in which I was able to make sections through the entire body, four septa were somewhat smaller than the eight others; and, finally, Strethill Wright has described a parasitic *Halcampa* living on Medusæ (*Halcampa fultoni*), in which we can distinguish four stronger and eight weaker septa (Ann. and Mag. Nat. Hist., ser. iii. vol. viii. p. 133, 1861). All this shows that an unequal development of the septa, and, consequently, a difference in their morphological value, is not unusual in *Halcampa*. If we assume that the eight stronger septa are homologous with the septa of *Edwardsia*, whilst the four other septa are new formations, then the genus *Halcampa* would present us with transition forms between the Edwardsiæ and the Hexactiniæ.

I shall not discuss the point in question further, but I wish to draw particular attention to the importance of a detailed investigation of the Ilyanthidæ for a phylogenetic study of the Actiniaria. I am of opinion that an investigation of the position of septa, extended not only over the mature animals, but also over the larvæ, would furnish us with very interesting explanations as to the manner in which the paired arrangement of the septa has been developed among the Actiniaria. Of course a mere enumeration of the septa would not suffice, but it would be necessary to lay down definite characters for the determination of the septa newly formed in the Ilyanthidæ, with special reference to the distribution of the muscles and the relations of position depending upon it.

Reproductive organs were present in all the septa; ovaries in the larger of the two specimens examined, testes in the smaller; they lay below the œsophagus, inwards from the longitudinal muscles. The ovaries were admirably preserved, so that I availed myself of the opportunity to make a more detailed examination of the origin of the ovicells and the structure of the filamental apparatus. The youngest ova are again portions of the epithelium (Pl. XII. fig. 11), and become surrounded very gradually by the supporting lamella; if the latter be strongly coloured, we see from ova of considerable size, such as that given in fig. 11, that they are not yet entirely surrounded by the supporting lamella, but that the interior of the follicle of the ovum still communicates with the epithelium by means of a wide, roundish opening. A fine hatching is visible on that portion of the ovum which closes the opening as though fine filaments were present on the surface; these are either processes of the ovum itself, which serve to connect it with the epithelium, or they are the bases of the epithelial cells. This point cannot be definitely determined after preservation in spirit, but would require material preserved in osmic acid.

After the ovum has passed into the supporting lamella, it still reaches the bases of the epithelial cells by means of a narrow process, the cells having undergone the modifications already described (fig. 8). The cells are fine filaments, with few granules, and compressed into a body shaped like a gustatory bulb; they are much more numerous than in *Corallimorphus*.

The part of the filamental apparatus formed of epithelial cells lies originally in the same plane as the opaque, granular, epithelial cells, but later, when the ova increase in size, it occupies the bottom of a depression in the epithelium, surrounded by the neighbouring cells which have increased in length. On the other hand, it never passes over into the mesoderm, so that the filamental apparatus remains in a condition which leaves room for further differentiation in *Corallimorphus*. On the larger ovicells there is a narrow cortical layer which is distinguished from the central parts by a structure only indistinctly preserved in spirit. Radial lines indicate, however, that the protoplasm has become divided into small rod-shaped pieces.

Whilst acontia are wanting, the configuration of the mesenteric filaments is the same as in other Actiniæ. I was able to make out a marginal stoma by the help of transverse sections in the upper part of the septa, but I could not determine whether a perioral stoma exists or not.

After the septa are free from their reproductive organs, their mesenteric filaments, and their stronger, specialized muscular cords, they still extend as far as the centre point of the rounded posterior end of the body. Two of the septa are connected in such a way as to form a partition wall separating the four septa on the one side from the six septa on the other (Pl. III. fig. 10). This arrangement precludes the existence of a central posterior pore, but in place of it I found numerous eccentric openings, which are, however, so small that they could not be perceived on the surface, even under a strong magnifying glass. I observed them by making sections transversely through the posterior body-wall of the larger animal, and parallel to the convex terminal surface of the smaller.

The openings are placed in a circular zone at a little distance from the centre point. In sections parallel to the surface I found two of them in the same radius, one outside the other, and I therefore presume that there are about twenty-four of them; each radial chamber probably containing two (Pl. XIII. fig. 5). This point cannot, however, be easily determined from preserved material, as in such a case the wall is pleated, and also from its convex curvature is not well adapted for making such sections.

If we prepare a series of transverse sections, we have a successive view of a large number of openings, often two in the same transverse section, placed symmetrically left and right from the middle; from the relation of their positions to the septa, which can also be seen in transverse section, we may assume that they are regularly distributed over the different radial chambers (fig. 6). There is always a distinct hole in the supporting lamella through which the ectodermal epithelium of the pedal disk sends a cellular mass projecting like a mushroom towards the gastric space above the surface of the endodermal epithelium. This epithelial mass completely closes the opening, but consists of two layers of cells, firmly pressed together; when these part asunder, which must be the case when the posterior body-end of the animal becomes distended, an open canal is formed in the epithelium, through which water can penetrate into the inside of the body. Similar arrangements probably exist in *Edwardsia;* the aboral section of this Actinia, being likewise separated from the preceding by a constriction, can be alternately distended and contracted, and during this process the openings might be of great service.

Tribe II. P A R A C T I N I Æ.

Actiniaria with septa united in pairs. Septa of each pair furnished with transverse muscular fibres on the sides turned from one another, and with longitudinal muscular fibres on the sides turned towards one another, excepting the two pairs of directive septa, which are opposite one another, and have longitudinal muscles on the sides turned from one another, and transverse muscles on the sides turned towards one another. Number of the septa not determined by the number six. Mouth fissure-shaped, œsophagus with two œsophageal grooves and two œsophageal lappets.

I have separated two forms from the Hexactiniæ because the number of their antimeres does not increase in multiples of six, and I have given them the name of "Paractiniæ" because they resemble the Hexactiniæ in the most important points, and therefore represent a parallel group. Above all, they are furnished with œsophageal grooves and have septa arranged in pairs, of which two pairs corresponding to the œsophageal grooves are placed opposite one another, have longitudinal muscles on the sides turned from one another, and are therefore true directive septa. The tentacles have undergone retrograde metamorphosis in both forms, which differ, however, so greatly from one another that I consider them as the representatives of two different families.

Family, SICYONIDÆ.

Sessile Paractiniæ with tetramerous arrangement of the septa; circular muscle mesodermal; tentacles transformed by retrograde metamorphosis into small knob-like stumps.

The most striking characteristic of the Sicyonidæ—apart from the retrograde metamorphosis of the tentacles, which is also met with among the Hexactiniæ—is the tetramerous arrangement of the septa. Hæckel, as we know, sought in his Generelle Morphologie for soft-membraned ancestors of the fossil Tetracorallia, and believed he had found one of their descendants in *Cerianthus.* Recent works on the anatomy of *Cerianthus* have greatly lessened the probability of Hæckel's view being correct, as in the mature animal the number of the septa is always even, but otherwise very variable. In *Sicyonis crassa*, on the other hand, we have before us an animal in which the number four is as persistent as the number six in the Hexactiniæ, and which, moreover, has the same paired arrangement of the septa as we meet with in the existing hexamerous corals. It is therefore quite possible that the Sicyonidæ and Tetracorallia may be closely related.

Sicyonis, n. gen.

Sicyonidæ, with discoid, flattened body, smooth wall, and alternating reproductive septa and muscular septa.

Sicyonis crassa, n. sp. (Pl. IV. figs. 1-9).

Sixty-four wart-like tentacles placed in two alternating rows ; circular muscle weak ; oral disk covered with numerous fine radial furrows.

Habitat.—Station 147. December 30, 1873. Lat. 46° 16′ S., long. 48° 27′ E. Depth, 1600 fathoms. One specimen.

Dimensions.—Height, 2 cm. Diameter of the pedal disk, 7 cm. ; of the oral disk, 9 cm.

The new species, which I have named *Sicyonis crassa*, is one of the most interesting Actiniæ dredged from great depths, both on account of the constitution of the tentacles and of the arrangement of the septa. The body of the single specimen before me is cake-shaped, as the transverse measurement of the pedal disk amounts to 7 cm., and that of the oral disk to 9 cm., whilst the height only amounts to 2 cm. The height would, however, certainly be greater in a natural state, as the animal had been very much compressed in the packing.

The body is tolerably tough, more, however, from the thickness of its walls than from the firmness of its tissue. The consistency of the latter is between that of cartilage and of gelatinous tissue, and consists in all parts of the body of a homogeneous fundamental substance enclosing numerous extremely small cells. The fundamental substance is also traversed by numerous bundles of fibrillæ, which become very distinct in preparations stained with carmine. These bundles have a wavy course, and become connected from time to time so as to form a reticulate framework. It was not possible to recognise the natural colour of the animal.

The pedal disk (fig. 2) is marked by radial furrows ; a large number, more than 100, begin at the margin, of which some reach the centre, whilst others do not extend so far. Their course is irregularly waved and indented, and they correspond to the insertions of the septa inside the animal.

The wall is small in height, and divided by a deep circular constriction into an upper and a lower half (fig. 9) ; it appears, on the whole, smooth and only furrowed irregularly on the surface in consequence of the contraction of the animal. The circular layer of fibres on the inside is very weak, both because the separate fibrillæ are very fine, and because the layer, formed by them, is only slightly pleated. The circular muscle at the margin of the peristome is also insignificant ; it lies immediately outside the tentacles, and produces about four or five narrow circular swellings on the inside of the wall (fig. 1). It belongs completely to the mesoderm, in which it is embedded as a very narrow streak, close under the endoderm. The fibrillæ, like those of the wall, are very fine, and united in small bundles which lie close to one another, and are only separated by a small amount of intervening substance. In transverse section, and under weak magnifying power, the muscular layer therefore presents the appearance of a finely granulated mass.

The most important parts for the definition of the species are the oral disk and its tentacles. The surface of the oral disk is marked by sixty-four radial furrows, which run from the swollen margin of the mouth towards the bases of the tentacles, and are caused by the attachments of the septa. They are, moreover, correlated with the arrangement of the radial muscles, the layer of which always either becomes thinner or is completely interrupted along a line below every furrow. The muscles are further mesodermal, and so deeply embedded in the supporting lamella that they lie at equal distances from the endodermal and the ectodermal surfaces. The separate fibrillæ (fig. 6) are very powerful, and the way in which they are grouped gives rise in transverse section to a figure recalling the conditions known in the vertebrata. A few fibrillæ are closely compacted into a primitive bundle, several such bundles unite to form a secondary bundle (fig. 8), and these again are united into larger groups. Each portion of the muscular layer lying between two radial furrows contains several groups of such bundles.

There are sixty-four tentacles in all, distributed in two alternating circles. They present a very unusual appearance, and are short knob-like elevations with a broad oval base, and are pierced by a wide opening at the point. This gives them the appearance of sucking cups, and on this account I have named the animal *Sicyonis*. The surface is repeatedly pleated, and the interior also shows distinct circular folds (fig. 9). The walls are very thick as far as a thin margin surrounding the terminal opening (fig. 3). The radial muscular fibres of the oral disk make their way as longitudinal cords into the tentacles, and have the same arrangement in the middle of the broad layer of connective tissue as we have already discussed in the description of the oral disk. Examined in transverse section (fig. 5), they are deposited in a ring, which, however, is interrupted on the side turned towards the margin of the peristome. There the layer of connective tissue is very thick, but only contains a few isolated bundles of muscular fibrillæ. We see, moreover, in longitudinal section (fig. 3), that the cords of muscular fibres do not make their way into the thin margin surrounding the opening in the tentacle, but terminate abruptly before they reach this point. The margin, therefore, merely consists of a lamella of connective substance, covered by two layers of epithelium passing into one another at the free edge.

On the œsophagus (fig. 4), the two œsophageal grooves at once strike the eye as deeply incised furrows, bounded by broad folds and running zig-zag, as secondary transverse folds project alternately left and right. The other longitudinal furrows, which run, ten in number, on either side between the œsophageal grooves, are less distinct. From the oral disk the œsophagus is separated by a thick lip-like swelling, divided into twenty-four parts corresponding to the number of the longitudinal furrows of the œsophagus.

The number of the pairs of septa amounts in all to sixty-four. Sixteen of these are of equal size and are inserted into the œsophagus; alternating with these we find sixteen other pairs only a little smaller, which end on the oral disk, but like the others are purely muscular septa. On the other hand the last thirty-two pairs of septa, which are equally distributed in the interspaces between the muscular septa, bear only the reproductive organs and are furnished merely with a very thin muscular layer. There is a very pronounced difference in size between the smallest muscular septa and the reproductive septa, such as I have already described in *Ophiodiscus*. In *Sicyonis* also the septa are merely thin-walled mesenteries for the reproductive organs, thick masses of which (testes) occupy the free margin of the fold; they only extend upwards to one-third the height of the animal, and are entirely wanting in the angle between the wall and the oral disk (fig. 9).

Fig. 9 shows the distribution of the muscles on the muscular septa. On the side of the longitudinal muscles a single cord radiates like a fan towards the œsophagus and the central parts of the oral disk; on the side of the transverse muscles the parietobasilar muscle extends half way up the wall, where it occasions the constriction already mentioned. In the perfect septa a small opening lies in the neighbourhood of the mouth. The muscular septa and genital septa are finally to be distinguished by the fact that the former only bear mesenteric filaments.

Sicyonis crassa has another character in common with *Ophiodiscus* besides the differentiation of the septa into reproductive and muscular,- viz., the relation in which the number of the pairs of septa stands to the number of the tentacles.

In the majority of Actiniæ there are at least twice as many tentacles as there are pairs of septa, so that each intraseptal and each interseptal space has its own special tentacle. In *Sicyonis* and *Ophiodiscus* there is an equal number of pairs of septa and of tentacles; the thirty-two intraseptal spaces of the muscular septa only have their own special tentacles, whilst the other tentacles belong in common to the thirty-two intraseptal spaces of the reproductive septa and the sixty-four adjacent interseptal spaces. This also shows the rudimentary character of the reproductive septa, since they are of so little importance in the constitution of the body of the Actinia that their appearance has not even been followed by an increase in the number of the tentacles.

Family, POLYOPIDÆ, Hertwig.

Paractiniæ, without pedal disk, posterior end of the body round and saccular, with aboral opening (?) ; tentacles transformed into stomidia by retrograde metamorphosis.

In earlier systems the Polyopidæ would have been placed among the Ilyanthidæ, to which family, apart from the absence of tentacles, they bear a strong external resemblance. It is quite possible that at some future time forms may be found which shall furnish a closer link between our Polyopidæ and the Edwardsiæ formerly described as Ilyanthidæ ; more especially as the Edwardsiæ occupy in some measure a central position in the midst of the Actiniæ, and send out lines of affinity in various directions. At present, however, it is more convenient to separate the Edwardsiæ and the Polyopidæ as the paired grouping of the septa, which is so pronounced in the latter, is still wanting in the former.

Polyopis, n. gen.

Polyopidæ with smooth wall, the surface having longitudinal furrows indicating the position of the septa ; circular muscle wanting.

Polyopis striata (Pl. II. fig. 11 ; Pl. XI. figs. 1–12).

Wall with thirty-six longitudinal lines ; oral disk with thirty-six strongly developed radial swellings and thirty-six marginal stomidia arranged in a circle.

Habitat.—Station 299. December 14, 1875. Lat. 33° 31′ S., long. 74° 43′ W. Depth, 2160 fathoms. One specimen.

Dimensions.—Height, nearly 2 cm. ; breadth, 2 cm.

Colour.—(Determined from the spirit specimen) wall saffron-yellow, oral disk whitish, œsophagus dark brown.

The small Actinia without tentacles, which I call *Polyopis striata* (ὀπή = opening), was probably sac-shaped during life ; its rounded posterior end probably stuck in the sand, whilst its broad anterior end formed by the oral disk projected freely. In consequence of packing, the animal was pressed quite flat, the oral disk and œsophagus turned out and very much injured, the septa consequently misplaced and torn. The difficulty of examining the septa was increased by the fact that from the hardening by alcohol, the septa had stuck together, and could not be easily separated by dissection. The preservation of the tissue was satisfactory, especially that of the epithelium on the oral disk, œsophagus, and septa.

The wall is of a delicate yellowish colour, which is contained in the endoderm, as the ectoderm is rubbed off and the mesoderm colourless and transparent after the epithelium is removed from the inside. The colour is caused by numerous small granules, which completely fill the endodermal epithelial cells.

The lower end of the sac-shaped body, the aboral pole of the longitudinal axis, is denoted by a small depression, which is equally visible on either side, and is caused, it seems to me, by a microscopically small opening found at this spot (Pl. XI. fig. 11). In order to settle this question by transverse sections, I cut out the portion of the wall containing the opening, and laid it to stain in carmine, but unfortunately it got lost.

On the exterior in the periphery of the aboral depression there are six shallow, radial furrows, which soon become less distinct as they run upwards. Instead of them, thirty-six longitudinal streaks begin, the external signs of the origins of the septa, which run at an equal distance from one another to the margin of the oral disk. The inside of the wall is covered with a smooth layer of circular muscular fibres, which are never compacted into a distinct sphincter, which explains why the upper end of the wall is not contracted at all.

The structure of the oral disk, which projected like a proboscis in the animal examined, requires a more detailed description. Thirty-six stomidia lie close to its peripheral margin; these are fine, longitudinal fissures enclosed by thickened lips, their greatest diameter extending in a radial direction. Through the stomidia we see the inside of the body, looking alternately into an intraseptal and an interseptal space; they therefore alternate with the septa which are inserted into the narrow portions of the oral disk, lying between two stomidia. Sections perpendicular to the surface of the disk and parallel to its margin through the region of the stomidia are, therefore, divided into as many pieces as there are septa, and each piece consists of a septum and the section of the oral disk belonging to it (Pl. XI. fig. 9).

Distinctly marked radial thickenings (Pl. II. fig. 11; Pl. XI. fig. 6), extending to close upon the oral opening, proceed inwards from the stomidia. They are broad and shallow in the middle of the oral disk, but rise towards the outside and towards the inside into narrow comb-like ridges, the outer ridges being divided into two small folds. These folds end near the stomidia and twist repeatedly during their course so as to produce S-shaped figures. Each two contiguous folds enclose a fissure along which we can pass a needle a little way into the interior of the corresponding radial thickening, which shows that the inner part of the thickening is hollowed out by a radial invagination.

From the varying relations of the different parts of the oral disk the transverse sections also present very different figures, according as they are made nearer to or further from the oral margin. Fig. 7 gives a section corresponding to the line δ in fig. 6. The supporting lamella is thickened in the middle between each two septa and covered by a repeatedly folded muscular layer. Inwards from this point, in the region of the line ε, above each radial chamber, the supporting lamella rises like a ridge which also bears a thickly pleated muscular lamella, as shown in fig. 5. The section given in fig. 3, whose position is determined by the line γ, shows the same figure, but with this difference, that in this case hollow spaces appear in the supporting lamella, which either lie as triangular gaps at the bases of the ridges, or force themselves as fissures into the ridges themselves. These hollow spaces, found in transverse section, correspond to the pouch-shaped invaginations, which extend into the peripheral part of each radial swelling; here and there I found accumulations of cells in the spaces,—the remains of the epithelium lining them, which unfortunately was badly preserved. In fig. 1 we have a transverse section taken through the small folds at the beginning of the radial thickenings, along the line *a*. The figures 1–3 show an irregular arrangement of the muscles, as they are sometimes divided perpendicularly, sometimes obliquely, sometimes parallel to their direction. This irregularity may be explained partly by the tortuous course taken by the beginning of the radial swelling, partly by the fact that the muscular fibres, which originally extended horizontally, have been slightly diverted from their straight direction by the comb-like elevations of the supporting lamella.

The œsophagus was too much injured to allow of its constitution being determined by means of dissection. I was able, however, to examine pieces of it, recognisable by their brown-violet colour, in a series of sections, and to make out openings which lie under the oral margin and lead into the radial chambers. It seemed to me that there was an opening surrounded by a swollen margin between every two insertions of the septa (fig. 4). The openings are not all of the same size, as many of them can be recognised in a whole series of transverse sections as long fissures, whilst others are only visible in three to four moderately thin successive sections. They can hardly be considered artificial productions, in the first place, because the surfaces of the epithelium of the two sides pass evenly into one another at the margin of the opening, and secondly, on account of the comportment of the muscular system. The œsophagus of *Polyopis striata* has exceptionally ectodermal longitudinal muscular fibres, which are only apparent in thin transverse sections, as they are extremely fine. The muscular layer is thickly pleated at the rounded margins of the openings, so that it may here be regarded as a sphincter capable of closing the opening.

The septa correspond to the longitudinal ridges on the surface of the wall, and are therefore thirty-six in number; they lie at perfectly equal distances from one another, but are in pairs notwithstanding, as may be seen from the arrangement of the muscles. Among them there are two pairs of directive septa (fig. 8) which are separated from one another by eight pairs of ordinary septa. The latter vary very much in size, although I was not able to observe any arrangement in cycles of unequal value; I consider it most probable that we have here a tetramerous arrangement of the septa, but that a pair of septa too many has been formed in one interspace on either side. Downwards the septa reach nearly as far as the aboral opening; they are, however, of different sizes, so as to present the figure given in fig. 11, β.

The longitudinal muscles are slightly pleated, the transverse muscles not at all. There is a special muscular cord on the same side as the transverse muscle, which extends close to the wall, becomes broader as it runs downwards, and is homologous in position with the parietobasilar muscle of other Actiniæ. Further, it appears to me that all the septa reach the œsophagus, are all furnished with reproductive organs (in the present instance with testes), and have all a small perioral and a very large marginal opening (fig. 12). Unfortunately I could not decide this point with any certainty, as only a few septa, such as that given in fig. 12, could be dissected out; most of them were sticking together so that the mode in which the reproductive organs were distributed on the septa was never clearly seen in transverse sections.

Tribe III. M O N A U L E Æ.

Actiniaria with paired septa, but with only one pair of directive septa.

The Monauleæ form the third and last group in which the paired arrangement of the septa is distinctly pronounced, and therefore come nearer to the Hexactiniæ and Paractiniæ than the Zoantheæ and Ceriantheæ. It is remarkable that there is only one pair of directive septa, a fact which may perhaps be explained by the obliteration of the second pair.

From the absence of the second pair of directive septa, it follows that the body is exactly bilaterally symmetrical, as it is divided into symmetrical halves by only one divisional plane which runs through the intraseptal space of the directive septa. This divisional plane passes through an interseptal space on the opposite side, and divides the remaining pairs of septa equally, half lying on its right and half on its left. The whole number of the pairs of septa is consequently unequal.

There is only one œsophageal groove, caused by the marked shortness of the directive septa, and on account of this I have chosen the name Monauleæ (αὐλός, a groove or tube). This groove was not very distinct, however, in transverse sections in the species examined; it would probably come out more clearly if looked at from the surface.

As I only know one species, it would be little to the purpose to give special diagnoses for the family and genus. I shall therefore proceed at once to discuss the species.

Family, MONAULIDÆ, Hertwig.

Scytophorus, n. gen.[1]

Scytophorus striatus, n. sp. (Pl. III. fig. 6 ; Pl. XIII. figs. 1, 3, 8).

Sessile Monaulidæ with seven pairs of septa and fourteen longitudinal furrows on the

---

[1] σκῦτος = leather.

wall ; the wall covered with a tough cuticle ; no circular muscle ; tentacles fourteen in number, of medium size, arranged in a single circle.

Habitat.—Station 150. February 2, 1874. Lat. 52° 4′ S., long. 71° 22′ E. Depth, 150 fathoms. Two specimens.

Dimensions.—Height, 2·7 cm. ; breadth, 0·8 cm.

Colour.—(Determined from the spirit material) brownish-yellow.

The Actiniæ without pedal disk and with rounded, aboral end mostly vary in the arrangement of their septa from the type predominating in the whole section, as was explained in the Introduction, but this is rarely the case with the sessile forms. *Scytophorus striatus*, which represents a new species, furnishes one of the few examples of this variation which have come under my observation. I found two specimens of it in the Challenger material, so that I was able to examine one of them thoroughly.

The body is very much elongated, and even in a state of contraction measures 2·7 cm. in length, whilst it is only 0·8 cm. in breadth (Pl. III. fig. 6). The upper part of the body is also inverted considerably (more than 0·5 cm.), as we see from the longitudinal sections, a formation recalling *Phellia pectinata*, which has, however, an entirely different structure. The surface is deeply incised by fourteen longitudinal furrows, which are the more distinct because the surface is not soft as in the majority of Actiniæ, but of a leather-like consistency. This is owing to the presence of a strong cuticle, whose structure and relation to the underlying epithelium are best understood by transverse sections (Pl. XIII. fig. 1).

The cuticle consists of two layers ; (1), a superficial layer, which hardly stains at all in carmine, but keeps its natural tint, to which is due the yellowish colour of the entire animal ; and (2), a deeper layer which becomes an intense red when treated with this reagent. The two layers are tolerably well defined, at some points even by a smooth line. The stratification parallel to the surface, usually found in cuticular secretions, can be recognised in the lower deposit, and striation perpendicular to the surface is also present at many points.

As the cuticle is of nearly equal thickness throughout, the longitudinal furrows of the body, which show in transverse sections as deep indentations, are caused entirely by the underlying epithelium and the supporting lamella. Both of these have an equal share in causing the difference of level. The supporting lamella, a homogeneous fundamental substance with scattered fusiform and branched cells, is very thick between each two furrows, and becomes thin below the indentations, and in the same way the epithelium is unusually high between the furrows, but reduced to an almost imperceptible layer below them. Where the epithelial cells are elongated they are separated from one another by interspaces ; they are easily torn in preparing transverse sections, so that an artificial hollow space arises between the cuticle and the supporting lamella.

The whole integument undergoes modification at numerous small, sharply defined spots. The supporting lamella projects like a papilla, and so reaches within a little distance of the cuticle, and the epithelial cells are shortened correspondingly, but thickly compacted ; their bases sink a little way into the supporting lamella, so that the contour of the latter is notched, whilst at the same time they converge from their broader basis towards a small spot of the cuticle which has a different appearance. The outer cuticular layer pierces the inner layer, and extends to the top of the epithelial cells ; it thus forms a conical projection, the central part of which is stained deep red by carmine, whilst the periphery only preserves the yellower colour, so on the whole it shows in transverse section the figure given in Plate XIII. fig. 1.

The cone of the outer cuticular layer is sometimes forced apart from the epithelium by a thin stratum of the inner layer (fig. 8), but in this case the projection of the supporting lamella is also wanting, and the epithelium has the same nature as usual.

I consider myself justified in explaining the conditions of structure of the cuticle described above by the supposition that the cuticle undergoes a periodical change, a kind of desquamation. The outer, yellow layer is the hardened cuticle ; this probably becomes detached after a time, and is replaced by the inner cuticle, which stains so easily in carmine. The circumscribed spots at which the yellow cuticle reaches the epithelium, indicate the points at which it is more firmly attached to the surface of the body ; they are the fastening nodes of the cuticle. The connection is gradually dissolved when the yellow layer is forced apart by a fresh layer, even from the points of attachment to the epithelium, in the manner just described.

The number of the fastening nodes in each transverse section is very large ; I counted more than twenty in one section, including those in process of retrograde formation, all on the whole of equal size. I also examined these peculiar formations in longitudinal sections, and found the same figures as in transverse sections. I lay stress on this fact as it proves that we are not dealing with long streaks.

The cuticle passes on to the inverted part of the wall, which in the contracted animal projects downwards more than 0·5 cm. into the inside of the body ; it becomes thinner, especially the superficial yellow layer.

A sharply defined circular muscle, such as I have described in most true Actiniæ, is wanting in *Scytophorus striatus;* instead of it, there is a peculiar differentiation of the endodermal layer of muscular fibres. The layer of fibrillæ is raised at short intervals into folds, which are strengthened by the supporting substance, and produce branched figures in transverse section. These bushes of muscles, which are covered by epithelium only, project freely into the gastric space : they are most strongly developed in the upper contracted and inverted section of the wall, where they are thickly branched and placed closely together so as to replace the absent sphincter.

The ectodermal muscular fibres of the small oral disk and its, to all appearance, equally small tentacles are very weak. The tentacles partly hang down into the œsophagus, are also partly invaginated and retracted into the radial chambers in a way which is more common among the Octocorallia than among the Hexacorallia ; in this case the sequence of the layers is inverted in transverse sections, as the ectoderm is turned inwards, the endoderm outwards. There are fourteen tentacles in all, each of them belonging to a radial chamber.

On the œsophagus there are alternately eight longitudinal furrows and eight longitudinal thickenings (Pl. XIII. fig. 3), but little can be said about their constitution, as it was plainly very much influenced by the contraction of the body. The deepest furrow belongs to the interspace between the two directive septa, and may be regarded as an œsophageal groove, even though I was not able to make out distinctly that it is covered by a specially constituted epithelium. The transverse section of the œsophagus is roundish, so that the flattening in the direction of the transverse axis, common to many Actiniæ, is wanting.

The septa are perfect without exception. They are thin lamellæ bearing a very strong muscular pennon, in the middle between the œsophagus and the wall. At this point the longitudinal muscles are pleated in a sharply defined space nearly as thickly as in *Tealia bunodiformis;* besides these, a special cord of longitudinal muscles runs along the wall and a rudimentary parietobasilar muscle lies in a similar position on the side of the transverse muscles. A wide marginal stoma can be seen in transverse section between the two longitudinal muscular cords.

The arrangement of the septa and the nature of the reproductive organs is of the highest importance. *Scytophorus striatus* is the only Actinia known at present, in which the number of the pairs of septa is unequal. This is not an accidental abnormality, as it is caused by the absence of the second pair of directive septa and not by irregular growth of the different parts of the body; this was clear from both the specimens under examination, as in each one wall was furnished with fourteen longitudinal furrows, corresponding exactly to the fourteen septa, i.e., to the seven pairs. The existing pair of directive septa is only distinguished from the other septa by the lamellæ being shorter, on which account the wall and the œsophagus approach nearest to one another at this point.

Scytophorus striatus belongs to the small number of Actiniæ in which hermaphroditism has been undeniably observed ; all the septa (the directive septa included) bear ova in their upper sections, many of which were almost mature in the specimen I examined, whilst the lower sections bear testes, though these were not so numerous as the ovicells.

Tribe IV. E D W A R D S I Æ.

Actiniaria with eight septa ; among which are two pairs of directive septa, whilst the remaining four septa are not paired ; all the septa furnished with reproductive organs ; tentacles simple, usually more numerous than the septa.

Though Quatrefages, the discoverer of the Edwardsiæ (Mémoire sur les Edwardsies, nouveau genre de la famille des Actinies, Annales d. Sc. Nat. Zool., ser. ii. vol. xviii. p. 65, 1842), observed correctly that these Actiniæ have only eight septa, this important character has not been sufficiently taken into account by most of the more recent writers. Milne-Edwards and Gosse, who attach too much importance to the external characteristics of the animal, had the absence of the pedal disk principally in view, and united the Edwardsiæ with similar forms, *Ilyanthus*, *Cerianthus*, &c., into the group of "Actinies pivotantes," or the family of the Ilyanthidæ. Allman was the first to draw attention in a short notice (Quart. Jour. Microsc. Sci., new ser., vol. xii. p. 394, 1872) to the detached position of the Edwardsiæ, as he maintained them to be forms which, in the distribution of the septa, more closely resemble the Alcyonaria and the extinct Tetracorallia. My brother and I have shown more recently, from a thorough anatomical examination of the position of the septa (Actinien, pp. 124 and 137), that the Edwardsiæ occupy an intermediate position between the larvæ of the Actiniæ with eight septa and the Alcyonaria. In the Alcyonaria the septa are arranged in such a way, that reckoned from one end of the sagittal axis, all the eight septa (four left and four right) bear longitudinal muscles on the faces turned away from the starting point, whilst in the larvæ Actiniæ the first four only (two left and two right) have longitudinal muscles on the faces turned away, and the four following on the faces turned towards the starting point, so that we find the same relative arrangement, whichever end of the sagittal axis we start from. In the Edwardsiæ we meet with the number six and two, *i.e.*, considered from one fixed end of the sagittal axis the first six septa are constituted like those of the Alcyonaria, the last two like those of the Actiniæ. As in the Actiniæ the two pairs of septa placed one at each end of the oral fissure form the directive septa, two pairs of the directive septa are therefore likewise present in the Edwardsiæ.

The correctness of the view, briefly recapitulated above, has been further corroborated by a newly published work of Angelo Andres (Intorno all' Edwardsia Claparedii ; Mittheil. der zoolog. Station zu Neapel, Bd. ii. p. 123) ; at the same time he pronounces in favour of Allman's view that the Edwardsiæ may bear the same relation to the Tetracorallia as the Actiniæ do to the skeleton-forming Hexacorallia. I do not agree with him on this point. Apart from the number of the calcareous septa, the formation of the skeleton is the same in the Hexacorallia and Tetracorallia, and it is therefore probable that similar relations have existed among the soft parts of the body, and that the paired arrangement of the septa was already developed in the Tetracorallia. As this is not the case in the Edwardsiæ, I am inclined to seek for points of connection with the Rugosa in such forms as *Sicyonis crassa*.

There was no true *Edwardsia* among the Challenger material ; but I was long duboius as to whether it might not be expedient to include among them those forms in which the paired arrangement and the number twelve of the septa begin to be developed, as for example *Halcampa clavus.* We may gather from this how closely the Edwardsiæ are connected by transition forms with the other Actiniæ, and how advisable it is to discuss them along with the latter, and to separate them from the Alcyonaria. From this point of view the constitution of the tentacles is of great importance, as they in no way resemble the tentacles of the Alcyonaria.

Tribe V. Z O A N T H E Æ.

Actiniaria with numerous septa of two different kinds, smaller, imperfect, sterile microsepta, and larger perfect macrosepta furnished with reproductive organs and mesenteric filaments; the two kinds usually placed alternately, so that each pair is composed of a larger and a smaller septum; two pairs of directive septa at the ends of the sagittal axis, one pair containing only macrosepta, the other only microsepta; only one œsophageal groove, corresponding to the larger directive septa; animals usually forming colonies; wall usually traversed by ectodermal canals, and having the outside encrusted with foreign bodies.

Zoologists differ very much in their opinions as to the limits and the definition of the Zoantheæ. Milne-Edwards (Hist. des. Corall., tom. i. p. 298) includes in this division only colonial, sessile forms which increase by basal gemmation and have a leather-like sheath hardened by encrustation with sand granules (faux polypiéroïde); Gosse agrees with him (Actinologia Britannica, p. 295), but considers the encrustation with sand granules as a secondary character. Most zoologists keep to the definition given by Milne-Edwards and Gosse.

In 1856, Steenstrup described an Actinia under the name *Sphenopus marsupialis,* which closely resembles the Zoantheæ, but is distinguished from them by not forming colonies and not being sessile. (Overs. Kongelige danske Videnskab. Selskabs Forhand., p. 37, 1856). As Gray (Proc. Zool. Soc., p. 235, 1867) included this Actinia among the Zoantheæ, he set aside the characters used by Milne-Edwards, viz., the formation of colonies and the sessile mode of life, but without replacing them in the diagnosis by new characters, which would be at once common to all Zoantheæ, and distinctive from other Actiniaria. To what degree the sharp limitation of the Zoantheæ suffered from this may be seen from the fact that Gray included in this tribe the genera *Edwardsia, Halcampa,* &c.

The discovery of *Sphenopus* led to difficulties as to the limitation of the Zoantheæ which were also not obviated by the fact that Verrill considered *Sphenopus* to be related to the Edwardsiæ, to which it has certainly a strong external resemblance. But anatomically *Sphenopus* agrees so thoroughly with the Zoantheæ that it cannot be separated from them. A study of the arrangement of the septa is the only possible means of discovering distinctive characters for the division.

Angelo Andres (Quart. Jour. Micros. Sci., new ser., vol. xvii. p. 221, 1877) and my brother and myself (Actinien, p. 127) had already pointed out that the position of the septa in the Zoanthew was regulated on an entirely different principle from that in other Actiniaria, though G. v. Koch was the first to find out the true nature of it. He discovered what I fully corroborate, that the septa present are of two different sizes (Morphol. Jahrb., Bd. vi. p. 359, 1880). The larger or macrosepta only reach the œsophagus and bear reproductive organs and mesenteric filaments, whilst the smaller or microsepta are sterile and end on the oral disk; the latter are not, as I formerly supposed, young septa destined to be developed into larger, but are really rudimentary formations.

Both the larger and the smaller septa bear muscles on both sides: one side bears longitudinal fibres, the layer of which is, however, only slightly pleated, the other side bears fibres which rise obliquely, and are homologous with the transverse muscular fibres of the other Actiniæ, though they can easily be mistaken for longitudinal fibres in transverse sections. There is here, therefore, a predisposition to the paired arrangement of the septa, the existence of which was first recognised by G. v. Koch. Each pair consists of a small and a large septum, having longitudinal muscles on the faces turned towards one another (Pl. XIV. fig. 2). The two pairs of directive septa form an exception, however, as one pair of them, the ventral, contains large septa only,—the other pair, the dorsal, only small septa; in some Zoanthew, we must also except two pairs of ordinary septa which lie right and left at a little distance from the small directive septa, and contain macrosepta only (Pl. XIV. fig. 3).

The manner in which the larger and smaller septa are distributed can be more accurately determined if we start from the directive septa, and disregard provisionally the grouping in pairs. In the Zoanthew, as in all Actiniæ, two kinds of septa alternate; in the septa of the one system the muscles are disposed in the same way as they are in the ventral pair of directive septa, whilst in the other system the case is reversed, and they have the same disposition as they have in the dorsal pair of directive septa. The septa which have the same arrangement of the muscles as the small dorsal directive septa, viz., the dorsal septa, are likewise small, whilst the others, the ventral septa, are strong; it is only in the neighbourhood of the small directive septa that the conditions are reversed as the dorsal septa are strong, and the ventral septa are weak. We can therefore divide the ordinary pairs of septa into two different regions; in the one (the larger, or ventral region), the ventral septa of the single pairs are macrosepta, and the dorsal septa are microsepta, whilst in the other (the dorsal region), the reverse is the case, and the dorsal septa are macrosepta. When all the pairs of septa are equally developed, the two regions are bounded on either side by microsepta, but those two microsepta are often wanting left and right, and in this way the pairs formed of macrosepta alone, which have been already mentioned, are produced: these contain two large dorsal septa of the dorsal region and two large ventral septa of the ventral region.

The correlation, which exists in all Actiniaria between the œsophageal grooves and the directive septa, is also shown in the Zoantheæ, for there is only one œsophageal groove, whilst the other is wanting, in correspondence with the rudimentary nature of the directive septa to which it should belong. The tentacles, on the other hand, are equally developed and placed in two circles, the inner of which belongs to the intraseptal spaces, the outer to the interseptal spaces.

All the characters taken into account by former naturalists in the diagnosis of the Zoantheæ are of subordinate value when compared with the peculiar conditions just mentioned. The animals are united into colonies either by means of branched stolons or by means of a broad basal plate, but there are also solitary forms which are embedded with their rounded aboral ends in the sand like the Edwardsiæ. The entire surface of the wall is often permeated with foreign bodies, though in many specimens such encrustations are wanting completely. Finally, the canals, which make their way from the ectoderm into the wall, where they become branched and connected into plexuses, are confined to certain forms only.

In the division of the Zoantheæ I agree chiefly with Verrill, who divided the species forming colonies into four genera; *Mammilifera*, *Zoanthus*, *Palythoa*, and *Epizoanthus*. The former two are distinguished from the latter by the absence of sand encrustations. *Zoanthus* and *Epizoanthus* are distinguished from *Mammilifera* and *Palythoa* by the fact that in the former two the polyps project plainly above the common basis, whilst in the latter two they are united up to the free end by the basal cœnenchyma. I have restricted the family Zoanthidæ to those genera which form colonies, and have associated all those which are solitary under the name Sphenopidæ.

Family ZOANTHIDÆ.

Zoantheæ forming colonies; the individuals of a colony connected with one another by endodermal canals, which run out from the gastric space at the lower end of each polyp.

Zoanthus, Cuvier, *pro parte.*

Zoanthus, Verrill.

Zoanthidæ without sand encrustations and with a slightly developed cœnenchyma consisting either of a plexus of stolons or of a thin plate; the single polyps projec to a considerable height above the cœnenchyma.

Zoanthus, sp. (?) (Pl. XIV. figs. 1–4 and 6).
Habitat.—Bermuda Islands.
Dimensions.—(Of the individual polyps): height, 0·1–1·3 cm. ; breadth, 0·1–0·4 cm.

Numerous species of the genus *Zoanthus* have been described which resemble one another closely, and probably only differ slightly in their anatomy, so that the species can only be determined by the colour, the number and arrangement of the tentacles, &c. This is the reason why I have not given any specific name to the single specimen of the genus *Zoanthus* found among the Challenger material, in which the colour of the body and the nature of the tentacles could not be made out, and why I have refrained from giving any diagnosis of species, as from insufficient knowledge of the closely allied species it is impossible to determine which characteristics belong to the whole genus and which to the individual species.

The colony, which was about 4 cm. long and 2 cm. broad, was firmly attached to a stone, and consisted of some thirty individuals varying greatly in size. The smallest of these are little knobs which hardly project 1 to 2 mm. above the cœnenchyma, the largest are long cylindrical tubes, more than 1 cm. in length. They lie so thickly compacted that the cœnenchyma is almost entirely covered, and only shows here and there as a thin plate. The cœnenchyma is abundantly developed on the margin into stolons, which are alternately broad and narrow.

I made a thorough anatomical examination of three individual polyps of different sizes, which were highly contracted like all the animals of the colony. The upper end of the wall is not only contracted but inverted a little; the only indication of the point at which we can reach the interior of the body is a small navel-like depression. Apart from the folds caused by contraction, the surface of the body is perfectly smooth.

The wall (Pl. XIV. fig. 4) is of considerable thickness, and consists histologically of a homogeneous fundamental substance, with fine fibres embedded in it. The fibres are hardly double contoured, are slightly waved, and run sometimes directly, sometimes obliquely, from one epithelial surface to the other. They begin at the endoderm with a granular enlargement which seems to pass directly into the epithelium; towards the ectoderm they branch repeatedly behind one another. They are furnished with nuclei, and therefore bear a strong resemblance to the muscular fibres of the Ctenophora, but their state of preservation did not admit of determining the histological value of the fibres.

The cells of the connective substance are strongly granulated bodies, either rounded or branched.

Finally, we find canals in the wall, such as do not exist in any other Actiniaria, though they are found in the Alcyonaria. These canals vary greatly in diameter; the smaller are simple cords of cells, and only the larger ones show a lumen surrounded by a layer of epithelium. As the canals repeatedly ramify and anastomose, they form a thick net-work, which extends from the endoderm to the ectoderm, but is thickest near the latter. Kölliker's observations show that in the Alcyonaria the canals are produced from the ectoderm, which is also the case in *Zoanthus*; I have repeatedly found that the epithelium of the body-surface sinks like a funnel into the mesoderm, where it is prolonged into a broad or narrow canal which soon begins to throw out branches (fig. 2).

The ectodermal epithelium is covered by a fibrous cuticle, which recalls the "epidermis" of *Phellia pectinata* and *Cereus spinosus*. The endodermal epithelium has produced a thin, circular muscular layer, and is traversed by small, roundish, sharply-contoured bodies. I consider these bodies as parasitic, unicellular organisms of the same kind as those which my brother and I have already observed in various species of Actiniæ. There was no visible trace of the usual yellowish and greenish colour, but this was probably owing to the preservation in spirit.

In the inverted part of the wall I found a sphincter of a very peculiar nature (Pl. XIV. fig. 1). It consists of two perfectly separate portions, a larger, which begins at the outer part of the wall, bends round at the inverted edge, and extends a little way into the invaginated part, and a smaller, which lies at the boundary between the wall and the oral disk. When the animal is expanded, this second portion of the sphincter will lie above the larger portion of the muscle; when the animal is contracted it occupies the lowest part of the invaginated wall. A space without muscles, which does not contract, and, therefore, becomes pleated, lies between the two portions.

Both parts of the sphincter are mesodermal and placed at an equal distance from the endoderm and the ectoderm; their bundles of fibrillæ are arranged irregularly and repeatedly crossed and interwoven in their course, so that the same transverse section passes obliquely through some, transversely through others. The bulk of them lies in the inverted part of the wall, whilst the muscles merely form a thin layer in the outer part of the wall.

The oral disk bears a double corona of small tentacles, corresponding in number to the septa, in that part of its periphery which is contiguous to the wall. The inner tentacles communicate with the intraseptal spaces, the outer tentacles with the interseptal spaces, the two are therefore placed alternately. The muscular system of the oral disk and of the tentacles is ectodermal and extended in a smooth layer.

The distribution of the muscles can be very well recognised in the septa of the strongly contracted polyps. The longitudinal muscular lamella is pleated both in the small rudimentary septa and in the large septa so as to form a small muscular pennon, whilst the fibrillæ which rise obliquely are less strongly developed (Pl. XIV. fig. 2). The paired grouping of the septa is consequently very distinct, and we can also easily distinguish the two pairs of directive septa from the ordinary pairs. The number of the latter varies according to the size of the animal. In the largest polyp examined, there were in all twenty-nine pairs of septa (Pl. XIV. fig. 3). Of the two pairs of opposite directive septa, one pair is rudimentary, does not bear mesenteric filaments, and does not reach the œsophagus, whilst the other pair is perfect, bears mesenteric filaments, and does reach the œsophagus.   The remaining twenty-seven pairs are distributed in the space to the right and left of the œsophagus, so that thirteen pairs lie on the one side and fourteen pairs on the other.   Each pair consists of a larger perfect macroseptum, and a smaller imperfect microseptum.

If we term the side marked by the larger pair of directive septa, the ventral side, we see that almost all the pairs of septa are placed in such a way that the larger, perfect septa are directed ventrad, the smaller imperfect septa dorsad ; the two pairs of septa next to the small dorsal pair of directive septa form the only exception to this rule as their dorsal septa are the larger, their ventral septa the smaller.   We can therefore distinguish two systems of pairs of septa, a dorsal and a ventral.   The result is the following perfectly regular arrangement of the septa : as a rule the larger and smaller septa alternate, but at three points two small septa lie between two large septa, viz., at the dorsal end where the small pair of directive septa lie, and a little way further right and left from the directive septa, where the dorsal and the ventral systems of septa are mutually bounded by small septa.

At the ventral end, on the other hand, we find three spaces between large septa, in which the small septa are wanting, viz., the intraseptal space of the large directive septa, and the two adjacent interseptal spaces.   To explain this more clearly I give formulæ for the dorsal (1), and for the ventral side (2), showing the distribution of the septa.

1. Dorsal side, { &c. *gk gk* ┊ *kg kg k* | *k gk gk* ┊ *kg kg* &c. }
2. Ventral side, { &c. *kg kg* *kg kg* <u>*g*</u> | <u>*g*</u> *gk gk* *gk gk* &c. }

In these formulæ the letter *g* indicates the large septa, *k* the small septa, the dotted lines the boundaries between the dorsal and ventral systems, the black lines the position of the sagittal axis, the underlining the directive septa.

Three of the twenty-seven pairs of septa are still imperfectly developed, and much smaller than the others ; the two pairs lying to the right and left of the ventral directive septa, and the extra pair of septa which is only present on the one side.   As I discovered from other polyps of the same *Zoanthus* colony, the two pairs named at first are the youngest in age.   Their macrosepta resemble on the whole the small septa of the other pairs ; they have no mesenteric filaments, and the uppermost section only reaches to the œsophagus.

I got an explanation of the manner and sequence in which the septa are developed from examination of a small polyp, only a few millimetres high.   It had forty-eight septa in all ; exclusive of the directive septa, there were twenty-one on one side and twenty-three on the other (Pl. XIV. fig. 6).   In the region of the smaller directive septa, the conditions were the same as in the developed polyps, but towards the ventral side the

septa all became smaller as they approached the larger directive septa ; on one side only
the first seven, on the other side only the first six, macrosepta reached the œsophagus, then
followed five other macrosepta which still decreased in size, so that the smallest, which
came next the ventral directive septa, hardly projected at all into the gastric space. The
microsepta left off still earlier, for they became smaller in exact proportion to the macrosepta, and as they were in general less they disappeared sooner. On the ventral side the
directive septa only were perfect, and were separated by a wide interspace from the septa
which were next in development.

Two facts may be deduced from the above observations : (1) The macrosepta and
microsepta can be distinguished from the first by the difference in size ; they develop
independently and at different periods, whilst in the Hexactiniæ and Paractiniæ the septa
of a pair start simultaneously and are of the same size from the first. (2) The septa are
not produced regularly in the periphery of the body of the Actinia, but within a limited,
ventral productive zone. The dorsal septa are therefore the oldest, the ventral septa the
youngest, with the exception of the directive septa, which are developed very early.

The third polyp was intermediate between the two specimens described, both in
the size and the number of its septa, which amounted to fifty-two. A more minute
description of it is therefore unnecessary, and I shall conclude my remarks on the
Zoantheæ with some details as to the structure of the septa.

A cellular cord, or a canal filled with cells, runs in the supporting lamella of the septa
in immediate proximity to the wall (Pl. XIV. fig. 2). It is usually divided into several
cords by commissures of the supporting lamella and is of such strength that the whole
septum becomes visibly and locally thickened. I never could make out any connection
between this septal canal and the ectodermal cords of the wall in any of the numerous sections which I prepared, and I am inclined to believe that it is produced from the endoderm.
My reason is that I have observed that the same roundish bodies which are to be found
in the endoderm, which I regard as parasitic, unicellular organisms, force their way into
the septal canal, but never into the canals of the wall. I attach less importance to the
origin of the canals, as they seem to be connected with the endoderm here and there where
the septa spring from the wall. However, the figures, which led me to consider such a
mode of connection as probable, did not furnish sufficient proof of its actual existence.

The structure of the mesenteric filaments is essentially the same as in the Actiniæ; during the greater part of their course they consist entirely of the median glandular streak,
and it is only a little way below the œsophagus that they are widened by the addition of
paired ciliated streaks, the surface of which is indented at regular intervals by transverse
furrows. This upper section of the mesenteric filaments appears to me identical with the
" flattened organs " described by Verrill as " having a curved or crescent form and a
transversely striated surface,—attached to the principal radiating lamellæ, near the base
of the stomach " (Trans. Connect. Acad., vol. i. p. 494). Verrill, Andres, and others

erroneously consider these organs as peculiar to the Zoantheæ, and explain them to be gills, a view which is, however, quite unwarranted.

I did not find reproductive organs either in the three polyps minutely examined or in several others which I only opened longitudinally.

The cœnenchyma consists of the same tissue as the wall of the polyps, but the proportions of the component parts are altered. The branched fibres are more scanty and crossed irregularly in every direction, whilst the cells of connective substance are remarkably abundant, and many of them have assimilated black granules, and so become branched pigment cells. The ectodermal canals are more numerous than usual, and form a thick net-work ; it is often difficult to distinguish them from the endodermal connective tubes, which run from one polyp to another, and which also may become branched into small vessels.

Epizoanthus, Gray.

Zoanthidæ, in which the outer layer of the body is encrusted with sand granules ; cœnenchyma a thin lamella usually stretched over Gasteropod shells which have been abandoned by their owners and are inhabited by *Paguri* ; polyps projecting considerably above the surface of the cœnenchyma.

Epizoanthus parasiticus (Pl. III. figs. 2, 9, 12 ; Pl. XIV. fig. 5).

Zoanthus parasiticus, Verrill, Memoirs Boston Soc., vol. i. p. 34.

The upper part of the wall of the polyps, which is a few millimetres broad, separated from the lower by a circular furrow, forming a shallow disk when contracted, and covered with forty radial ridges; tentacles seventy to eighty, filament-shaped, arranged in two rows. Colony parasitic upon a Gasteropod shell, the calcareous components of which have been absorbed and replaced by the cœnenchyma.

Habitat.—Station 235. June 4, 1875. Lat. 34° 7' N., long. 138° 0' E. Depth, 565 fathoms. Two specimens.

Dimensions.—Height of the individual polyps, 1·5–2·5 cm. ; breadth, 1·4–1·7 cm.

Epizoanthus parasiticus, of which there were two specimens among the Challenger material, belongs to those Actiniaria which settle as parasites on shells inhabited by hermit crabs. As Verrill, who was the first to give a detailed account of *Epizoanthus*, observed, the Gasteropod shell is almost entirely dissolved, even the columella being completely replaced by the cœnenchyma of the parasite. The form of the shell, however, is still retained, and the hermit crab continues to live comfortably inside, undisturbed by the changes which his home has undergone. The snail shell can only be recognised externally by the wide opening and the point which projects as a stumpy knob.

The number of the individual polyps and their arrangement on the surface of the body is almost the same in both the colonies investigated. Eight polyps are uniformly distributed along that circumference which divides the upper half of the shell from the lower when the *Pagurus* is crawling about on the bottom ; the polyps just mentioned are the largest and most powerful of the colony, and are plainly most favourably placed for acquiring nutriment, as they are always at a little distance from the bottom (Pl. III. fig. 2). A medium-sized polyp rises nearly in the middle of the convex upper side of the colony, and in one colony a second smaller polyp lay close beside it. On the lower side an obviously rudimentary polyp grows on the posterior margin of the opening of the shell (fig. 9) ; it has the best position on the lower side, which is on the whole disadvantageous to development, as it is raised from the bottom as long as the *Pagurus* is crawling about, and only lies upon it when the *Pagurus* has retreated into the shell. In the colony consisting of eleven individuals there was the indication of a twelfth between the eight marginal polyps. It may be taken as a general rule that the distribution of the polyps on the surface of the colony is not accidental, but that those spots are preferred in which the animal has room for free development, and also a convenient position for acquiring nutriment.

The whole surface of the colony is covered by a dirty yellow substance permeated by sand granules, which can be easily scraped off; underneath this the fundamental substance of the wall becomes visible, which resembles cartilage in consistency and colour, and is also hardened superficially by sand granules. This hardened layer is so thin that it can be removed by sections parallel to the surface, and yet leave sufficient fundamental substance both in the cœnenchyma and the wall for transverse sections. These conditions were extremely favourable to examination, so that I regretted the more that the colonies were not better preserved.

The large marginal polyps were 2–2·5 cm. high, 1·4–1·7 cm. broad, and slightly flattened from above downwards. The upper part of the wall is inverted, and forms a horizontal roof ; this might be taken at first sight for the oral disk, as it is separated from the bulk of the wall by a circular furrow, and also differs in its structure, being furnished with numerous (about forty) radial ridges, already observed by Verrill, which are broad where they begin at the margin and become narrower as they run inwards. The radially striated part of the wall is distinguished from the oral disk by being encrusted with sand granules like the rest of the wall. In the middle of this horizontal roof is a fissure running parallel to the margin of the colony, through which, in many polyps, the points of the incompletely retracted tentacles peep out. Through this fissure we may reach the inside of the polyp, first passing through the space lying above the oral disk.

The fundamental substance of the wall is homogeneous, but in transverse and longitudinal sections it shows a striation parallel to the surface of the body, which looks as if it were deposited in layers (Pl. XIV. fig. 5). The striated layers are crossed by fine fibres, which end in repeated branches under the ectoderm like those of *Zoanthus*, but are more numerous, more sharply contoured and waved repeatedly in their course. Besides the branched corpuscles of connective tissue, small and large islands of cells lie in the supporting substance; I presume that these islands of cells represent the system of cellular cords which are always found in *Zoanthus*, but are wanting in *Epizoanthus*. At certain points they are prolonged into longish sausage-shaped cords, several of which may also become united into a dendritic figure. In many parts of the coenenchyma I still found the remains of a branched vascular system, which formed very small meshes, especially about the endodermal connective tubes. I therefore feel justified in my conjecture that the oval islands of cells are caused by the unsatisfactory state of preservation, and are produced by the disintegration of a system of anastomosing cords.

A powerful circular muscle lies in the horizontally inverted part of the wall; it is broad at the beginning of the oral disk and becomes narrower from within outwards. The imperfect state of preservation did not allow me to give any histological description of its bundles of fibrillæ which run in the mesoderm between the ectoderm and endoderm. I could not make out that it was divided into a larger and a smaller part as in *Zoanthus*.

The large size of the individual polyps of *Epizoanthus parasiticus* renders them admirably suited for dissection by means of knife and scissors. If we cut open the animal longitudinally and spread it out by turning back the upper end of the wall (Pl. III. fig. 12), we find adjacent to the latter, the double corona of long, filamentous tentacles, the aggregate number of which amounts to seventy or eighty. The tentacles of the inner row alternate with those of the outer. The oral disk extends far down, and is covered with shallow radial furrows corresponding to the tentacles. It is divided by a distinct thickening from the œsophagus, in which our attention is at once attracted to the single œsophageal groove. When spread out the œsophageal groove forms a scutiform plate, separated from the adjacent parts of the œsophagus by longitudinal furrows, and divided by a more distinct median furrow into a right and a left half; it is prolonged far below the lower margin of the œsophagus, so that it is almost twice its length. The triangular lappet formed in this way is likewise divided into two by the prolonged longitudinal furrow, and deeply indented at the end.

Below the lower margin of the œsophagus there are seen thirty-two to thirty-four septa, the zigzag margins of which are caused by the reproductive organs; these are macrosepta, the microsepta only becoming visible when the others are folded back. I examined the mutual relations of the two kinds of septa in transverse sections and with essentially the same result as G. v. Koch in *Epizoanthus axinellæ* (Morphol. Jahrb., Bd. vi. p. 359, 1880). Two pairs of directive septa lie at the ends of the sagittal axis, the dorsal pair consisting of microsepta, the ventral of macrosepta; the latter only reach the œsophagus and are attached close to the œsophageal groove, which is also ventral. Besides these there are fifteen pairs of septa on either side (if the aggregate number of pairs of septa is increased to thirty-three, there are sixteen on one side and fifteen on the other), which consist of (1), a pair of septa adjoining the dorsal directive pair, and having the dorsal septum larger than the ventral ; (2), thirteen pairs of septa situated towards the ventral aspect of the body, and having the ventral septum larger than the dorsal ; and (3), a pair consisting of two macrosepta and lying between the two above mentioned groups. The distinction then between *Epizoanthus parasiticus* and *Epizoanthus axinellæ* on the one hand and the true *Zoanthus* on the other, is that in the latter the two systems are separated by microsepta, in the former by macrosepta, so that a pair of septa is made up of one septum from either system.

The remarks made by me on the septal canals and mesenteric filaments of *Zoanthus* apply equally to *Epizoanthus parasiticus*. The reproductive organs were well developed, and seemed to lie only on the macrosepta, and that without exception ; they were testes in the specimen which I examined in transverse section.

The individual animals of the *Epizoanthus* colony were united at the base by a tolerably thick crust, in which numerous canals run from one polyp to another ; all the canals extend with repeated anastomosis in one and the same layer of the cœnenchyma. Hence if we cut a colony through longitudinally, the cœnenchyma is separated by the vascular stratum into a broader external and a narrower internal layer ; the character of the tissue is the same in both, except that the inner layer is without branched fibres. The gastric spaces of all the polyps reach as far as the vascular stratum, in which lies a very large canal surrounding the opening of the shell like a ring (Pl. III. fig. 9).

The hollow of the shell enclosed by the cœnenchyma is lined by a chitinous membrane, which lies firmly attached to the thin layer of the cœnenchyma, and has a structure of its own. Two lamellæ are separated from one another by an interspace, and are connected by perpendicular septa parallel to one another which divide the interspace into numerous tubes and smaller prismatic spaces. I leave it an open question whether this chitinous membrane is the last remains of the Gasteropod shell or a cuticular formation secreted by the superficial epithelium of the *Epizoanthus*.

The mode of life of *Epizoanthus parasiticus* is the same as that of *Epizoanthus papillosus* and *Epizoanthus cancrisocius*, the former of which was described by Gray in the Proceedings of the Zoological Society, 1867, p. 237, the latter by Studer in the Monatsberichten der Berliner Academie, Jahrg., 1878, p. 547. Both forms settle on Gasteropod shells, occupied by a hermit crab, and completely absorb the calcareous parts of the shell. The upper section of the wall of *Epizoanthus papillosus* appears to be of the same nature as that of *Epizoanthus parasiticus*. I draw this inference from Gray's words in the description given of the individual polyps, " The apex when expanded is flat, with close, radiating white lines." It is therefore still a question whether these are merely allied species or whether *Epizoanthus papillosus* and *Epizoanthus cancrisocius* are identical with *Epizoanthus parasiticus.*

Family SPHENOPIDÆ.

Solitary Zoantheæ with the posterior end of the body rounded.

Sphenopus, Steenstrup.

Sphenopidæ with thick wall, the uppermost layers of which are encrusted with sand granules ; with strong mesodermal sphincter.

Gray, in his system of the Zoantheæ (Proc. Zool. Soc., 1867, p. 236), has erected several genera, in which the individual polyps remain solitary, and are either firmly attached to the bottom or stick in the sand by means of the rounded body-end, viz., the genera *Isaurus, Pales, Orinia,* and *Sphenopus.* As no thorough anatomical studies have been made as yet of all these forms, it is doubtful in the meantime whether they ought to be placed among the Zoantheæ or not. *Sphenopus* is the only one of which I can affirm that it belongs to the Zoantheæ, as the macrosepta and microsepta are visible in regular order, and the œsophagus has only one œsophageal groove.

Sphenopus arenaceus, n. sp. (Pl. II. fig. 10, Pl. XIV. fig. 8).

The greater part of the wall is encrusted with sand granules, and so transformed into a kind of carapace ; tentacles small and pointed, about sixty in number, distributed in two rows ; thirty macrosepta and the same number of microsepta.

Habitat.—Cape York. (? The title of the label enclosed with the preparation was nearly entirely destroyed by the rough surface of the animal, and could not be exactly made out.) One specimen.

Dimensions.—Length, 4·5 cm. ; breadth, 2·8 cm.

Colour.—(Determined from the spirit specimen) brown-red.

The wall of *Sphenopus arenaceus,* a new species, which I erect here from a single specimen among the Challenger material, is encrusted with foreign bodies to a degree which I have never found in any other Zoanthea ; it forms a firm unyielding capsule, in which the soft parts are completely concealed when the animal is strongly contracted. The form of the *Sphenopus* then becomes irregularly oval, rather smaller at the rounded posterior end of the body than at the anterior. The wall is inverted a little way at the anterior end, though its nature does not undergo any change.

The surface is regularly rough like shagreen, as the sand granules are nearly all of equal size. The granules force their way so deeply into the wall that only a thin layer of soft tissue remains on the endodermal side ; it is broadest in the front, and becomes narrower as it runs backwards, till the wall at the aboral body-pole consists almost entirely of a layer of sand 5 millimetres thick (even in Pl. II. fig. 10 the soft part of the wall is too large in proportion to the layer of sand granules). Where the sand grains are absent the fundamental substance is homogeneous and furnished with two different forms of cells, small branched cells and larger roundish ones, the latter being entirely filled with strongly refractive concrement-like granules. The tissue between the sand granules (Pl. XIV. fig. 8), on the other hand, appears rather fibrous, and even the corpuscles of connective tissue are fusiform in shape. The direction of the fibres and the fusiform cells is parallel to the surface of the body. In most parts the sand granules are so thickly compacted that the fundamental substance is entirely covered.

There are no ectodermal vessels in the wall, but the supporting fibres are very numerous; they are richly furnished with granular protoplasm, are very fine and branched on the endodermal side, whilst towards the ectoderm they become lost among the sand granules.

The mesodermal circular muscle, which is strongly developed as in the other Zoantheæ, is not confined merely to the inverted part of the wall, but extends a good way down into the outer section. It is strongest where it begins close to the oral disk and lies in the non-encrusted section of the wall, it then becomes narrower and gradually approaches the endoderm, till the lower end almost touches the epithelium. It consists of bundles of fibrillæ, which give repeatedly waved figures in transverse section; several bundles are united into roundish bundles of the second order, which remain farther apart from one another.

Whilst the wall is very thick and firm, all the inner parts consist of delicate, easily torn lamellæ. The oral disk only is tolerably strong, and foreign bodies (sponge spicules, sand granules) are enclosed here and there in its supporting lamella. It is covered by a smooth layer of ectodermal radial muscles, and the margin bears two rows of tentacles; I could not determine the number of the tentacles accurately because of the strong contraction, but there were probably about sixty of them.

Before the oral disk passes into the œsophagus, which is of considerable size, it rises into a thin, sharp-margined lip, which is repeatedly indented at the edge. A large number of longitudinal ridges of the œsophagus, which correspond to the origins of the perfect septa, spring from these indentations.

The œsophageal groove is remarkably distinct; it is distinguished by its depth, and is enclosed by two broad folds, almost as hard as cartilage. Gray probably had these folds in mind when he specially mentions that in *Sphenopus marsupialis* "the laminæ of the stomach have a cartilaginous edge." They extend a little way beyond the lower margin of the stomach and form a projection, resembling the prow of a boat.

The arrangement of the septa agrees essentially with that already described in detail for *Zoanthus*, sp.? Two small directive septa lie at the dorsal end of the œsophagus, two large directive septa at the ventral end, which is easily recognised by the œsophageal groove ; two pairs, with dorsal macrosepta and ventral microsepta, adjoin the former on either side ; twelve pairs, with ventral macrosepta and dorsal microsepta, adjoin the latter. The small dorsal and the large ventral septal regions are therefore separated on either side by microsepta.   There are in all thirty macrosepta and thirty microsepta.

The following observations seem to me to justify these statements. From the dissection of individual septa, it was evident to me that the œsophagus is surrounded by two kinds of septa, viz., macrosepta, which are attached along the entire length of the œsophagus ; and microsepta, which end on the oral disk before it becomes raised into the oral lip. In all of them the muscular fibres which rise obliquely are very distinct, the longitudinal fibres less so.

The only example of *Sphenopus arenaceus* which I was able to examine was bisected longitudinally parallel to the sagittal plane, so that only the one half (Pl. II. fig. 10) contained the œsophageal groove and the septa fastened to it. At the end of the œsophageal groove three macrosepta followed one another before I liberated the first microseptum by dissection, whilst the adjoining part of the other half begins with a microseptum, and the macrosepta and microsepta come alternately. If we then compare the transverse section through *Zoanthus* (Pl. XIV. fig. 3), we find a similar arragement of the septa in the region of the œsophageal groove, except that in *Sphenopus* the outermost of the four macrosepta placed in a row in *Zoanthus* is wanting. As it falls in the line through which the section has been taken in dividing the animal, it has most likely been destroyed.

At the dorsal end we first meet with a microseptum, then with a macroseptum ; after which, on dissection, I found the septa arranged in the following order, two microsepta, one macroseptum, one microseptum, one macroseptum, one microseptum, one macroseptum. In the adjoining portion of the other half, I found one microseptum, one macroseptum, one microseptum, one macroseptum, two microsepta, one macroseptum. If we compare this arrangement with fig. 3 of *Zoanthus*, and consider the two pairs of microsepta discovered by dissection to be homologous with the two lateral pairs of microsepta in *Zoanthus*, we should likewise meet with the same corresponding conditions if we assume that one of the small directive septa and the adjoining macroseptum have been destroyed in making the section.

Finally, as regards the number of the septa, I determined them according to the lines of insertion which shone through the œsophagus ; in this way we can settle the number of the macrosepta, with which the number of microsepta corresponds, presupposing, of course, that they are arranged in the same way as in *Zoanthus*. I found this to be the case in at least half of the septa dissected.

The reproductive organs and mesenteric filaments were cemented by mucus into a badly preserved mass, and were not adapted for examination.

Tribe VI. CERIANTHEÆ.

Actiniaria with numerous unpaired septa and a single ventral œsophageal groove; the septa are longest on the ventral side and gradually diminish towards the dorsal aspect; the two septa attached to the bottom of the œsophageal groove (directive septa) are remarkably small, and are distinguished in this way from the other ventral septa.

I have made no further anatomical investigations of the Ceriantheæ, and cannot even complete the statements which were formerly made by von Heider (Sitzungber. d. Wiener Akad. Math. Naturw. Cl., Bd. lxxix. Abth. 1, p. 204, Jahrg., 1879), and my brother and myself (Actinien, p. 107). From these we cannot even certainly determine what position the animals occupy in the circle of the Actiniaria, and whether or not they ought to be placed in one of the known principal divisions. They are distinguished from all the forms previously discussed, except the Edwardsiæ, by the fact that they want the paired arrangement of the septa—at least up to the present it has not been observed in them. They come nearest the Zoantheæ, as they have only one œsophageal groove; the septa also appear not to be disposed in a circle, but in the region of a limited zone of growth, which, however, lies dorsally, not ventrally as in the Zoantheæ. In this case the largest septa are found in the region of the œsophageal groove, and the septa gradually decrease in size from that point to the opposite end of the sagittal axis; two pairs of very small septa lie under the œsophageal groove, to which the name of directive septa is given more from their position than from their anatomical constitution.

Family CERIANTHIDÆ.

Ceriantheæ with a double corona of tentacles, marginal principal tentacles and circum-oral accessory tentacles, posterior end of the body rounded, without sphincter.

Cerianthus, Delle Chiaje.

Cerianthidæ with aboral pore, with a sheath consisting of mud, sand granules, and nematocysts, in which the posterior end of the animal lies as if in a case.

Cerianthus americanus.

Cerianthus americanus, Verrill, Memoirs Boston Soc., vol. i. p. 32, 1866.

Habitat.—Station 321. February 25, 1876. Lat. 35° 2′ S., long. 55° 15′ W. Depth, 13 fathoms. One specimen.

Dimensions.—Length of the animal (in the contracted condition), 12 cm.; breadth of the oral disk, 3·5 cm.; length of the inner tentacles, 2–2·5 cm.; of the outer tentacles, 4–5 cm.

Most species of the genus *Cerianthus* are far surpassed in size by *Cerianthus americanus*, which Verrill only has hitherto described. His account of it is as follows :
" Column very long, cylindrical, expanded at the top, tapering gradually below ; in expansion, often two feet or more long, in contraction, six or eight inches. Body enclosed in a loosely investing tube, buried in the mud. Tentacles long and numerous, the outer series (125 or more) are from 1·25 to 1·50 inches long, slender, very flexile, usually much curled at the ends; inner series similar, about ·75 long, nearly the same as the former in appearance ; often brought together and spirally twisted in a central bundle. Base with a small but distinct opening.

" Color of column dark cinnamon-brown, lined longitudinally with a lighter tint of the same ; outer tentacles cinnamon-brown, lighter at the bases ; inner series darker, marked with white longitudinal lines ; disk bright yellow, the central portion brown ; at the bases of the tentacles spotted with dark brown."

I consider the single specimen of the genus *Cerianthus* dredged by the Challenger as identical with *Cerianthus americanus*. As it is more than 12 cm. long, it may easily have measured more than 50 cm. when alive. The number of the outer tentacles, which I reckoned at about two hundred, is larger than in the specimens examined by Verrill, whilst their length is about the same. The distribution of colour on the tentacles was no longer recognisable, as the whole colour of the animal had been changed by the spirit. I did not attempt an anatomical examination, as I did not wish to destroy the unique specimen.

APPENDIX.

By way of appendix I shall describe some forms whose systematic position I was unable to determine, as their state of preservation did not admit of an anatomical investigation of the inner parts, especially of the septa.

Two of them seemed to me to be closely related and to belong to the same genus *Porponia*, and I shall discuss them in detail as interesting species, though I have not done so in the case of the others.

Porponia, n. gen.

Actiniaria (Hexactiniæ ?) with two œsophageal grooves, without circular muscle, with thin-walled tentacles, the bases of which are supported on the outer side by clasp-like prolongations of the wall.

Porponia elongata, n. sp. (Pl. I. figs. 1, 2).

Body elongated, sessile, wall cartilage-like, small, upper end terminated by twenty-seven knobs forming supporting clasps for the outer sides of the same number of long, thin-walled tentacles ; twenty-seven additional tentacles placed in an inner second row, and alternating with the outer tentacles.

Habitat.—Station 160. March 13, 1874. Lat. 42° 42′ S., long. 134° 10′ E. Depth, 2600 fathoms. Two specimens.

Dimensions.—Height, 5·5 cm.; breadth of the base, 2·5–3·5 cm.; breadth of the oral disk, 3·0–4·0 cm. ; length of the tentacles, 1·5–2·5 cm.

Whilst the majority of Actiniæ, especially those from great depths, form a short column, and are frequently flattened into a disk, the body form of *Porponia elongata*, a new species taken from a depth of 2600 fathoms, approximates that of the elongated Cerianthidæ. In both specimens examined the body, though contracted, was twice as long as high. It is broadest in the region of the oral disk, below which it becomes a little narrower, and then becomes broader again at the pedal disk, by which it is firmly attached to the bottom. It was impossible to recognise the original colour of the animal, but this was partly owing to the fact that the ectoderm was completely macerated away.

The pedal disk is thin and the insertions of the septa shine through it as whitish, radial lines. There are altogether about thirty-two to thirty-four such lines, some of which, however, only project a little way towards the centre of the pedal disk. Setting these aside, we can count in both cases twenty-eight almost equally distinct lines, which appear to be grouped in pairs.

Contrasted with the pedal disk the wall is very thick, as it measures 2–3 mm. in transverse section, and by reason of its cartilaginous hardness forms at the same time a most powerful protection for the parts covered by it. The surface is smooth and only traversed here and there by furrows, which may, however, be absent in the living animal; the upper margin ends in pointed knobs which project like battlements above the enclosed oral disk. The number of the knobs appears to be constant, as it amounted to twenty-seven in both the larger and the smaller specimen examined, though they differed in size. The larger and smaller knobs are placed irregularly, so that sometimes both kinds alternate, sometimes several knobs of the same size lie beside one another.

The oral disk, which springs from the wall at the base of the knobs, is as thin as tissue paper and correspondingly transparent. Numerous (probably fifty-four) white radial streaks denote the insertions of the underlying septa.

The tentacles, like the oral disk, are very thin-walled and delicate, and are 1·5–2·5 cm. long. The base is of medium breadth; they then diminish rapidly in size, and run out into a long fine point, through which even pressure cannot expel the contents of the tentacles, thus showing the absence of the terminal opening common to many Actiniæ. They are placed in two alternating rows of twenty-seven tentacles each. The outer tentacles spring immediately on the inside of the twenty-seven knobs of the wall, which may therefore be regarded as clasp-like thickenings of their basal sections; the inner tentacles alternate with the outer, and are placed so close to them that their bases are partially inserted into the interspaces between the outer tentacles.

The oral disk is covered by a thin ectodermal slightly pleated layer of radial muscular fibres, which extend as longitudinal fibres into the tentacles; in many places it had fallen away along with the epithelium lying above it. There were still fewer of the circular endodermal muscular fibres preserved.

The oral angle and the œsophageal grooves are very distinct in the oral fissure and the œsophagus. The œsophageal grooves are only a little longer than the rest of the œsophagus, but on the other hand they are of considerable breadth, and occupy about two-fifths of the whole extent of the œsophagus. The side walls of the grooves are repeatedly folded in a transverse direction. Longitudinal folds, nine in the one case, eleven in the other, which begin with the same number of knobs at the margin of the oral fissure, run on the two intermediate portions of the œsophageal wall. The oral margin itself projects as a ridge, just as the oral disk in *Sphenopus arenaceus* is very much raised before it passes at an acute angle into the œsophagus.

There are, altogether, twenty-eight septa inserted into the œsophagus—veil-like, extremely delicate, easily torn membranes, never pierced by septal stomata. It was impossible to arrive at any decided opinion as to their structure and arrangement, both specimens having been badly preserved. As both the ectodermal epithelium and muscles were almost entirely macerated away, so also all the endodermal parts formed a disintegrated mass in the radial chambers. The muscles of the septa were nowhere preserved, so that I could only form an idea of their course from the furrows on the surface of the supporting lamellæ. These were, however, not very distinct, as the muscles of the septa, like the muscles of all the other organs, are extremely weakly developed ; as far as I could make out each septum bears longitudinal muscles on the one side, and transverse muscles on the other, as in other Actiniæ.

All the septa are furnished in the section below the œsophagus with reproductive organs which reach like long, broad, folded bands almost as far as the pedal disk, but the mesenteric filaments were macerated away and nowhere to be found.

Besides the twenty-eight perfect septa there are imperfect septa, which only reach as far as the middle of the oral disk, and do not bear reproductive organs. I did not determine the number of them by direct observation, as in order to do this I should have been obliged to dissect the entire animal, and I could not make up my mind to this, considering how insufficiently it was preserved. I estimate them at twenty-six, as in the majority of Actiniaria the aggregate number of the tentacles nearly corresponds to that of the septa.

Though the anatomical description here given is but deficient, I consider myself justified in regarding *Porponia elongata* as a form systematically interesting. The position of the tentacles in a double row, the presence of perfect reproductive septa (macrosepta) and imperfect sterile septa (microsepta) are characteristics which recall the Zoantheæ ; the numbers of the tentacles and the septa likewise agree with those of this group, as they are neither multiples of the number six, as in the Hexactiniæ, nor of the number four, as in the Paractiniæ. On the other hand, having two œsophageal grooves, *Porponia elongata* comes closer to the Hexactiniæ, among which, as I have already specially observed (p. 30), it most resembles the Antheomorphidæ. I therefore consider it most likely that *Porponia elongata* is an intermediate form between the Hexactiniæ and the Zoantheæ.

Porponia robusta (Pl. I. fig. 10).

Body compressed, as high as broad, sessile ; wall tough, the upper end prolonged into numerous scimitar-shaped processes, which support the outer walls of the long, thin-walled saccular tentacles.

Habitat.—Station 237. June 17, 1875. Lat. 34° 37′ N., long. 140° 32′ E. Depth, 1875 fathoms. One specimen.

Dimensions.—Height, 4 cm. ; breadth of the oral disk, 4 cm. ; breadth of the pedal disk, 3 cm.

The single specimen of *Porponia robusta* had unfortunately been preserved in chromic acid, and had therefore become so brittle that I must confine myself to a description of the external form of the body. The animal is shaped like a short, compressed cylinder; it becomes a little broader towards the pedal disk, but very markedly so in the upper half, so that the margin of the oral disk is turned outwards even when the animal is fully contracted.

The pedal disk and oral disk are thin-walled, but the wall itself is of considerable thickness; its upper surface is smooth, for though there are oblique and longitudinal wrinkles and furrows they are plainly owing to contraction. There is no circular muscle, as may be gathered from the form of the anterior end of the body. A single row of tentacles stands on the margin between the oral disk and wall; they look like long, wide, thin, membraned sacs, and do not become smaller at the ends. A firm clasp, quite 1 cm. long, runs on the outer wall of the tentacles, as a prolongation of the body-wall; it is broadest and thickest at the base, and gradually becomes narrower and thinner towards the end. As the tentacles, in consequence of contraction, are turned over towards the oral disk, the tentacle clasps are also bent inwards like a scimitar, many of them so much so that they lie obliquely above the oral disk. I was unable to determine the exact number of the tentacles, as they were bent confusedly over one another, and the friable nature of their clasps prevented me from trying to separate them. They amounted, however, to more than forty.

Besides the longitudinal ridges, I found two œsophageal grooves on the œsophagus, one of them much more strongly developed than the other. After I had removed the pedal disk by a horizontal section, I was able to count the septa, of which there were thirty-eight, separated from one another by interspaces of equal size. They appeared to me all to bear reproductive organs, but only to extend partially to the œsophagus. They also projected more or less towards the centre of the pedal disk.

In this appendix I have still three forms of Actiniæ to consider besides the *Porponiæ*. The first was taken at Tristan da Cunha, at a depth of 1000 fathoms, and appears to be a *Phellia*. The body, 1·3 cm. long and 1·0 cm. broad, is covered with a finely granulated, brownish, leather-like cuticle, which is wanting on the short inverted part of the wall. A strong circular muscle, which contracts the wall to such an extent that the entrance to the oral disk is completely closed, lies in the inverted portion of the wall. I can say nothing as to the number of the very small tentacles, and I was also unable to examine the number and nature of the septa more minutely.

The two other forms of Actiniæ were taken along with the four specimens of *Cereus spinosus* and the single specimen of *Porponia robusta*, at a depth of 1875 fathoms, on June 17, 1875, at station 237 (lat. 34° 37′ N., long. 140° 32′ E.); like the Actiniæ just mentioned, they had been placed in chromic acid, and were therefore but little adapted for examination.

In the one instance I had to do with an Actinia, which so strongly resembled the *Dysactis crassicornis* described on page 44, that I was long inclined to consider it as the same species. As in *Dysactis crassicornis*, the muscles on the oral disk and tentacles are mesodermal; the strong sphincter, which is also enclosed in the mesoderm, lies close under the endoderm, and contracts the wall so strongly that the surface becomes arranged in ridge-like, projecting folds. The tentacles only are different; they are placed in four alternating rows, are equal to one another in size, and are much longer and more powerful than in *Dysactis crassicornis*, so that even when contracted they form slightly curved horns 3 cm. long. The most striking point, however, is the wide, gaping opening at the free end, from which one might give the animal the specific name *tubulifera*. This Actinia probably belongs to the genus *Paractis*, the smooth surface of the wall, the mesodermal circular muscle, and the equality of size in the tentacles of the individual rows being common to both. The two specimens of this Actinia before me are both 3 cm. high and 6 cm. broad at the pedal disk; they become smaller towards the upper end, the diameter of which only amounts to 2·5 cm.

The last Actinia to be considered belongs to the forms in which the tentacles have undergone retrograde formation, on account of which I have named it *Liponema multiporum*. The only specimen of it was hardened in chromic acid and also greatly injured, a combination most unfavourable for examination. The pedal disk and the lower part of the wall were torn, the œsophagus forcibly protruded and also torn, so that the oral disk was stretched and misplaced; it formed the side walls of the body, and this led me at first to take it for the wall and the wall for the pedal disk, till I discovered my mistake in examining it histologically.

The oral disk is devoid of freely moving tentacles, but has instead numerous, small stomidia, roundish openings not measuring more than 2 mm. in diameter. The tentacles in *Liponema multiporum* have undergone retrograde formation to a greater extent than in any other Actinia, as there are not the smallest remains of their walls, while in *Polyopis* these can still be recognised as thickened ridges surrounding the openings (Pl. XIV. fig. 7).

Part of the stomidia, which number several hundreds, are arranged on the margin of the oral disk in a repeatedly waved circle, the remainder lie at short distances from one another on the oral disk, on which they are distributed nearly to the oral opening. After dissecting a number of septa I became convinced that more than one stomidium communicates with each radial chamber; in fact, I believe that the marginal openings must be considered principal stomidia, the others accessory stomidia. We therefore have here the same conditions as in the Discosomidæ and Corallimorphidæ, if we consider the tentacles to be replaced by the stomidia. The oral disk is covered with numerous fine ridges which wind between the accessory stomidia and so have a very sinuous course. The radial muscles are ectodermal and borne by fine supporting folds, having the same constitution as in *Cerianthus*. I have also examined the circular muscular system of the wall; I found it thickly pleated in the whole upper region of the wall, especially in the part adjoining the oral disk, where it formed a kind of sphincter. The pleating ceases rather suddenly at the outer margin of the principal stomidia. The muscular folds of the layer of circular muscles are very long, and thickly branched only at the base, so that a principal fold soon becomes divided into numerous parallel secondary folds.

SURVEY OF THE ACTINIÆ EXAMINED.

Family.	Genus.	Species.	Depth in Fathoms.	Station.	Habitat.	If New		Number of Specimens.
						Species.	Genus.	
Corallimorphidæ	Corallimorphus	profundus	2025	293	39° S. 105° W.	n. sp.	n. g.	1
"	"	"	1375	300	33° S. 78° W.	n. sp.	n. g.	1
"	"	rigidus	1375	146	46° S. 45° E.	n. sp.	n. g.	3
"	"	"	1950	157	53° S. 108° E.	n. sp.	n. g.	1
"	"	"	1425	195	4° S. 129° E.	n. sp.	n. g.	1
Antheomorphidæ	Antheomorphe	elegans	2900	244	35° N. 169° E.	n. sp.	n. g.	3
Antheadæ	Comactis	flagellifera	25	...	30° S. 20° E.	...	...	1
Tealidæ	Tealia	bunodiformis	Shore.	...	37° S. 12° W.	n. sp.	...	3
"	Leiotealia	nymphæa	120	149	49° S. 70° E.	...	...	1
Paractidæ	Dysactis	crassicornis	10	312	53° S. 70° W.	n. sp.	...	1
"	"	"	55	313	52° S. 68° W.	n. sp.	...	4
"	"	rhodora	55	313	52° S. 68° W.	...	...	2
"	Paractis	tubulifera	1875	237	34° N. 140° E.	n. sp.	...	2
"	"	excavata	1375	300	33° S. 78° W.	n. sp.	...	1
"	Tealidium	cingulatum	1800	158	50° S. 123° E	n. sp.	...	1
"	Antholoba	reticulata	55	313	52° S. 68° W.	...	...	3
"	Ophiodiscus	annulatus	2160	299	33° S. 74° W.	n. sp.	n. g.	4
"	"	sulcatus	1375	300	33° S. 78° W.	n. sp.	n. g.	1
Liponemidæ	Polysiphonia	tuberosa	565	235	34° N. 138° E.	n. sp.	n. g.	20
"	Polystomidium	patens	1825	296	38° S. 88° W.	n. sp.	n. g.	1
"	Liponema	multiporum	1875	237	34° N. 140° E.	n. sp.	n. g.	1
Sagartidæ	Sagartia	sp. (?)	360	194	4° S. 129° E.	...	...	1
"	Calliactis	polypus	18	208	11° N. 123° E.	...	...	3
"	"	"	...	...	17° N. 27° W.	...	...	6
"	Cereus	spinosus	1950	157	53° S. 108° E.	n. sp.	...	1
"	"	"	1875	237	34° N. 140° E.	n. sp.	...	4
"	Phellia	pectinata	147	307	49° S. 74° W.	n. sp.	...	1
"	"	sp. (?)	1000	...	...	?	...	1
"	Bunodes	minuta	1600	147	46° S. 48° E.	n. sp.	...	1
Amphianthidæ	Stephanactis	tuberculata	345	232	35° N. 139° E.	n. sp.	n. g.	1
"	"	abyssicola	1350	46	40° N. 66° W.	n. sp.	n. g.	2
"	Amphianthus	bathybium	2300	241	35° N. 157° E.	n. sp.	n. g.	1
Ilyanthidæ	Halcampa	clavus	25	149	49° S. 70° E.	...	...	2
"	"	"	120	149	...	...	...	1
Sicyonidæ	Sicyonis	crassa	1600	147	46° S. 48° E.	n. sp.	n. g	1
Polyopidæ	Polyopis	striata	2160	299	33° S. 74° W.	n. sp.	n. g.	1
Monaulidæ	Scytophorus	striatus	150	150	52° S. 71° E.	n. sp.	n. g.	2
Zoanthidæ	Zoanthus	sp. (?)	...	...	...	...	...	1
"	Epizoanthus	parasiticus	565	235	34° N. 138° E.	...	...	2
Sphenopidæ	Sphenopus	arenaceus	...	...	...	n. sp.	...	1
Cerianthidæ	Cerianthus	americanus	13	321	35° S. 55° W.	...	...	1
...	Porponia	elongata	2600	160	42° S. 134° E.	n. sp.	n. g.	2
...	"	robusta	1875	237	34° N. 140° E.	n. sp.	n. g.	1

NOTE.—The reader is reminded that this is not a complete list of the Challenger Actiniæ. A number of specimens, which did not reach Professor Hertwig till after this Memoir was in type, will be described in a Supplementary Report.—J. M.

Concluding Remarks.

In the Introduction I have given a sketch of the structure of the Actiniaria, and also at the same time a short summary of the most important morphological results furnished by the Challenger material; all that remains is for me to discuss how far the results of the Challenger expedition have furthered our knowledge of the manner in which the group in question is distributed. I have therefore made out a tabular survey (p. 130) of the Actiniæ described and their habitats, and have also stated whether or not they are new species and genera. It follows, of course, that I have only enumerated as new, such species as have been actually described for the first time by Moseley and myself, whilst I have included among the known animals those forms to which, since we know their anatomy more thoroughly, it has been necessary to give new names, especially new generic names.

The table in question gives no determinate results as to the geographical distribution of the animals; it was, indeed, evident from the first that the Challenger material was neither sufficient nor suitable for this purpose. The number of hauls made by the dredge was utterly disproportioned to the vast tracts traversed by the ship in her voyage round the world; the individual faunatic regions especially have been very irregularly examined. As the ship was mostly on the high seas, the coasts, which would have furnished the richest spoils, were of necessity almost entirely neglected, and in this way we only find one littoral species in the list.

On the other hand, we must take into special consideration the manner in which the Actiniæ are distributed in the different depths of sea. How far is the number of the Actiniæ diminished by the increase of the depth? How far does the deep-sea fauna vary from the fauna of the coasts and the shallows? Has life in the depths exercised, as in other cases, a visible influence on the organisation of the animal? These are questions which may be partially solved from the tolerably wide range of material furnished by the Challenger collection.

As a rule the number of the Actiniæ decreases as the depth increases; up to the present they have not been observed even in the Challenger expedition at a depth of over 2900 fathoms, though the decrease does not take place so rapidly as might be expected. In proof of this I contrast the results given by the hauls with the dredge in 10–500 fathoms, with those in 500–2900 fathoms. The net was let down ninety-seven times in depths of 10–500 fathoms, and eleven times with some result, i.e., with the capture of some twenty specimens distributed over thirteen different species. There were one hundred and sixty-five hauls with the dredge at depths of 500–2900 fathoms, fourteen of these furnished about sixty specimens, representing twenty-one different species. These numbers cannot of course be compared off hand, as the hauls made by the dredge in great depths lasted much longer, and consequently extended over a larger tract, but at the same time we can see from this that the deep-sea Actiniæ are by no means exceptionally rare.

The relative abundance of the Actiniæ among the deep-sea fauna is shown by the fact that several species and several specimens of the same species were not unfrequently found at the same station. Station 235 furnished the largest number of individuals, viz., twenty specimens of *Polysiphonia tuberosa* and two colonies of *Epizoanthus parasiticus* were taken at a depth of 565 fathoms. Stations 237 and 300 were distinguished by the diversity of the forms dredged; at the former four specimens of *Cereus spinosus*, two of *Paractis tubulifera*, one of *Porponia robusta*, and one of *Liponema multiporum* were taken at a depth of 1875 fathoms, at the latter one *Corallimorphus profundus*, one *Paractis excavata* and one *Ophiodiscus sulcatus* were taken at 1375 fathoms. The following stations yielded also good results :—Station 299 ; depth, 2160 fathoms ; one *Ophiodiscus annulatus* and one *Polyopis striata*. Station 157 ; depth, 1950 fathoms ; one *Cereus spinosus* and one *Corallimorphus rigidus*. Station 147 ; depth, 1600 fathoms ; one *Bunodes minuta* and one *Sicyonis crassa*.

The stations in shallow water are far behind as regards the results of the dredgings. The only stations worthy of special mention are Station 143, depth 120 fathoms, which contributed two *Halcampa clavus* and one *Leiotealia nymphæa* to the Challenger material ; and Station 313, depth 55 fathoms, which contributed three *Antholoba reticulata*, four *Dysactis crassicornis*, and two *Dysactis rhodora*.

As regards the relation in which the fauna of the different depths stand to one another, it may already be safely asserted that the greater the depth, the more the fauna varies from that of the coast. I will make only two divisions, and compare, on the one hand, the Actiniæ from 10–500 fathoms, and on the other, the Actiniæ from 500–2900 fathoms with the known forms essentially belonging to the coast. The first region gives on the whole thirteen species and twelve genera, of which five species and two genera (*Scytophorus* and *Stephanactis*) are new. The remaining twenty-one species and seventeen genera belong to the second region (two genera, *Phellia* and *Stephanactis*, are represented in both divisions), of which not less than twenty species and eleven genera are new. The depths of 500–3000 fathoms are therefore inhabited by entirely different Actiniæ, as even the only species which cannot be considered as new, *Epizoanthus parasiticus*, approached the first region, as it was taken at a depth of 565 fathoms.

The varying character of the deep-sea fauna leads us to the third question already started, viz., has life in the great depths a visible influence on the organisation of the Actiniæ ? This influence can be distinctly recognised in many forms, and is shown by the nature of the tentacles which have undergone retrograde formation, and are transformed first into tubes, and afterwards into simple openings in the oral disk. In *Paractis tubulifera* (depth 1875 fathoms) the tentacles have the same constitution as in the majority of Actiniæ, except in one point, that the terminal opening, which is usually small or entirely wanting, gapes widely. In *Polysiphonia tuberosa* (565 fathoms) the tentacles have become short, slightly movable, wide-mouthed tubes; in *Sicyonis crassa* (1600 fathoms) they are small, wart-like rings, and in *Polystomidium patens* (1825 fathoms) and *Polyopis striata* (2160 fathoms) the walls have almost entirely disappeared, so that the terminal opening forms a fissure in the oral disk, the last remains of the tentacle being represented by a circular margin surrounding the fissure, and so we come finally to the genus *Liponema* (1875 fathoms), in which the points at which the tentacles were actually placed are merely indicated by openings in the oral disk. Of the twenty-one forms from 500–3000 fathoms here described, no less than six species have therefore undergone modifications of the tentacles in the same sense, whilst it has never been observed in a single one of the forms of the coast fauna, which greatly exceed the deep-sea fauna in number.

The view that the retrograde formation of the tentacles is connected with life in greater depths is not only supported by the fact observed, that the character is limited in its distribution to the deep-sea Actiniæ, but also by the way in which it appears in the different groups of Actiniæ. The six forms named in the last paragraph show conditions allied to those in families of Actiniæ lying widely apart from one another. Of the three genera united as Liponemidæ, *Liponema* comes near the Discosomidæ, as its stomidia may be divided into principal and accessory stomidia ; *Polystomidium patens* resembles the Antheadæ in having an endodermal muscle and marginal spherules, and *Polysiphonia* with its mesodermal circular muscle resembles the Paractidæ, to which *Paractis tubulifera* undeniably belongs. It might therefore perhaps be advisable to do away with the family Liponemidæ, and to distribute its members among the Discosomidæ, Antheadæ, and Paractidæ. Finally, *Sicyonis crassa* and *Polyopis striata* vary entirely from other Actiniæ, and are at the same time forms which differ entirely one from another. It is most probable that a character which appears in forms which vary so remarkably, but exist under the same conditions, is the consequence of these conditions of existence.

There is another point in the mode of life of the deep-sea Actiniæ which seems to me to favour the transformation of the tentacles into tubes and openings. The nutriment of the deep-sea animals probably consists chiefly of material which is already disintegrated, and of a soft nature when obtained. The animals often ingest sand, impregnated with nutriment, from which they extract what is digestible ; at least I have repeatedly found the interior of the deep-sea Actiniæ full of mud. In such a mode of nutrition the long prehensile tentacles would not be of the same use as they are in the littoral Actiniæ, which lie in wait for booty, whilst on the other hand it would be a decided advantage to the animals to be furnished with numerous inhalent tubes and openings through which they can absorb semi-liquid nourishment. This then is the advantage of the stomidia and tubular tentacles.

The retrograde formation of the tentacles is by no means the only point to be taken into consideration in the varying character of the deep-sea Actiniæ, the position of the septa being equally important. The arrangement of the septa typical of the Hex-actiniæ is only present in thirteen genera, among which I reckon *Ophiodiscus* and *Poly-stomidium*, in which we meet with the differentiation of muscular and genital septa which is otherwise unknown, and the genera *Stephanactis* and *Amphianthus*, in which we find some approach to the Antipatharia. The other four genera differ from one another as well as from the Hexactiniæ in the arrangement of the septa. They swell the number of the varying forms represented in shallow water by the Zoanthew, Ceriantheœ, and Edwardsiæ, and therefore seem to indicate that the diversity in the structure of the Anthozoa was formerly much greater than it is at present, and that the remains of this diversity have been more extensively preserved in the depths of the sea than in the shallow waters. In this way we can recognise peculiarities in deep-sea Actiniæ which are common to the whole deep-sea fauna.

TABLE OF CONTENTS.

PLATE I.

PLATE I.

The lettering is the same in all the figures.

— — —

All the figures are of natural size.

Fig. 1. *Porponia elongata.*

Fig. 2. *Porponia elongata*, opened by a longitudinal incision; and the pedal disk split up by repeated radial incisions. In the lettering on the plate for *so* read *sr*.

Fig. 3. *Cereus spinosus.*

Fig. 4. *Cereus spinosus;* the half of a sextant prepared by cutting into separate pieces; in the left-hand portion one of the principal septa (*h¹*) reaching to the œsophagus, with mesenteric filament and acontia but without reproductive organs; then follow a pair of septa of the fourth order (*h⁴*) and a pair of septa of the third order (*h³*). The right-hand portion begins with the next following pair of small septa of the fourth order (*h⁴*), and the much larger pair of septa of the second order (*h²*). All the accessory septa have mesenteric filaments, acontia and reproductive organs, but do not reach the œsophagus which hangs over them like an apron. A portion of the œsophagus has been removed in the left-hand portion. Only the septa of the second order have coiled mesenteric filaments like the principal septa. The three tentacles of the first row (*t¹*) belong to the pairs of septa of the first to the third order, the two of the second row (*t²*) to the pairs of septa of the fourth order, the four of the third row (*t³*) to the interseptal spaces.

Fig. 5. *Cereus spinosus*, opened by a longitudinal incision, which has run between a septum of the third and a septum of the fourth order. The principal septa (*h¹*) project with their coiled mesenteric filaments below the lower margin of the œsophagus; the septa of the second order (*h²*) project with smooth edges as their coiled mesenteric filaments, and their reproductive organs are covered by the œsophagus; the septa of the third order (*h³*) project with their reproductive organs. The septa of the fourth order (*h⁴*) are only visible at the side.

Fig. 6. *Paractis excavata*, one-third of the animal has been cut out in order to show the arrangement of the oral disk and the corona of tentacles; the section is directed so as to show two principal septa.

Fig. 7. *Phellia pectinata*, opened longitudinally; the section runs between two principal septa of the same pair; the principal septa project with their coiled mesenteric filaments below the œsophagus.

Fig. 8. *Anthromorphe elegans.*

Fig. 9. *Antholoba reticulata.*

Fig. 10. *Porponia robusta;* fig. 10, *a*, a separate tentacle.

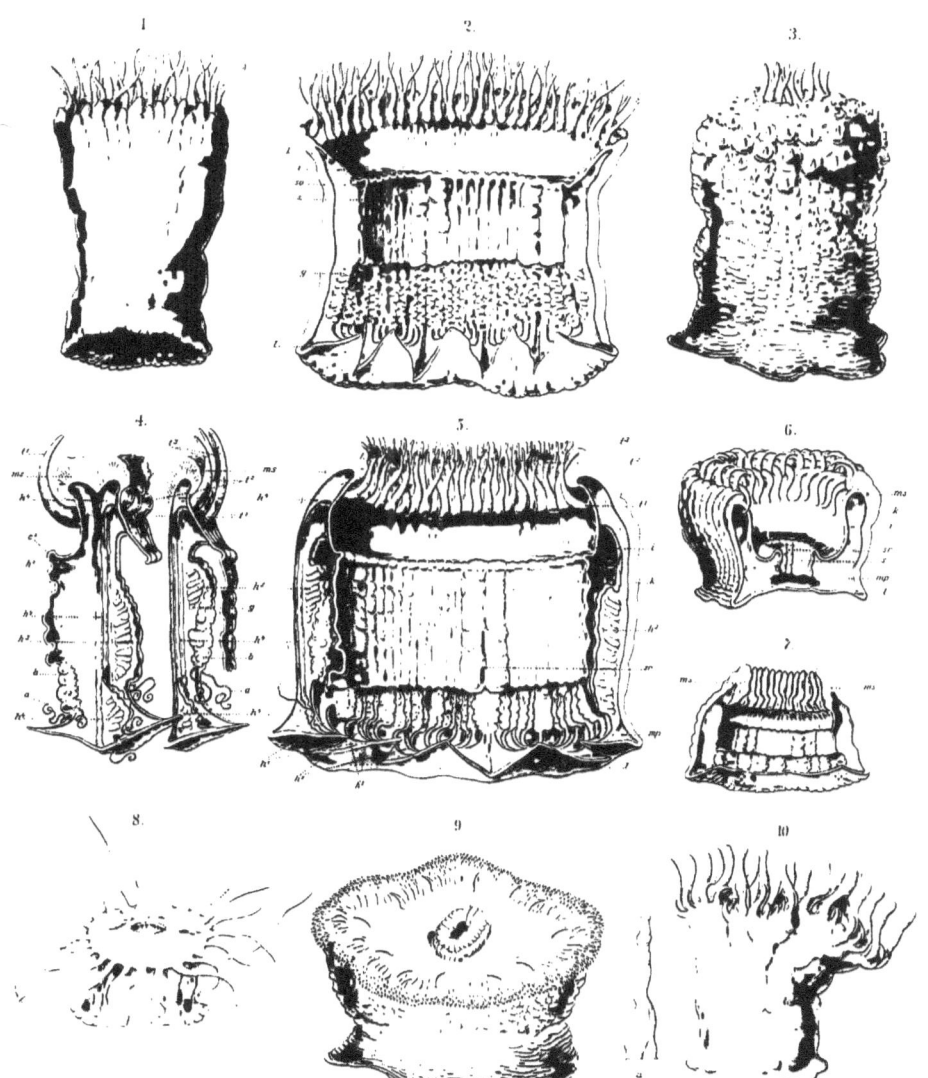

PLATE II.

PLATE II.

Fig. 1. *Corallimorphus rigidus,* seen from the oral disk ; one half the natural size.

Fig. 2. *Corallimorphus profundus,* seen from the pedal disk ; one half the natural size.

Fig. 3.   ,,   ,,   seen from the oral disk ; one half the natural size.

Fig. 4. Lateral view of a portion of *Corallimorphus rigidus;* natural size.

Fig. 5. Half of the pedal disk of *Corallimorphus rigidus;* natural size.

Fig. 6. A septum with two tentacles, running out from the corresponding intraseptal space ; seen from the side of the intraseptal space.

Fig. 7. *Polysiphonia tuberosa,* lateral view ; natural size.

Fig. 8. *Polysiphonia tuberosa,* a part of the margin of the oral disk, the tentacles having been cut away at their bases.

Fig. 9. *Polysiphonia tuberosa,* seen from the oral disk.

Fig. 10. *Sphenopus arenaceus,* bisected longitudinally ; natural size. (By an oversight the microseptum has been omitted on the left-hand side.)

Fig. 11. *Polyopis striata,* twice the natural size.

Fig. 12, *a. Bunodes minuta,* natural size.

Fig. 12, *b. Bunodes minuta,* bisected longitudinally.

Fig. 13. *Stephanactis abyssicola,* one and a half times the natural size ; seen from the oral disk.

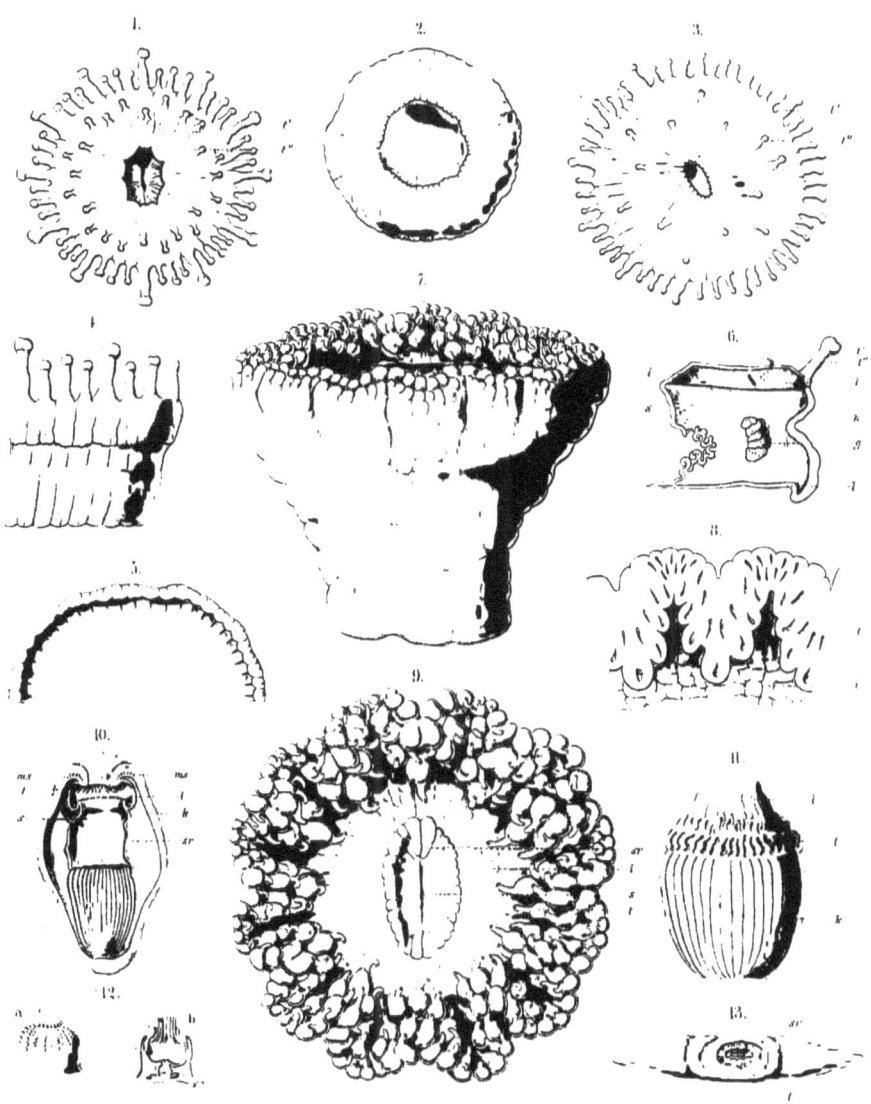

PLATE III.

PLATE III.

The lettering is the same in all the figures.

a Acontia.
b Mesenteric filaments.
c Stomata in the septa.
c¹ Perioral stomata.
c² Marginal stomata.
cu Cuticle.
d Glandular streaks of the mesenteric filaments.
e Ciliated streaks of the mesenteric filaments.
ek Ectoderm.
en Entoderm.
g Reproductive organs.
h Septa. *rh* Directive septa.
i Oral disk.

k Wall.
l Pedal disk.
m Muscles.
mm Mesodermal muscles.
ml Longitudinal muscles of the septa.
ml¹ Retractor.
mp Parietobasilar muscle.
mt Transverse muscles.
mr Radial muscles of the oral disk and longitudinal muscles of the tentacles
ms Circular muscle of the wall.
me Mesoderm.
n Urticating cells.
o Ovicells.

p Filamental apparatus of the ovicells.
p¹ Process of the ovicell.
p² Apical set of epithelial cells.
r Marginal spherules.
rh Directive septa.
s Œsophagus.
so Openings of the œsophagus into the radial chambers.
sr Œsophageal grooves.
ss Lappets of the œsophagus.
t Tentacles and the openings homologous with them.
t¹ Principal tentacles.
t² Accessory tentacles.
v Openings of the pedal disk.

All statements given as to magnifying powers have reference to Zeiss's system. The magnifying powers amount to

	Oc. 1.	Oc. 2.		Oc. 1.	Oc. 2.
a¹	6	10	D	195	240
A	55	70	F	410	550
C	95	125	J	470	530

A with unscrewed front lens (unscr. A) magnifies with Oc. 1 : 30 times; with Oc. 2 : 40 times.

Fig. 1. *Halcampa clavus*, bisected longitudinally so that the plane of division has opened two intraseptal spaces; twice the natural size.

Fig. 1, *a*. Half of the upper end of the body seen from the oral side; tentacles bent inwards; twice the natural size.

Fig. 1, *b*. Upper end of the body with expanded tentacles; twice the natural size.

Fig. 2. *Epizoanthus parasiticus*; natural size.

Fig. 3. *Tealidium cingulatum*, in a contracted condition, seen from the upper end of the body; twice the natural size.

Fig. 4. *Halcampa clavus*; natural size.

Fig. 5. *Comactis flagellifera*; twice the natural size.

Fig. 6. *Scytophorus striatus*; natural size.

Fig. 7. *Stephanactis tuberculata*, lateral view; natural size.

Fig. 7, *a*. *Stephanactis tuberculata*, from the oral side; natural size.

Fig. 7, *b*. *Stephanactis tuberculata*, lateral portion of the body with the œsophageal groove.

Fig. 8. *Ophiodiscus sulcatus*; natural size; greatly restored.

Fig. 9. A colony of *Epizoanthus parasiticus*, divided longitudinally; natural size.

Fig. 10. Pedal disk of *Halcampa clavus* detached and seen from the inside. A, Oc. 1.

Fig. 11. *Amphianthus bathybium*, seen from the surface; natural size.

Fig. 11, *a*. *Amphianthus bathybium*, a piece of the wall; slightly enlarged.

Fig. 11, *b*. *Amphianthus bathybium*, the margins of the pedal disk enclosing the *Mopsea*; slightly enlarged.

Fig. 11, *c*. *Amphianthus bathybium*, lateral view; natural size.

Fig. 12. Individual of a colony of *Epizoanthus*, opened longitudinally, and expanded; twice the natural size.

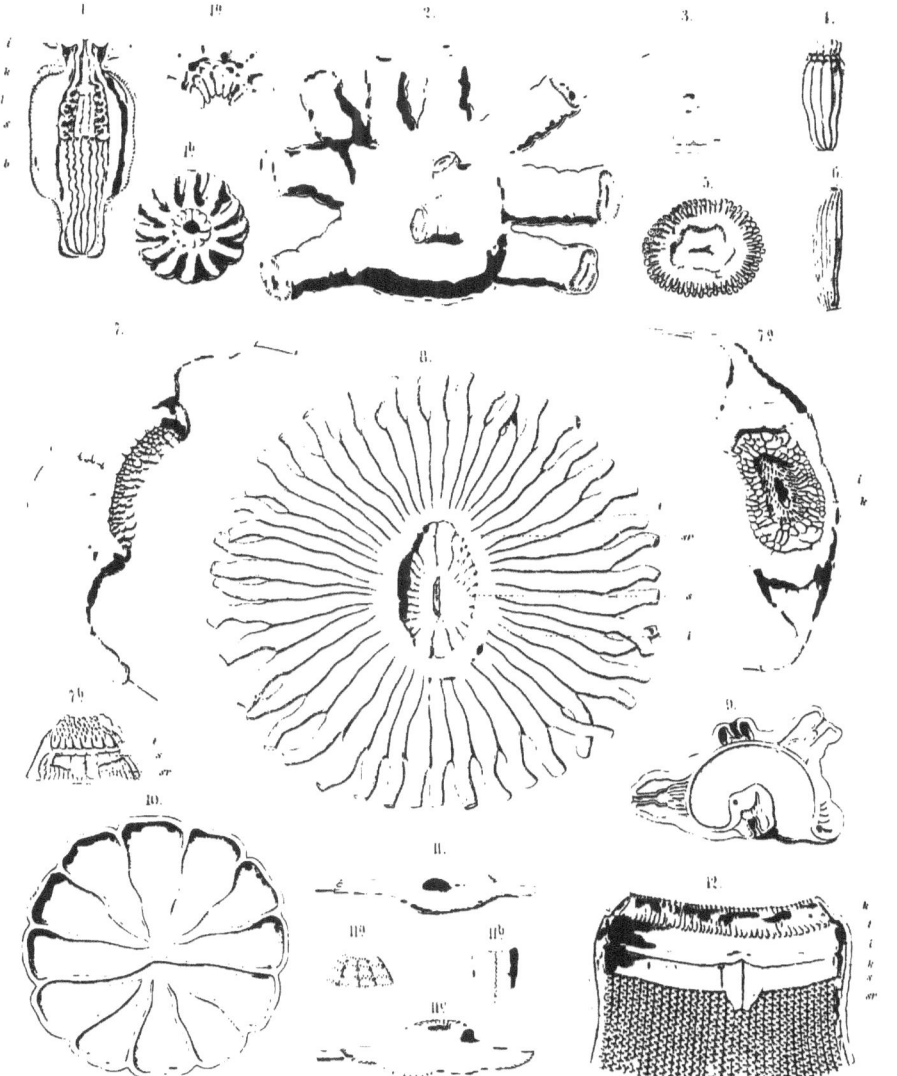

PLATE IV.

PLATE IV.

The lettering is the same in all the figures.

a Acontia.
b Mesenteric filaments.
c Stomata in the septa.
c¹ Perioral stomata.
c² Marginal stomata.
cn Cuticle.
d Glandular streaks of the mesenteric filaments.
e Ciliated streaks of the mesenteric filaments.
ek Ectoderm.
en Endoderm.
g Reproductive organs.
h Septa. rh Directive septa.
i Oral disk.

k Wall.
l Pedal disk.
m Muscles.
mm Mesodermal muscles.
ml Longitudinal muscles of the septa.
ml⁰ Retractor.
mp Parietobasilar muscle.
mt Transverse muscles.
mr Radial muscles of the oral disk and longitudinal muscles of the tentacles
ms Circular muscle of the wall.
mc Mesoderm.
n Urticating cells.
o Ovicells.

p Filamental apparatus of the ovicells.
p¹ Process of the ovicell.
p² Apical set of epithelial cells.
r Marginal spherules.
rh Directive septa.
s Œsophagus.
so Openings of the œsophagus into the radial chambers.
sr Œsophageal grooves.
sz Lappets of the œsophagus.
t Tentacles and the openings homologous with them.
t¹ Principal tentacles.
t² Accessory tentacles.
v Openings of the pedal disk.

All statements given as to magnifying powers have reference to Zeiss's system.   The magnifying powers amount to

	Oc. 1.	Oc. 2.		Oc. 1.	Oc. 2.
a¹	6	10	D	195	240
A	55	70	F	410	550
C	95	125	J	470	580

A with unscrewed front lens (unscr. A) magnifies with Oc. 1 : 30 times; with Oc. 2 : 40 times.

Sicyonis crassa.

Fig. 1. Transverse section through the upper end of the wall and the circular muscle situated there. Ten times the natural size, but drawn with unscr. A, Oc. 2. On the right hand side of the figure for ek read en.

Fig. 2. A sector of the pedal disk ; natural size.

Fig. 3. Longitudinal section through the wall of a wart-like tentacle. Unscr. A, Oc. 2.

Fig. 4. The entire animal, seen from the oral side ; natural size.

Fig. 5. Transverse section through the basal portion of a tentacle ; about six times the natural size.

Fig. 6. Part of a transverse section through the radial muscles of the oral disk. D, Oc. 2.

Fig. 7. Part of a transverse section through the circular muscle ; enlarged more than the preceding. D, Oc. 2.

Fig. 8. Transverse section through the oral disk, and insertion of a septum. Unscr. A, Oc. 2.

Fig. 9. Septum ; natural size.

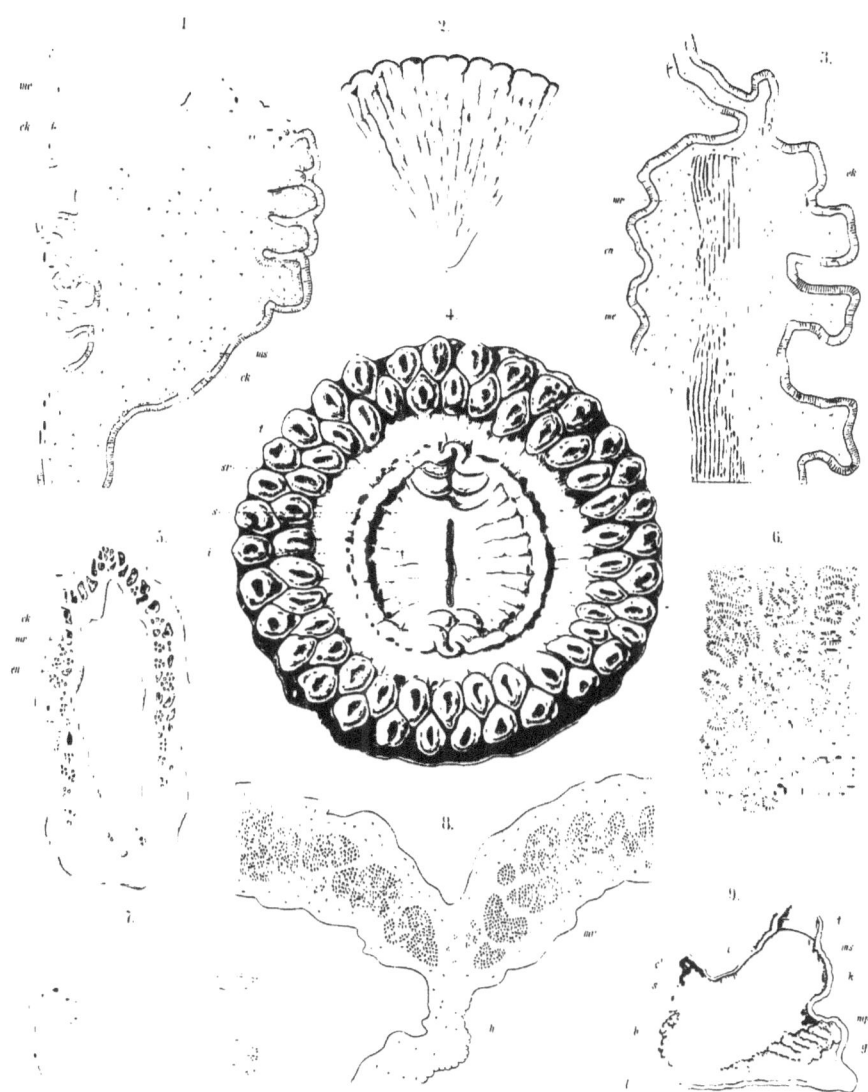

Richard Hertwig del.

F.A.Funke,Leipzig,Lithogr

PLATE V.

PLATE V.

The lettering is the same in all the figures.

a Acontia.
b Mesenteric filaments.
c Stomata in the septa.
c¹ Periforal stomata.
c² Marginal stomata.
cu Cuticle.
d Glandular streaks of the mesenteric filaments.
e Ciliated streaks of the mesenteric filaments.
ek Ectoderm.
en Endoderm.
g Reproductive organs.
h Septa.   *rh* Directive septa.
i Oral disk.

k Wall.
l Pedal disk.
m Muscles.
mm Mesodermal muscles.
ml Longitudinal muscles of the septa.
ml² Retractor.
mp Parietobasilar muscle.
mt Transverse muscles.
mr Radial muscles of the oral disk and longitudinal muscles of the tentacles
ms Circular muscle of the wall.
me Mesoderm.
n Urticating cells.
o Ovicells.

p Filamental apparatus of the ovicells.
p¹ Process of the ovicell.
p² Apical set of epithelial cells.
r Marginal spherules.
rh Directive septa.
s Œsophagus.
so Openings of the œsophagus into the radial chambers.
sr Œsophageal grooves.
sz Lappets of the œsophagus.
t Tentacles and the openings homologous with them.
t¹ Principal tentacles.
t² Accessory tentacles.
v Openings of the pedal disk.

All statements given as to magnifying powers have reference to Zeiss's system.   The magnifying powers amount to

	Oc. 1.	Oc. 2.			Oc. 1.	Oc. 2.
a¹	6	10	D		195	240
A	55	70	F		410	550
C	95	125	J		470	550

A with unscrewed front lens (unscr. A) magnifies with Oc. 1 : 30 times; with Oc. 2 : 40 times.

Polystomidium patens.

Fig. 1. The portion of the œsophagus, contiguous to the labial margin, with the openings leading into the radial chambers ; three times the natural size.

Fig. 2. Septum with pedal disk, wall, oral disk, œsophagus, and mesenteric filament ; natural size.

Fig. 3. Half of the animal seen from the aboral side ; natural size.

Fig. 4. Transverse section through the oral disk, near the oral margin.   C, Oc. 2.

Fig. 5. Transverse section through a mesenteric filament in the upper part of its course.   C, Oc. 1.

Fig. 6. The entire animal, seen from the oral side ; natural size.   As the only specimen sent for examination was greatly injured, some restoration has been necessary.

Fig. 7. Transverse section through the oral disk, near the stomidia.   C, Oc. 2.

Fig. 8. Longitudinal section through the upper end of the wall, the circular muscle running in it and a marginal spherule.   Unscr. A, Oc. 2.

Fig. 9. Longitudinal section through the circular muscle.   D, Oc. 2.

Fig. 10. Longitudinal section through the lower end of the wall.   A, Oc. 2.

Fig. 11. Horizontal section through the circular muscle.   A, Oc. 2.

Fig. 12. Transverse section through a septum.   Unscr. A, Oc. 2.

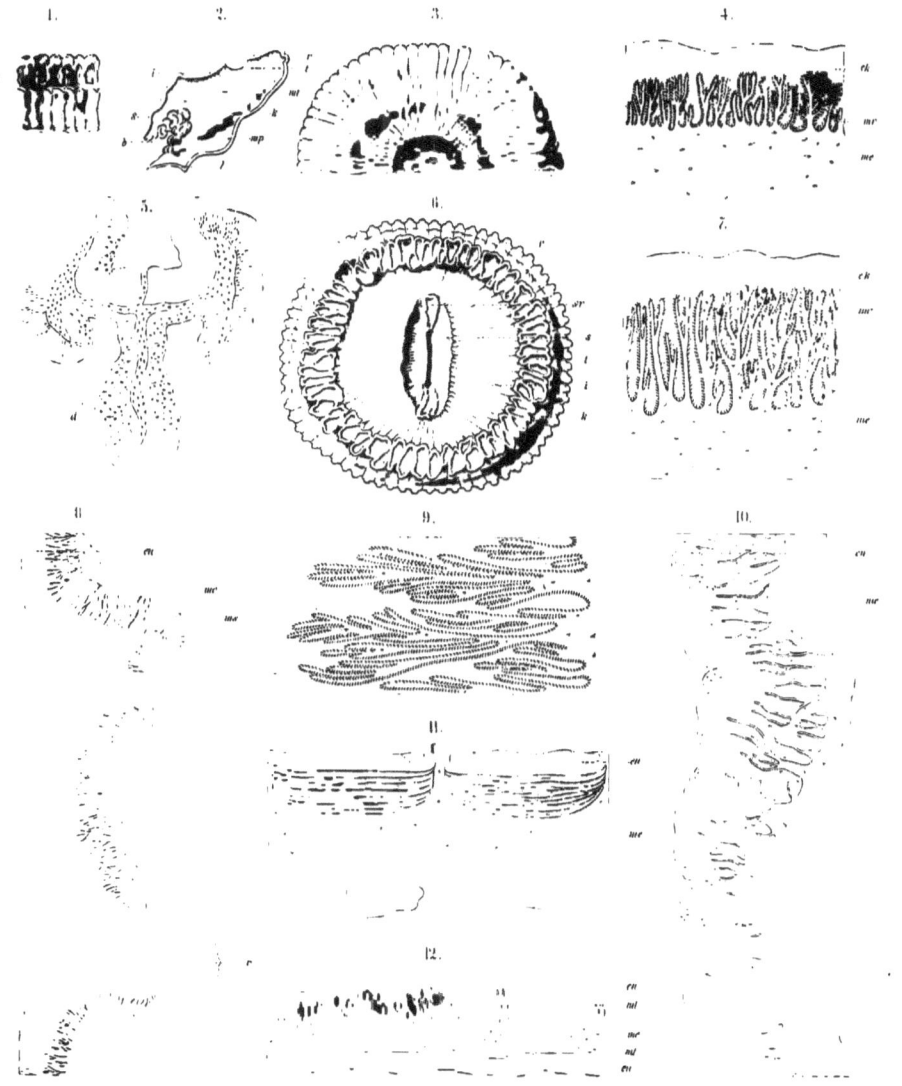

PLATE VI.

PLATE VI.

The lettering is the same in all the figures.

a Acontia.	*k* Wall.	*p* Filamental apparatus of the ovicells.
b Mesenteric filaments.	*l* Pedal disk.	*p¹* Process of the ovicell.
c Stomata in the septa.	*m* Muscles.	*p²* Apical set of epithelial cells.
e¹ Perioral stomata.	*mm* Mesodermal muscles.	*r* Marginal spherules.
c² Marginal stomata.	*ml* Longitudinal muscles of the septa.	*rh* Directive septa.
cu Cuticle.	*ml¹* Retractor.	*s* Œsophagus.
d Glandular streaks of the mesenteric filaments.	*mp* Parietobasilar muscle.	*so* Openings of the œsophagus into the radial chambers.
e Ciliated streaks of the mesenteric filaments.	*mt* Transverse muscles.	*sr* Œsophageal grooves.
ck Ectoderm.	*mr* Radial muscles of the oral disk and longitudinal muscles of the tentacles	*sz* Lappets of the œsophagus.
en Endoderm.	*ms* Circular muscle of the wall.	*t* Tentacles and the openings homologous with them.
g Reproductive organs.	*me* Mesoderm.	*t¹* Principal tentacles.
h Septa. *rh* Directive septa.	*n* Urticating cells.	*t²* Accessory tentacles.
i Oral disk.	*o* Ovicells.	*v* Openings of the pedal disk.

All statements given as to magnifying powers have reference to Zeiss's system. The magnifying powers amount to

	Oc. 1.	Oc. 2.					Oc. 1.	Oc. 2.
a¹	6	10		D			195	240
A	55	70		F			410	550
C	95	125		J			470	580

A with unscrewed front lens (unscr. A) magnifies with Oc. 1 : 30 times; with Oc. 2 : 40 times.

Transverse sections through different forms of the circular muscle.

Fig. 1. Circular muscle of *Cereus spinosus*.   a¹, Oc. 1.

Fig. 2.   „   „   *Tealidium cingulatum*.   C, Oc. 2.

Fig. 3.   „   „   *Polysiphonia tuberosa*.   a¹, Oc. 2.

Fig. 4.   „   „   *Tealia bunodiformis*.   C, Oc. 2.

Fig. 5.   „   „   *Phellia pectinata*.   a¹, Oc. 2.

Fig. 6.   „   „   *Comactis flagellifera*.   C, Oc. 2.

PLATE VII.

PLATE VII.

The lettering is the same in all the figures.

a Acontia.	*k* Wall.	*p* Filamental apparatus of the ovicells.
b Mesenteric filaments.	*l* Pedal disk.	*p¹* Process of the ovicell.
c Stomata in the septa.	*m* Muscles.	*p²* Apical set of epithelial cells.
c¹ Perioral stomata.	*mm* Mesodermal muscles.	*r* Marginal spherules.
c² Marginal stomata.	*ml* Longitudinal muscles of the septa.	*rh* Directive septa.
cu Cuticle.	*ml¹* Retractor.	*s* Œsophagus.
d Glandular streaks of the mesenteric filaments.	*mp* Parietobasilar muscle.	*so* Openings of the œsophagus into the radial chambers.
e Ciliated streaks of the mesenteric filaments.	*mt* Transverse muscles.	*sr* Œsophageal grooves.
ek Ectoderm.	*mr* Radial muscles of the oral disk and longitudinal muscles of the tentacles	*sz* Lappets of the œsophagus.
en Endoderm.	*mw* Circular muscle of the wall.	*t* Tentacles and the openings homologous with them.
g Reproductive organs.	*me* Mesoderm.	*t¹* Principal tentacles.
h Septa. *rh* Directive septa.	*n* Urticating cells.	*t²* Accessory tentacles.
i Oral disk.	*o* Ovicells.	*v* Openings of the pedal disk.

All statements given as to magnifying powers have reference to Zeiss's system. The magnifying powers amount to

	Oc. 1.	Oc. 2.			Oc. 1.	Oc. 2.
a¹	6	10	D		195	240
A	55	70	F		410	550
C	95	125	J		470	550

A with unscrewed front lens (unscr. A) magnifies with Oc. 1 : 30 times; with Oc. 2 : 40 times.

Leiotealia nymphœa (figs. 1–5).

Fig. 1. Transverse section through the oral disk. A, Oc. 2.

Fig. 2. Radial section through the anterior end of the body, the wall with upper and lower (*ms'*) circular muscles, and the oral disk with a tentacle. Unscr. A, Oc. 2. For *l* in the lettering of the plate read *t*.

Fig. 3. Transverse section through the septum at about one-third the height of the animal, passing perpendicularly through the parietobasilar muscle and longitudinal muscle. A, Oc. 1.

Fig. 4. Half a transverse section of the upper circular muscle. C, Oc. 1.

Fig. 5. Septum ; natural size.

Dysactis crassicornis (figs. 6–12).

Fig. 6. Transverse section through a septum. A, Oc. 1.

Fig. 7. Transverse section through the upper end of the wall. Unscr. A, Oc. 2 diminished two-thirds.

Fig. 8. Part of a transverse section through the circular muscle, more highly magnified. D, Oc. 1.

Fig. 9. Section through the circular muscle parallel to the course of the fibrillæ. A, Oc. 2.

Fig. 10. Transverse section through the oral disk of an old animal. Unscr. A, Oc. 2.

Fig. 11. Transverse section through the oral disk of a young animal. Unscr. A, Oc. 2.

Fig. 12. Septum ; natural size. The circular muscle appears rather too large in the drawing.

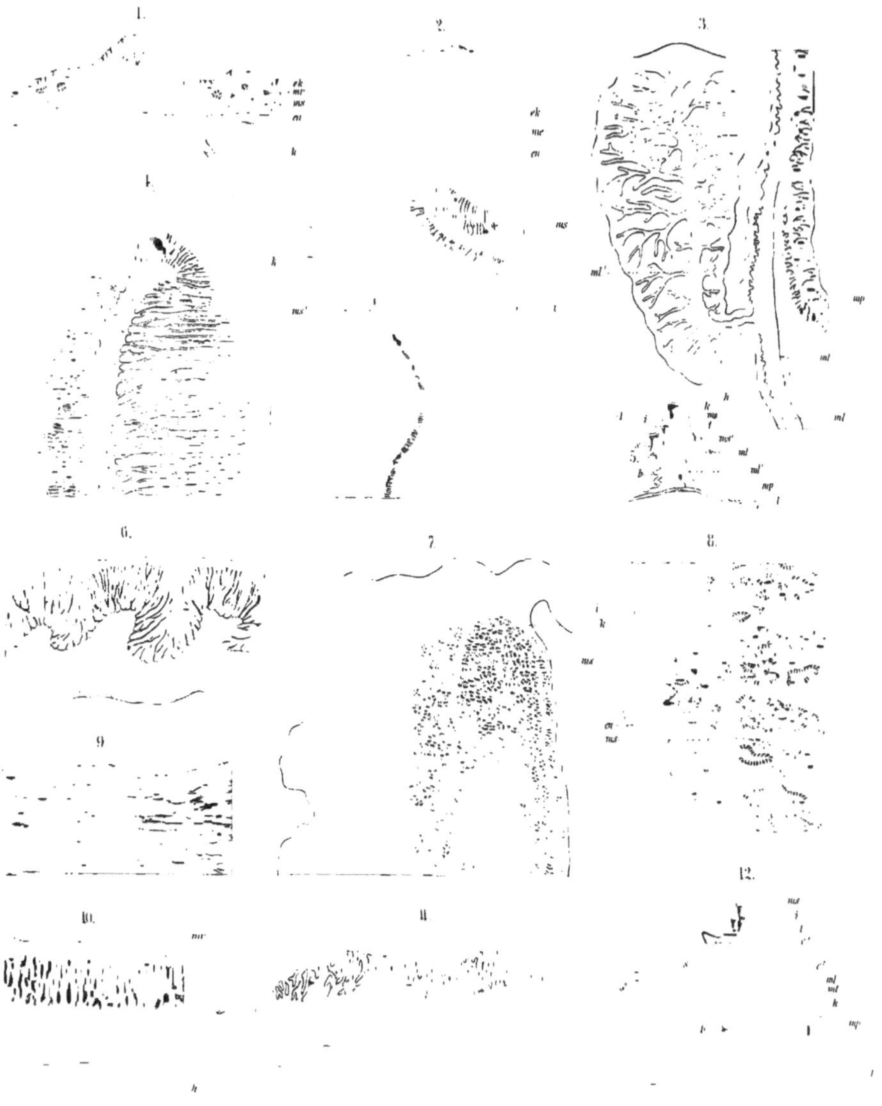
1.
2.
3.
4.
5.
6.
7.
8.
9.
10.
11.
12.
ek
me
ms
en
h
ml
mp

PLATE VIII.

PLATE VIII.

The lettering is the same in all the figures.

a Acontia.
b Mesenteric filaments.
c Stomata in the septa.
*e*¹ Perioral stomata.
*e*² Marginal stomata.
cu Cuticle.
d Glandular streaks of the mesenteric filaments.
e Ciliated streaks of the mesenteric filaments.
ek Ectoderm.
en Endoderm.
g Reproductive organs.
h Septa. *rh* Directive septa.
i Oral disk.

k Wall.
l Pedal disk.
m Muscles.
mm Mesodermal muscles.
ml Longitudinal muscles of the septa.
*ml*¹ Retractor.
mp Parietobasilar muscle.
mt Transverse muscles.
mr Radial muscles of the oral disk and longitudinal muscles of the tentacles
ms Circular muscle of the wall.
me Mesoderm.
n Urticating cells.
o Ovicells.

p Filamental apparatus of the ovicells.
*p*¹ Process of the ovicell.
*p*² Apical set of epithelial cells.
r Marginal spherules.
rh Directive septa.
s Œsophagus.
so Openings of the œsophagus into the radial chambers.
sr Œsophageal grooves.
sz Lappets of the œsophagus.
t Tentacles and the openings homologous with them.
*t*¹ Principal tentacles.
*t*² Accessory tentacles.
v Openings of the pedal disk.

All statements given as to magnifying powers have reference to Zeiss's system. The magnifying powers amount to

	Oc. 1.	Oc. 2.		Oc. 1.	Oc. 2.
a¹	6	10	D	195	240
A	55	70	F	410	550
C	95	125	J	470	550

A with unscrewed front lens (unscr. A) magnifies with Oc. 1 : 30 times; with Oc. 2 : 40 times.

Fig. 1. Transverse section through the wall of *Phellia pectinata*. D, Oc. 2.

Fig. 2. Transverse section through the directive septa of *Phellia pectinata* below the œsophagus. A, Oc. 2.

Fig. 3. Part of a transverse section through the longitudinal muscular swelling (retractor) of a septum of *Tealia bunodiformis*. C, Oc. 2.

Fig. 4. Longitudinal section through the wall of *Tealia bunodiformis* with endodermal saccules. A, Oc. 2.

Fig. 5. Part of a transverse section through the œsophagus, the wall, the directive septa, and the adjoining septa of *Tealia bunodiformis*. a¹, Oc. 1.

Fig. 6. Transverse section through the wall of *Cereus spinosus*. Fig. *a*, a portion of the cuticule, drawn out like a tube. D, Oc. 2.

Figs. 7, 8. Portions of the circular muscle of *Tealidium cingulatum*, taken at different points. J, Oc. 2.

Fig. 9. Endodermal muscles of the oral disk of *Comactis flagellifera*. D, Oc. 2.

Fig. 10. Portion of a transverse section through the circular muscle of *Phellia pectinata*. D, Oc. 1.

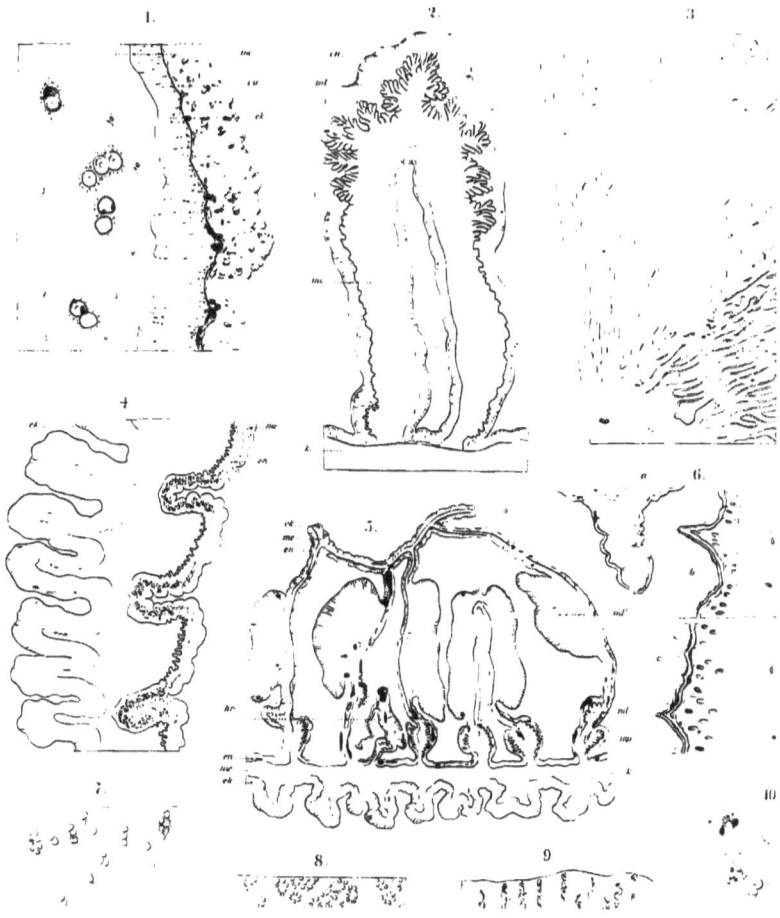

PLATE IX.

PLATE IX.

The lettering is the same in all the figures.

a Acontia.
b Mesenteric filaments.
c Stomata in the septa.
c^1 Perioral stomata.
c^2 Marginal stomata.
cu Cuticle.
d Glandular streaks of the mesenteric filaments.
e Ciliated streaks of the mesenteric filaments.
ek Ectoderm.
en Endoderm.
g Reproductive organs.
h Septa.   rh Directive septa.
i Oral disk.

k Wall.
l Pedal disk.
m Muscles.
mm Mesodermal muscles.
ml Longitudinal muscles of the septa.
ml^1 Retractor.
mp Parietobasilar muscle.
mt Transverse muscles.
mr Radial muscles of the oral disk and longitudinal muscles of the tentacles
ms Circular muscle of the wall.
me Mesoderm.
n Urticating cells.
o Ovicells.

p Filamental apparatus of the ovicells.
p^1 Process of the ovicell.
p^2 Apical set of epithelial cells.
r Marginal spherules.
rh Directive septa.
s Œsophagus.
so Openings of the œsophagus into the radial chambers.
sr Œsophageal grooves.
sz Lappets of the œsophagus.
t Tentacles and the openings homologous with them.
t^1 Principal tentacles.
t^2 Accessory tentacles.
v Openings of the pedal disk.

All statements given as to magnifying powers have reference to Zeiss's system. The magnifying powers amount to

			Oc. 1.	Oc. 2.					Oc. 1.	Oc. 2.
a^1	...	...	6	10	D	...	...	...	195	240
A	...	...	55	70	F	...	...	...	410	550
C	...	...	95	125	J	...	...	...	470	580

A with unscrewed front lens (unscr. A) magnifies with Oc. 1 : 30 times; with Oc. 2 : 40 times.

Polysiphonia tuberosa (figs. 1–10).

Fig. 1. Transverse section through the pedal disk, showing the muscular fibres which pass on to the furrows. A, Oc. 2.

Fig. 2. Transverse section through a tentacle bulb. a^1, Oc. 1.

Fig. 3. Horizontal section through the pedal disk. The upper part of the diagram is near the outer surface; the lower shows the section passing transversely through the bases of two septa. A, Oc. 2.

Fig. 4. Radial section through the pedal disk. C, Oc. 2.

Fig. 5. Pedal disk, natural size, seen from the lower side ; about one-sixth of it shown.

Fig. 6. Transverse section through the tentacle near the point. a^1, Oc. 1.

Fig. 7. Part of a transverse section through the pedal disk (fig. 1) more highly magnified. C, Oc. 2.

Fig. 8. Tentacles seen from the side ; natural size.

Fig. 9. A tentacle divided longitudinally ; natural size.

Fig. 10. Bottom of a radial furrow of the pedal disk, with the adjacent muscular fibres ; seen in transverse section. C, Oc. 1.

Corallimorphus rigidus (figs. 11 and 12).

Figs. 11 and 12. Transverse sections through the wall.

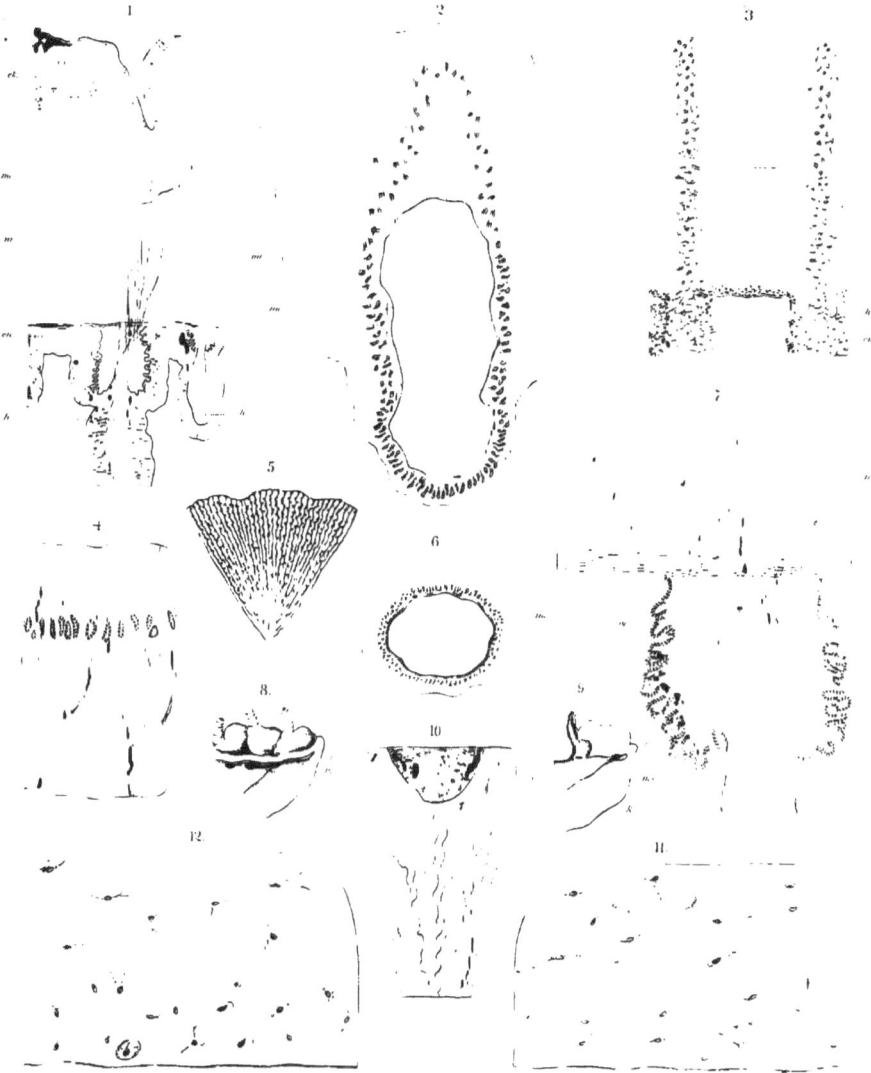

PLATE X.

PLATE X.

The lettering is the same in all the figures.

a Acontia.	*k* Wall.	*p* Filamental apparatus of the ovicells.
b Mesenteric filaments.	*l* Pedal disk.	*p*¹ Process of the ovicell.
c Stomata in the septa.	*m* Muscles.	*p*² Apical set of epithelial cells.
*c*¹ Perioral stomata.	*mm* Mesodermal muscles.	*r* Marginal spherules.
*c*² Marginal stomata.	*ml* Longitudinal muscles of the septa.	*rh* Directive septa.
eu Cuticle.	*ml*¹ Retractor.	*s* Œsophagus.
d Glandular streaks of the mesenteric filaments.	*mp* Parietobasilar muscle.	*so* Openings of the œsophagus into the radial chambers.
e Ciliated streaks of the mesenteric filaments.	*mt* Transverse muscles.	*sr* Œsophageal grooves.
	mr Radial muscles of the oral disk and longitudinal muscles of the tentacles	*sz* Lappets of the œsophagus.
ek Ectoderm.		*t* Tentacles and the openings homologous with them.
en Endoderm.	*ms* Circular muscle of the wall.	
g Reproductive organs.	*mv* Mesoderm.	*t*¹ Principal tentacles.
h Septa. *rh* Directive septa.	*u* Urticating cells.	*t*² Accessory tentacles.
i Oral disk.	*v* Ovicells.	*v* Openings of the pedal disk.

All statements given as to magnifying powers have reference to Zeiss's system. The magnifying powers amount to

	Oc. 1.	Oc. 2.					Oc. 1.	Oc. 2.
d	..	... 6	10	D	...	... ..	195	240
A	...	... 55	70	F	...	... ...	410	550
C	...	 95	125	J	...	... ...	470	530

A with unscrewed front lens (unscr. A) magnifies with Oc. 1 : 30 times; with Oc. 2 : 40 times.

Ophiodiscus annulatus (figs. 1–10).

Fig. 1. A portion of the animal, seen from the side; magnified a little.

Fig. 2. Transverse section through a tentacle near the base. Unscr. A, Oc. 2.

Fig. 3. A portion of the animal seen from the oral side; natural size.

Fig. 4. A principal septum with the two adjoining genital septa; magnified a little.

Fig. 5. Transverse section through the oral disk at the insertion of a septum. A. Oc. 2.

Fig. 6. Transverse sections through different parts of the circular muscle : *a* through the upper part, δ through the lower end. Unscr. A, Oc. 2.

Fig. 7. Portions of the circular muscle, more highly magnified ; *a* from the upper, *β* from the lower end. D, Oc. 2.

Fig. 8. Pseudo-tentacle, slightly magnified.

Fig. 9. Some terminal branches of the pseudo-tentacle, ten times the natural size.

Fig. 10. Longitudinal section through a branch of the pseudo-tentacle. J, Oc. 1 ; and reduced one half.

Antholoba reticulata (figs. 11 and 12).

Fig. 11. Transverse section through the circular muscle. D, Oc. 2.

Fig. 12. Transverse section through the oral disk. C, Oc. 1.

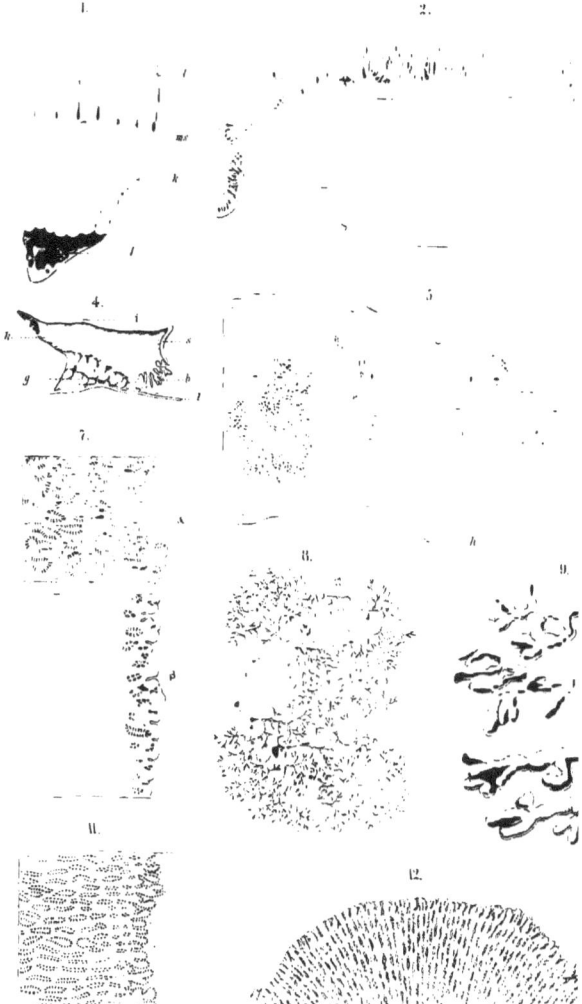

PLATE XI.

PLATE XI.

a Acontia.
b Mesenteric filaments.
c Stomata in the septa.
c¹ Perioral stomata.
c² Marginal stomata.
cu Cuticle.
d Glandular streaks of the mesenteric filaments.
e Ciliated streaks of the mesenteric filaments.
ek Ectoderm.
en Endoderm.
g Reproductive organs.
h Septa, *rh* Directive septa.
i Oral disk.

k Wall.
l Pedal disk.
m Muscles.
mm Mesodermal muscles.
ml Longitudinal muscles of the septa.
ml¹ Retractor.
mp Parietobasilar muscle.
mt Transverse muscles.
mr Radial muscles of the oral disk and longitudinal muscles of the tentacles.
mw Circular muscle of the wall.
me Mesoderm.
n Urticating cells.
o Ovicells.

p Filamental apparatus of the ovicells.
p¹ Process of the ovicell.
p² Apical set of epithelial cells.
r Marginal spherules.
rh Directive septa.
s Œsophagus.
so Openings of the œsophagus into the radial chambers.
sr Œsophageal grooves.
ss Lappets of the œsophagus.
t Tentacles and the openings homologous with them.
t¹ Principal tentacles.
t² Accessory tentacles.
v Openings of the pedal disk.

All statements given as to magnifying powers have reference to Zeiss's system. The magnifying powers amount to

	Oc. 1.	Oc. 2.		Oc. 1.	Oc. 2.
a¹	6	10	D	195	240
A	55	70	F	410	550
C	95	125	J	470	580

A with unscrewed front lens (unscr. A) magnifies with Oc. 1 : 30 times; with Oc. 2 : 40 times.

Polyopis striata (figs. 1–12).

(Figs. 1–8, Unscr. A, Oc. 1.)

Fig. 1. Transverse section through the oral disk near the stomidia, corresponding to line *a* in fig. 6.

Fig. 2. Transverse section through the oral disk, rather more towards the centre, corresponding to line β.

Fig. 3. Transverse section through the oral disk, still more towards the centre, corresponding to line γ.

Fig. 4. Transverse section through the upper part of the œsophagus and the openings lying in it.

Fig. 5. Transverse section through the oral disk, near the oral opening, corresponding to line ε.

Fig. 6. Surface view of a part of the oral disk. Unscr. A, Oc. 1, and reduced to one-eighth.

Fig. 7. Transverse section through the oral disk, nearly midway between figs. 3 and 5, corresponding to line δ.

Fig. 8. Transverse section through the lower part of two directive septa.

Fig. 9. Transverse section through a septum and the oral disk in the region of the stomidia. A, Oc. 2.

Fig. 10. Radial section through the oral disk, endodermal side. C, Oc. 2.

Fig. 11. The lower end of the body-wall *a* seen from the ectodermal side, β seen from the gastric side, about twice the natural size.

Fig. 12. Septum with adjacent portion of the wall, oral disk and œsophagus ; natural size.

Paractis excavata (figs. 13 and 14).

Fig. 13. Transverse sections through a tentacle, *a* at the point, *b* in the middle, *c* at the base. Unscr. A, Oc. 1.

Fig. 14. Part of a similar transverse section more highly magnified. D, Oc. 1.

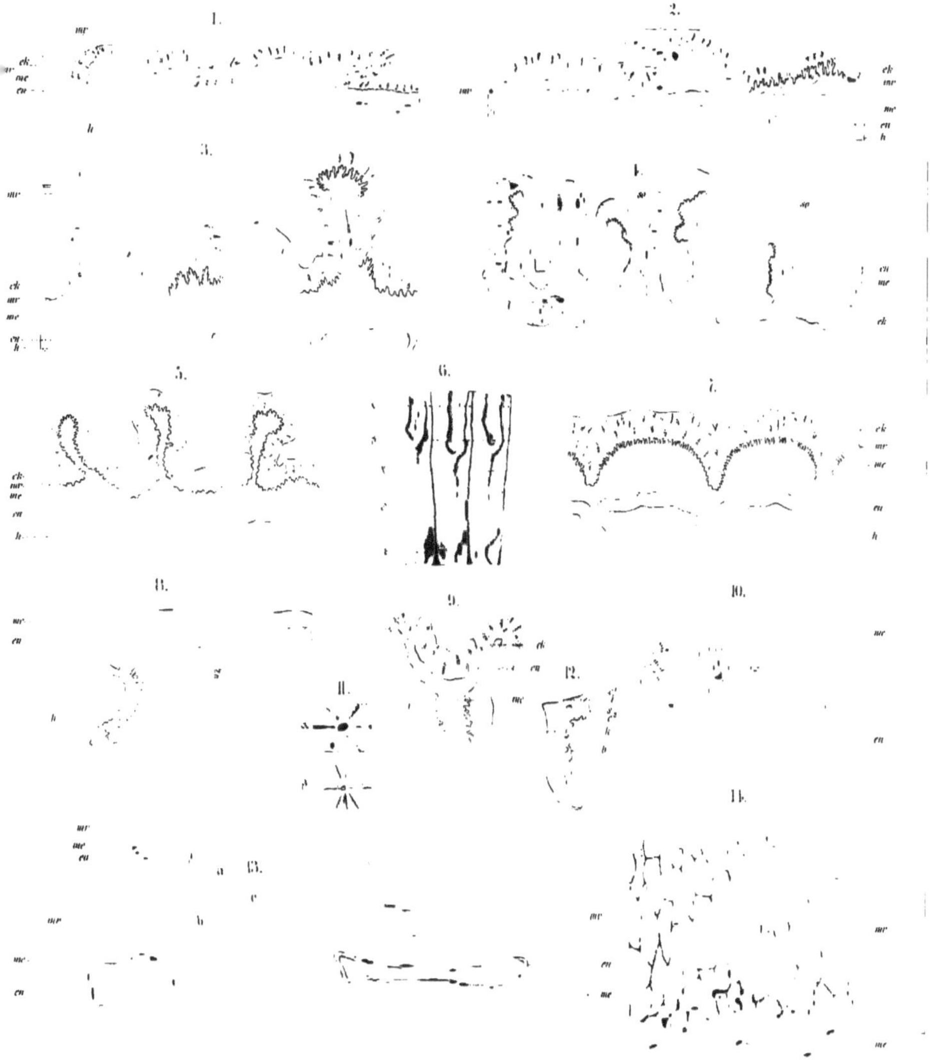
1.
2.
3.
4.
5.
6.
7.
8.
9.
10.
11.
12.
13.
14.
ek
mr
me
en
h

PLATE XII.

PLATE XII.

The lettering is the same in all the figures.

Corallimorphus rigidus. D, Oc. 2 (figs. 1–7).

Figs. 1–4. Young ovicells in the endoderm ; in figs. 2 and 3 two cells depicted in the act of migrating into the mesoderm.

Fig. 5. Ovicells with filamental apparatus; the epithelial cells of the filamental apparatus still lie completely in the epithelium.

Fig. 6. Ovicells with filamental apparatus; the epithelial cells of the filamental apparatus migrating into the mesoderm.

Fig. 7. Ovicells with filamental apparatus.

Halcampa clavus. D, Oc. 1 (figs. 8, 9, 11).

Figs. 8 and 9. Two ovicells of different ages with the epithelial apparatus.

Fig. 11. Ovicells which lie partly in the endoderm, partly in the mesoderm.

Cereus spinosus (fig. 10).

Fig. 10. Transverse section through an acontium of *Cereus spinosus.* C, Oc. 2.

PLATE XIII.

PLATE XIII.

The lettering is the same in all the figures.

All statements given as to magnifying powers have reference to Zeiss's system. The magnifying powers amount to

	Oc. 1.	Oc. 2.				Oc. 1.	Oc. 2.
a¹	6	10		D		195	240
A	55	70		F		410	550
C	95	125		J		470	550

A with unscrewed front lens (unscr. A) magnifies with Oc. 1 : 30 times; with Oc. 2 : 40 times.

Fig. 1. Transverse section through the mesoderm, ectodermal epithelium, and cuticle of *Scytophorus striatus*. D, Oc. 2.

Fig. 2. Longitudinal section through the pleated circular muscles of the wall at the lower end of *Halcampa clavus*. A, Oc. 1.

Fig. 3. Transverse section through the body of *Scytophorus striatus* passing through the œsophagus. a¹, Oc. 1.

Fig. 4. Transverse section through the body of *Halcampa clavus*, passing through the œsophagus. a¹, Oc. 1.

Fig. 5. Section parallel to the surface through the pedal disk of *Halcampa clavus*. C, Oc. 1.

Fig. 6. Transverse section through the pedal disk of *Halcampa clavus*. C, Oc. 1.

Fig. 7. Half a transverse section through the lower extremity of *Halcampa clavus*. a¹, Oc. 1.

Fig. 8. Transverse section through the cuticle of *Scytophorus striatus*. D, Oc. 2.

Fig. 9. Septum of the first order of *Antholoba reticulata*; natural size.

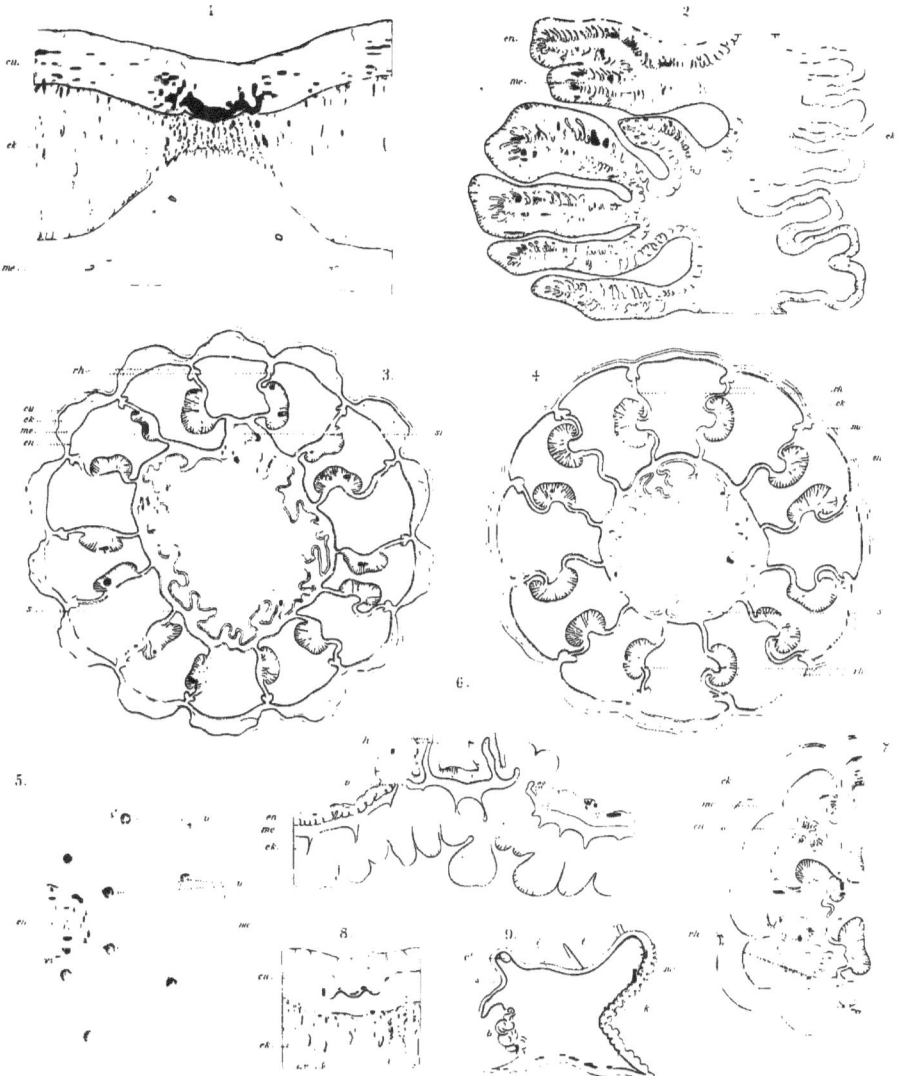

PLATE XIV.

PLATE XIV.

The lettering is the same in all the figures.

a Acontia.
b Mesenteric filaments.
c Stomata in the septa.
c[1] Perioral stomata.
c[2] Marginal stomata.
cu Cuticle.
d Glandular streaks of the mesenteric filaments.
e Ciliated streaks of the mesenteric filaments.
ek Ectoderm.
en Endoderm.
g Reproductive organs.
h Septa. *rh* Directive septa.
i Oral disk.

k Wall.
l Pedal disk.
m Muscles.
mm Mesodermal muscles.
ml Longitudinal muscles of the septa.
ml[2] Retractor.
mp Parietobasilar muscle.
mt Transverse muscles.
mr Radial muscles of the oral disk and longitudinal muscles of the tentacles
ms Circular muscle of the wall.
me Mesoderm.
n Urticating cells.
o Ovicells.

p Filamental apparatus of the ovicells.
p[1] Process of the ovicell.
p[2] Apical set of epithelial cells.
r Marginal spherules.
rh Directive septa.
s Œsophagus.
so Openings of the œsophagus into the radial chambers.
sr Œsophageal grooves.
sz Lappets of the œsophagus.
t Tentacles and the openings homologous with them.
t[1] Principal tentacles.
t[2] Accessory tentacles.
v Openings of the pedal disk.

All statements given as to magnifying powers have reference to Zeiss's system.   The magnifying powers amount to

	Oc. 1.	Oc. 2.			Oc. 1.	Oc. 2.
a¹	6	10	D		195	210
A	55	70	F		410	550
C	95	125	J		470	530

A with unscrewed front lens (unscr. A) magnifies with Oc. 1 : 30 times; with Oc. 2 : 40 times.

Zoanthus, sp. ? (figs. 1–4 and 6).

Fig. 1. Longitudinal section through the upper end of the wall and the circular muscle running in it.   Unscr. A, Oc. 2.

Fig. 2. Transverse section through the wall, œsophagus, macrosepta and microsepta. A, Oc. 2.

Fig. 3. Transverse section through an individual of a *Zoanthus* colony.   The figure is composite, the left-hand half representing a transverse section on a level with the œsophagus, the right-hand half a transverse section situated rather further down. a¹, Oc. 2.

Fig. 4. Part of a transverse section through the wall.   D, Oc. 2.

Fig. 6. Transverse section through a small individual of a *Zoanthus* colony, passing through the œsophagus. a¹, Oc. 2.

Epizoanthus parasiticus (fig. 5).

Fig. 5. Part of a transverse section through the wall of *Epizoanthus parasiticus*. D, Oc. 2.

Liponema multiporum (fig. 7).

Fig. 7. Marginal portion of the oral disk of *Liponema multiporum* ; twice the natural size.

Sphenopus arenaceus (fig. 8).

Fig. 8. Transverse section through the wall of *Sphenopus arenaceus*.   D, Oc. 2.

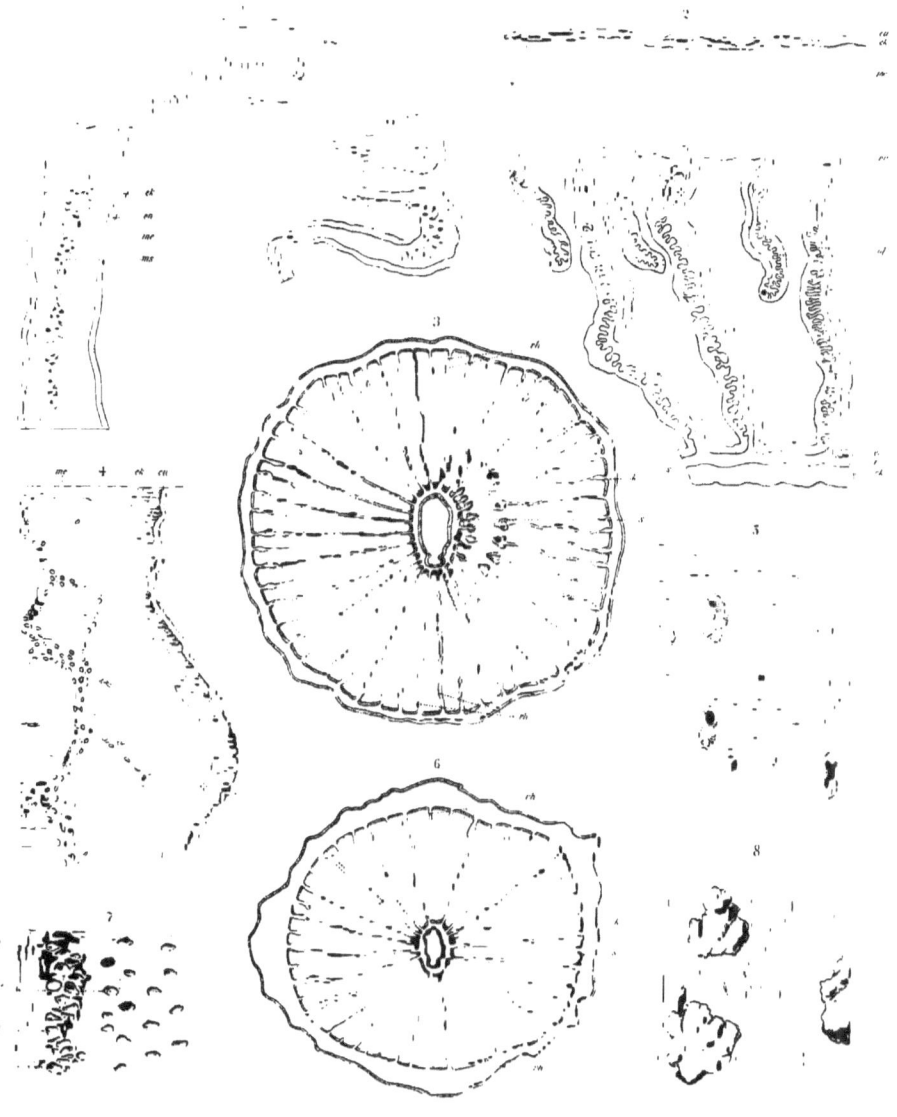